Not Just a Witch
Dial A Ghost

Eva Ibbotson writes for both adults and children. Born in Vienna, she now lives in the north of England. She has a daughter and three sons, now grown up, who showed her that children like to read about ghosts, wizards and witches 'because they are just like people but madder and more interesting'. She has written five other ghostly adventures for children. *Which Witch?* was runner-up for the Carnegie Medal and *The Secret of Platform 13* was shortlisted for the Smarties Prize.

Not Just a Witch

Dial A Ghost

Eva Ibbotson

MACMILLAN CHILDREN'S BOOKS

Not Just a Witch
First published 1989 by Macmillan Children's Books
This edition published 2001 by Macmillan Children's Books

Dial A Ghost
First published 1996 by Macmillan Children's Books
This edition published 2001 by Macmillan Children's Books

This double edition published 2002 by Macmillan Children's Books
a division of Macmillan Publishers Limited
20 New Wharf Road, London N1 9RR
Basingstoke and Oxford
www.panmacmillan.com

Associated companies throughout the world

ISBN 0 330 41471 2

1 3 5 7 9 8 6 4 2

A CIP catalogue record for this book is available from
the British Library.

Phototypeset by Intype London Ltd
Printed and bound in Great Britain by Mackays of Chatham plc, Kent

Not Just a Witch

for
Bertie, Freddie, Theo
and Octavia

Chapter One

When people quarrel it is bad, but when witches quarrel it is terrible.

Heckie was an animal witch. This didn't mean of course that she was a witch who was an animal; it meant that she did animal magic. Her full name was Hecate Tenbury-Smith and she had started when she was still a child, turning the boring noses of her mother's friends into interesting whiskery snouts or covering the cold ears of traffic wardens with thick black fur. She was a kind girl and only wanted to be helpful, but when she gave the swimming bath attendant red spots and a fishy tail so that he could pretend to be a trout if he wanted to, her parents sent her away to a well-known school for witches.

It was a school for making *good* witches. The motto the girls wore on their blazers said WITCHES AGAINST WICKEDNESS and the headmistress was choosy about whom she took.

Heckie was very happy there. She made a lot of friends, but her best friend was a stone witch called Dora Mayberry. Dora wasn't *made* of stone, but she could turn anything *into* stone. When Dora was still in her high chair, she had looked at a raspberry jelly out of her round little eyes and it turned into something you couldn't cut up even with a carving knife. And when she started turning the toothpaste

1

solid in its tube and filling the fridge with statues of pork chops, she too was sent away to school.

It takes thirty years to train a witch and during all that time, Heckie and Dora were friends. Heckie was tall and thin with frizzy hair, pop eyes and teeth which stuck out, giving her an eager look. Dora was squat and solid and had muscles like a footballer because it is heavy work dealing in stone. They shared their secrets and got each other out of scrapes, and at night in the dormitory they talked about how they were going to use their magic to make the world a better place.

By this time Heckie could change any person into whatever animal she pleased by touching him with her Knuckle of Power (though for the best results she liked to use her Toe of Transformation also) and Dora could turn anybody into stone by squinting at him out of her small round eyes. And then, when they had been friends for thirty years, Heckie and Dora quarrelled.

It happened at the Graduation Party where all the witches were to get their diplomas and get ready to go out into the world. The party, of course, was very special, and both Heckie and Dora went separately to the hat shop kept by a milliner witch and ordered hats.

Obviously a witch on the most important day of her life is not going to turn up in a straw hat trimmed with daisies or a bonnet threaded with sky-blue lace. Heckie thought for a long time and then she ordered a hat made of living snakes.

The snakes were mixed. The crown of the hat was made of Ribbon Snakes most delicately woven;

edging the brim were King Snakes striped in red and black and a single Black Mamba, coiled in the shape of a bow, hung low over Heckie's forehead.

Heckie tried it on and it looked lovely. The snakes hissed and spat and shimmered; the flickering tongues made the hat marvellously alive. Snake hats are not only beautiful, they are useful: when you take them off you just put them in a tank and feed them a few dead mice and a boiled egg or two and they last for years.

The day of the party came. Heckie put on her batskin robe, fixed a bunch of black whiskers on to her chin – and lowered the hat carefully on to her curls. Then she set off across the lawn to the tent where the refreshments were.

But what should happen then? Coming towards her was her friend Dora – and she was wearing exactly the same hat!

It wasn't roughly the same. It was exactly the same. The same Ribbon Snakes heaving and hissing on the crown; the same King Snakes writhing round the brim; the same poisonous Mamba tied into a bow!

The two witches stopped dead and glared at each other and the other witches stood round to see what would happen.

'How dare you copy my hat?' cried Heckie. She was really dreadfully upset. How could Dora, who was her best friend, hurt her like this?

But Dora was just as upset. 'How dare *you* copy *my* hat?' she roared, sticking out her jaw.

'I chose this hat first. I am an animal witch. It is my *right* to wear a hat of living snakes.'

3

'Oh, really? I suppose you've heard of my great-great-great-grandmother who was a Gorgon and had serpents growing from her scalp? It is *my* right to wear living snakes.'

But showing off about your relatives never works. Heckie only became angrier. 'The only thing you've got a right to wear on your head is a bucket,' she shrieked.

This was how the quarrel started, but soon the witches were throwing all sorts of insults at each other. They brought up old grudges: the time Dora had turned Heckie's hot-water bottle to cement so that Heckie woke up with her stomach completely squashed. The time Heckie borrowed three warts from Dora's make-up box and got cocoa on them . . .

From shouting at each other, the witches went on to tug at each other's hats. Dora tugged a Ribbon Snake out of Heckie's brim and hung it on a laurel bush. Heckie pulled at the end of Dora's Black Mamba and undid the bow. And all the time they screamed at each other as though they were spoilt little brats, not respectable middle-aged witches.

Ten minutes later both their hats were in ruins and a friendship which had lasted all their school-days was over.

The witches had planned to go and live close together in the same town. They were each going to buy a business where they could earn their living like ordinary ladies, but all their spare time would be spent in Doing Good.

Now Heckie went by herself to the town of Wellbridge, but Dora went off to a different town.

It was without her best friend, therefore, that Heckie began to try and make the world a better place.

Chapter Two

It was a boy called Daniel who found out that a witch had come to live in Wellbridge.

He found out the night he went to babysit for Mr and Mrs Boothroyd at The Towers. Mr Boothroyd owned a factory on the edge of the town which made bath plugs and he was very rich. Unfortunately he was also very mean and so was his wife. As for his baby, which was called Basil, it was quite the most unpleasant baby you could imagine. Most babies have *something* about them which is all right. The ones that look like shrivelled chimpanzees often have nice fingernails; the ones that look like half-baked buns often smile very sweetly. But Basil was an out and out disaster. When Basil wasn't screaming he was kicking; when he wasn't kicking he was throwing up his food and when he wasn't doing that he was holding his breath and turning blue.

Daniel was really too young to babysit and so was Sumi who was his friend. But Sumi, whose parents had come over from India to run the grocery shop in the street behind Daniel's house, was so sensible and so used to minding her three little brothers that the Boothroyds knew she would be fit to look after Basil while they went to the Town Hall to have dinner with the Lord Mayor. What's more, they knew they would have to pay her much less than they would have to pay a grown-up for looking after their son.

And Sumi had suggested that Daniel came along. 'I'll ask you your spellings,' she said, because she knew how cross Daniel's parents got when he didn't do brilliantly at school.

Daniel's parents were professors. Both of them. His father was called Professor Trent and if only Daniel had been dead and buried in some interesting tomb somewhere, the Professor would have been delighted with him. He was an archaeologist who studied ancient tribes and in particular their burial customs and he was incredibly clever. But Daniel wasn't mummified or covered in clay so the Professor didn't have much time for him. Daniel's mother (who was also called Professor Trent) was a philosopher who had written no less than seven books on The Meaning of Meaning and she too was terribly clever and found it hard to understand that her son was just an ordinary boy who sometimes got his sums wrong and liked to play football.

The house they lived in was tall and grey and rather dismal, and looked out across the river to the university where both the professors worked, and to the zoo. As often as not when Daniel came home from school there was nobody there, just notes propped against the teapot telling him what to unfreeze for supper and not to forget to do his piano practice.

When you know you are a disappointment to your parents, your schoolfriends become very important. Fortunately Daniel had plenty of these. There was Joe whose father was a keeper in the Wellbridge

Zoo, and Henry whose mother worked as a chambermaid in the Queen's Hotel. And there was Sumi who was so gentle and so clever and never showed off even though she knew the answers to everything. And because it was Sumi who asked him, he went along to babysit at The Towers.

The Boothroyds' house was across the river in a wide, tree-lined street between the university and the zoo. They had been quite old when Basil was born and they dressed him like babies were dressed years ago. Basil slept in a barred cot with a muslin canopy and blue bows; his pillow was edged with lace and he had a silken quilt. And there he sat, in a long white nightdress, steaming away like a red and angry boil.

The Boothroyds left. Sumi and Daniel settled down on the sitting-room sofa. Sumi took out the list of spellings.

'Separate,' she said, and Daniel sighed. He was not very fond of separate.

But it didn't matter because at that moment Basil began to scream.

He screamed as though he was being stuck all over with red-hot skewers and by the time they got upstairs he had turned an unpleasant shade of puce and was banging his head against the side of the cot.

Sumi managed to gather him up. Daniel ran to warm his bottle under the tap. Sumi gave it to him and he bit off the teat. Daniel ran to fetch another. Basil took a few windy gulps, then swivelled round and knocked the bottle out of Sumi's hand.

It took a quarter of an hour to clean up the mess

8

and by the time they got downstairs again, Sumi had a long scratch across her cheek.

'Separate,' she said wearily, picking up the list.

'S . . . E . . . P . . .' began Daniel – and was wondering whether to try an A or an E when Basil began again.

This time he had been sick all over the pillow. Sumi fetched a clean pillow-case and Basil took a deep breath and filled his nappy. She managed to change him, kicking and struggling, and put on a fresh one. Basil waited till it was properly fastened, squinted – and filled it again.

It went on like this for the next hour. Sumi never lost her patience, but she was looking desperately tired and Daniel, who knew how early she got up each day to mind her little brothers and help tidy the shop before school, could gladly have murdered Basil Boothroyd.

At eight o'clock they gave up and left him. Basil went on screaming for a while and then – miracle of miracles – he fell silent. But when Daniel looked across at Sumi for another dose of spelling he saw that she was lying back against the sofa cushions. Her long dark hair streamed across her face and she was fast asleep.

Daniel should now have felt much better. Sumi was asleep, there was no need to spell separate and Basil was quiet. And for about ten minutes he did.

Then he began to worry. *Why* was Basil so quiet? Had he choked? Had he bitten his tongue out and bled to death?

Daniel waited a little longer. Then he crept upstairs and stood listening by the door.

Basil wasn't dead. He was snoring. Daniel was about to go downstairs again when something about the noise that Basil was making caught his attention. Basil was snoring, but he was snoring... nicely. Daniel couldn't think of any other way of putting it. It was a cosy, snuffling snore and it surprised Daniel because he didn't think that Basil could make any noise that wasn't horrid.

Daniel put his head round the door ... took a few steps into the room.

And stopped dead.

At first he simply didn't believe it. What had happened was so amazing, so absolutely wonderful, that it couldn't be real. Only it *was* real. Daniel blinked and rubbed his eyes and shook himself, but it was still there, curled up on the silken quilt: not a screaming, disagreeable baby, but the most enchanting bulldog puppy with a flat, wet nose, a furrowed forehead and a blob of a tail.

Daniel stood looking down at it, feeling quite light-headed with happiness, and the puppy opened its eyes. They were the colour of liquorice and brimming with soul. There are people who say that dogs don't smile, but people who say that are silly. The bulldog grinned. It sat up and wagged its tail. It licked Daniel's hands.

'Oh, I do so like you,' said Daniel to the little, wrinkled dog.

And the dog liked Daniel. He lay on his back so that Daniel could scratch his stomach; he jumped up to try and lick Daniel's face, but his legs were too short and he collapsed again. Daniel had longed and longed for a dog to keep him company in that tall,

10

grey house to which his parents came back so late. Now it seemed like a miracle, finding this funny, loving, squashed-looking little dog in place of that horrible baby.

Because Basil had gone. There was no doubt about it. He wasn't in the cot and he wasn't under it. He wasn't anywhere. Daniel searched the bathroom, the other bedrooms ... Nothing. Someone must have come in and taken Basil and put the little dog there instead. A kidnapper? Someone wanting to hold Basil to ransom? But why leave the little dog? The Boothroyds might not be very bright, but they could tell the difference between their baby and a dog.

I must go and tell Sumi, he thought, and it was only then that he became frightened, seeing what was to come. The screaming parents, the police, the accusations. Perhaps they'd be sent to prison for not looking after Basil properly. And where *was* Basil? He might be an awful baby, but nobody wanted him harmed.

Daniel tore himself away from the bulldog and studied the room.

How could the kidnappers have got in? The front door was locked, so was the back and the window was bolted. He walked over to the fireplace. It was the old-fashioned kind with a wide chimney. But that was ridiculous – even if the kidnappers had managed to come down it, how could they have got the baby off the roof?

Then he caught sight of something spilled in the empty grate: a yellowish coarse powder, like bread-crumbs.

He scooped some up, felt it between his fingers,

11

put it to his nose. Not breadcrumbs. Goldfish food. He knew because the only pet his parents had allowed him to keep was a goldfish he'd won in a fair, and it had died almost at once because of fungus on its fins. And he knew too where the goldfish food came from: the corner pet shop, two streets away from his house. The old man who kept it made it himself; it had red flecks in it and always smelled very odd.

Daniel stood there and his forehead was almost as wrinkled as the little dog's. For the pet shop had been sold a week ago to a queer-looking woman. Daniel had seen her moving about among the animals and talking to herself. She'd been quite alone, just the sort of woman who might snatch a baby to keep her company. He'd read about women like that taking babies from their prams while their mothers were inside a supermarket. The police usually caught them – they weren't so much evil as crazy.

Daniel gave the puppy a last pat and went downstairs. Sumi was still asleep, one hand trailing over the side of the sofa. For a moment he wondered whether to wake her. Then he let himself very quietly out of the house and began to run.

Chapter Three

He ran across the bridge, turned into Park Avenue where his house was, then plunged into the maze of small streets that led between the river and the market place. Sumi's parents' shop was in one of these, and close by, on the corner, was the pet shop.

Daniel had been inside it often when the old man owned it, but now he stood in front of it, badly out of breath and very frightened. It was dusk, the street-lamps had just been lit and he could see the notice above the door.

UNDER NEW MANAGEMENT, it said. PROPRIETOR; MISS H. TENBURY-SMITH.

There was no one downstairs; the blinds were drawn, but upstairs, he could see one lighted window.

Daniel put his hand up to ring the bell and dropped it again. His knees shook, his heart was pounding. Suddenly it seemed to him that he was quite mad coming here. If the woman in the shop had taken Basil, she was certainly not going to hand him over to a schoolboy. She was much more likely to kidnap him too or even murder him so that he couldn't tell the police.

He was just turning away, ready to run for it, when the door suddenly opened and a woman stood in the hallway. She was tall with frizzy hair and

13

looked brisk and eager like a hockey mistress in an old-fashioned girls' school. And she was smiling!

'Come in, come in,' said Miss Tenbury-Smith. 'I've been expecting you.'

Daniel stared at her. 'But how . . .' he stammered. 'I mean, I've come—'

'I know why you've come, dear boy. You've come to thank me. How people can say that children nowadays are not polite, I cannot understand. I expect you'd like some tea?'

Quite stunned by all this, Daniel followed her through the dark shop, with its rustlings and squeakings, and up a narrow flight of stairs. Miss Tenbury-Smith's flat was cosy. A gas fire hissed in the grate, there were pictures of middle-aged ladies in school blazers, and on the mantelpiece, a framed photograph with its face turned to the wall.

'Unless you'd rather have fruit juice?' she went on. And as Daniel continued to stare at her, 'You're admiring my dressing-gown. It's pure batskin – a thousand bats went into its making. And in case you're wondering – *every single one of those bats died in its sleep*. I would never, never wear the skin of an animal that had not passed away peacefully from old age. Never!'

But now Daniel felt he had to get to the point. 'Actually, it's about the Boothroyd baby that I've come,' he said urgently.

'Well, of course it is, dear boy. What else?' said Miss Tenbury-Smith. 'You're quite certain that tea would suit you?'

'Yes . . . tea would be fine. Only, please, Miss Tenbury-Smith, my friend is in such trouble. We're

14

babysitting and the Boothroyds are due back any minute and there'll be such a row, so could you possibly give Basil back? Just this once?'

'Give him back? Give him *back*?' Her voice had risen to an outraged squeak.

'Well, you swapped him . . . didn't you? You kidnapped him?' But Daniel's voice trailed away, suddenly uncertain.

Miss Tenbury-Smith put down the teapot. Her slightly protruding eyes had turned stony. Her eyebrows rose. 'I . . . *kidnapped* . . . Basil Boothroyd?' she repeated, stunned. Her long nose twitched and she looked very sad. 'I was so sure we were going to be friends, Daniel,' she said, and he looked up, amazed that she should know his name. 'And now this!' She sighed. 'Now listen carefully. When you have kidnapped somebody you have got him. You agree with that? He is with you. He is part of your life.'

'Yes.'

'And would you imagine that a person in their right mind would want to have Basil? Even for five minutes? Or are you suggesting that I am *not* in my right mind?'

'No . . . no . . . But—'

'I came to Wellbridge to Do Good, Daniel. It's my mission in life to make the world a better place.' She tapped the side of her long nose. 'It hurts, you know, to be misunderstood.'

'So you didn't swap Basil for the little dog?'

'Swapped him? Of course I didn't swap him. Oh, I had so *hoped* that you would be my friend. I'm really very fond of boys with thin faces and big eyes.

15

Some people would say your ears are on the large side, but personally I like large ears. But I can't be doing with a friend who is stupid.'

'I want to be your friend,' said Daniel, who did indeed want it very much. 'But I don't understand. You're ... Are you ...? Yes, of course; I see. You're a witch!'

Miss Tenbury-Smith began to pour out the tea, but she had forgotten the tea-bags.

'Well, I'm glad you see something,' she said. 'But the point is, I'm not just a witch; I'm a witch who means to make the world a better place. Now let me ask you a question. Have you ever seen a kangaroo throwing a bomb into a supermarket, killing little children?'

'No, I haven't.'

'Good. Have you ever seen an anteater hijack an aeroplane?'

'No.'

'Or a hamster go round knocking old ladies on the head and stealing their handbags? Have you ever seen a coshing hamster?'

'No.'

'Exactly. It's very simple. Animals are not wicked. It is people who are wicked. So you might think wicked people should be killed.'

'Yes ... I suppose so.'

'However, killing is bad. It is wicked. And I'm not a wicked witch, I'm a good witch. And I do good by turning wicked people into animals.'

She leant back, pleased with herself, and took a sip of hot water.

Daniel stared at her. 'You mean . . . you changed Basil into a dog? Into that lovely dog?'

'Yes, I did. I'm so glad you liked it. I adore bull-dogs; the way they snuffle and snort, and those deep chests. When you take a bulldog on a ship, you have to face them upwind because their noses are so flat. It's the only way they can breathe. Of course, when I changed that dreadful baby, I was just limbering up. Wellbridge is a little damp, being so low-lying, and I wasn't sure how it would affect my Knuckle of Power.' She stuck out her left hand and showed him a purple swelling on the joint. 'If you get rheu-matism on your knuckle it can make things very tricky. But it all went like a dream. I really did it for that pretty friend of yours – so polite, and such a nice shop her parents keep with everything higgledy-piggledy, not like those boring supermarkets. Poor children, I thought, they're going to have such a horrible evening.'

'Yes, but you see it's going to be much more hor-rible if the Boothroyds come and find Basil gone. There'll be such trouble. So, please, could you change Basil back? If you can?'

'If I *can*?' said the witch, looking offended. 'Really, Daniel, you go too far. And actually I was going to change Basil back in any case, sooner or later, because babies aren't really wicked. To be wicked you have to know right from wrong and choose wrong, and babies can't do that. But I cannot believe that the Boothroyds wouldn't rather have the little dog for a night or two. He's completely house-trained, did you know?'

17

'Honestly, Miss Tenbury-Smith, I'm sure they wouldn't. I'm really sure.'

'Extraordinary,' said the witch, shaking her head to and fro. 'Well, in that case, let's see what we can do. Just wait while I change my clothes.'

Chapter Four

'Well, you seem to be right,' said Heckie as they approached The Towers. 'The dear Boothroyds do not sound happy.'

All the lights were on and one could hear Mrs Boothroyd's screams halfway down the street.

'Oh, poor Sumi!'

'Now don't worry,' said the witch, who had changed into her school blazer and pleated skirt. 'I shall pretend to be a social worker. That always goes down well. Just follow me.'

Inside the Boothroyds' sitting-room, a fat policeman was writing things in a notebook and a thin policeman was talking to headquarters on his walkie-talkie. Mrs Boothroyd was yelling and hiccupping and gulping by turns, and Mr Boothroyd was blustering and threatening to do awful things to Sumi's family. Sumi sat crouched on the sofa, her head in her hands. Between her shoes one could just see the dark, wet nose of the bewildered little dog.

'Now, my dear good people, what is all this about?' enquired Heckie briskly. 'I found this poor boy wandering about in the street quite beside himself.' She pointed to the letters WAW on her blazer. 'I am from the Wellbridge Association for Welfare,' she went on, 'and we cannot be doing with that kind of thing.'

'My baby's been kidnapped! My little treasure! My bobbikins!' screeched Mrs Boothroyd.

'And it's all these children's fault!' roared Mr Boothroyd.

'Nonsense,' said Heckie. 'He'll just have got mislaid somewhere. It often happens with babies.'

'We've searched high and low, Miss,' said the fat policeman.

But the little bulldog had heard Heckie's voice. He crawled out from under the sofa and as she crouched down to him, he leapt on to her lap.

'Who let that brute in again?' raged Mr Boothroyd – and Sumi blushed and turned her head away.

'Dogs give you fleas! They give you worms behind the eyeballs,' screeched Mrs Boothroyd.

Heckie looked hard at the Boothroyds. She was angry, but she was also amazed. In spite of what Daniel had said, she hadn't really believed that they would prefer Basil to the little dog. Then she gathered up the puppy and went to the door which Daniel was holding open for her, and out into the garden.

For an animal witch, turning nice animals into silly people is much harder than the other way round. Heckie's eyes were sad as she shook off her left shoe so that her Toe of Transformation could suck power from the earth. Then she spoke softly to the bulldog, waiting till his tail stopped wagging and his eyes were closed. Only when he slept did she touch him with her Knuckle of Power and say her spells.

Ten minutes later, Heckie returned to the drawing-room. She had held the puppy close to her chest, but she carried Basil at arm's length like a tray. His nightdress was covered in black streaks, he was bawling – but he was quite unharmed.

'My lambkin, my prettikins, my darling!' shrieked Mrs Boothroyd, covering him with squelchy kisses.

'My son, my boy!' slobbered Mr Boothroyd.

'Where was he, Miss?' asked the fat policeman.

'At the back of the coalshed,' said Heckie. 'The obvious place to look for a baby, I'd have thought.'

'But how did he get there?'

Heckie felt sorry for the fat policeman who so much wanted to have something to put in his notebook. 'You want to look for a tall man with red hair, blue eyes, a black moustache, an orange anorak and purple socks. I saw him climbing over the garden wall. It'll be him who put Basil among the coals.'

'But what would be the motive?' asked the policeman with the walkie-talkie.

'Oh, that's easy,' said Heckie. 'Revenge. Someone getting their own back. He'll have bought one of Mr Boothroyd's bath plugs and found it leaked. You know what it's like when all the hot water drains away and you're sitting in an empty tub all cold and blue with goosepimples . . .'

But when they had dropped Sumi off in the taxi Mr Boothroyd had been forced to pay for, Heckie turned to Daniel, looking thoughtful and serious.

'You know, Daniel, I shall have to change my plans entirely. I had no idea people would make such a fuss and be so unreasonable. I thought they'd come to me and say: "Please, Heckie, would you turn my drunken husband into a dear chimpanzee?" Or: "We feel that Uncle Phillip, who is a handbag snatcher, would do better as a Two-toed Sloth." That kind of

21

thing. But now I see it isn't so. I shall have to work in the *strictest* secrecy. Evil-doers will have to be *flushed out*!' She peered at Daniel. 'Might one ask why you are snivelling? Is it because there's no one at home?'

Sumi's parents had been there to welcome her, but Daniel's house, as the taxi drew up, was silent and dark.

Daniel shook his head. 'I don't mind being alone.' He wiped away the tear in the corner of his eye. 'It's that lovely bulldog. I miss him so *much*!'

Heckie examined his face in the light of the lamp. 'You know, you have the right ideas. Yes, I think I might be able to use you. For I have to tell you, Daniel, that I have just had a vision. I see a band of Wickedness Hunters! Children and witches together, uniting to rid Wellbridge of Wickedness! Yes, yes, I see it all. But first, dear boy, I must get myself a familiar. What a good thing that tomorrow is Sunday. Come after breakfast and we'll go to the zoo!'

Chapter Five

When Daniel called at the shop the following morning, he found Heckie feeding her hat.

After the quarrel with Dora Mayberry, Heckie had crept back and gathered up her Ribbon Snakes and King Snakes and the Black Mamba, and they now lived in a tank in a room behind the shop, eating boiled eggs and hissing and not being a trouble to anyone. It would have been easy for her to weave them together again and wear them on her head, but she hadn't the heart, and because she knew that Daniel was a boy who could be trusted with people's sorrows, she told him what had happened and how dreadfully she missed her friend.

'We had such plans, Dora and I. She was going to have a little business making garden gnomes and nice things like that, and gradually fill the park with interesting statues. Only statues of wicked people, of course. Dora was Good, like me. Come and see her picture.'

She took Daniel up to the sitting-room and showed him the photo of Dora which she had turned with its face to the wall. The stone witch, with her square jaw and piggy eyes, was not beautiful, but Daniel said she looked interesting, like a prize fighter.

'Yes, indeed,' said Heckie, and sighed. 'And you should have seen her on the netball field! But it's all over between us.' And she turned the photo back to face the wall.

When they had fed the other animals in the shop, Heckie went to the larder to fetch a carrot. The carrot was about half a metre long and as thick as a thigh and scarcely fitted into the shopping basket, which was a tartan one on wheels, but Heckie said it would do for their lunch.

'My friend grows them for me. She's a garden witch – there's nothing she can't do with vegetables, but they do come out rather big.'

'What I was wondering,' said Daniel as they wheeled the carrot towards the zoo, 'was why you *need* a familiar? I mean, they're animals that help witches to do their magic, aren't they – and you changed Basil all right without one?'

'I don't *need* one, but I *want* one. And nothing ordinary like black cats or toads. I bet Dora's trailing round with a bontebok by now at the very least.'

Wellbridge Zoo was small, but pretty and well-kept, with flower-beds between the cages. Daniel went there often because his friend Joe, whose father was a keeper in the ape house, could get him in free.

'Now to business,' said Heckie when they had paid and gone through the turnstile. 'You know what we're looking for?'

'An animal that's fierce?'

'Well, not so much fierce as powerful. Mean. Strange and perhaps a little throbbing; that kind of thing.'

But the sea lions, lying about like old sofas, did not look very mean or throbbing and nor did the giraffes with their knock knees and film-star eyes.

24

They passed the aviary and though the cassowary looked interesting with its flabby black wattles and dirty feet, Heckie did not think she really wanted a bird.

'All that flapping is not very good for magic, I have found.'

But when they got to the hyena, pacing up and down in its cage, Heckie's face lit up. 'Now that is something! The way its back end just trails away and those sinister spots, and the *smell*!'

She wrote something in her notebook and they crossed over to the big enclosure which housed the kangaroos and wallabies – great, rat-coloured beasts with huge feet and mad, twitchy ears which Heckie liked enormously. 'Oh, I wish I was an Australian witch,' she cried. 'Everything over there is so queer and extinct-looking!'

The animal houses were closer together now and Heckie was running from cage to cage, as excited as a child in a toy shop. There were penguins jumping from rock to rock with their feet together like loopy waiters; there was a rusty numbat shovelling up ants – and there was a camel in front of which she stood for a long time. It was a bull camel, tall and sneery with lumpy knees and a lower lip full of froth. Bits of dirty straw stuck to its hump, and a low rumble like thunder came from its throat.

'I want this camel,' said Heckie. 'I want it terribly. But I'm going to be sensible. I'm going to be practical. I'm going to be *brave*.'

Daniel could see how hard it was for her to tear herself away from the camel, but in the reptile house she cheered up again. It was a silent, sinister place

25

and every one of the animals looked as though it would help one to do magic: the crocodile, smiling in its sleep, the Bearded Basilisk, the iguana like a shrunken dinosaur . . .

In the ape house, they saw what seemed to be a very small ape in blue jeans forking fresh straw on to the floor. This turned out to be Daniel's school-friend Joe, helping his father clean out the cages.

Joe's mother had died when he was born and his father had reared Joe like he reared one of his orphaned apes, carrying him round in a blanket, feeding him on bottles of milk and bananas. Joe's hair was ginger like the orang-utans' and fell over his face; there was no tree he couldn't climb, and when anyone annoyed him, he stuck out his lower lip and glowered exactly like a gorilla.

Daniel introduced him to Heckie who was very interested to hear that his father was a keeper.

'Tell me,' she said, 'are there any empty cages in this zoo? Spare cages? In case someone was to send in some animals in a hurry? Unexpectedly?'

Joe gave her a sharp look from under his hair and said, yes, there were. 'They're over by the West Gate, behind the tea place.'

He went on staring at Heckie as she talked to the monkeys and the apes. Joe understood animals almost as well as his father and he knew that the way they came up to Heckie and laid their faces against the bars and tried to take her hand was quite out of the ordinary.

'Is she an animal trainer or something?' he asked Daniel, and Daniel said that perhaps in a way she was.

'We'll just have our picnic now and have a think,' said Heckie when they had been right round the zoo. 'Perhaps your nice friend will lend us a saw to cut up this interesting carrot. Or shall we just go across the road to The Copper Kettle?'

Daniel thought this was a good idea and soon they were sitting at a corner table, eating cucumber sandwiches and looking at Heckie's list.

'Of course, the baboons are unbeatable. Those red and blue behinds!' Her eyes glinted. 'But I like the orang-utans too: the way their hair hangs down from their armpits . . .' She bit into her sandwich. 'You notice I'm being brave about the camel?'

Daniel nodded and suggested the Bearded Basilisk. 'It might fit better into the flat?'

'Yes, but reptiles are dreadfully snooty. Cold-blooded, you know. Oh dear, this is so *difficult*.'

Heckie was very quiet as they wheeled the carrot back across the river and the tip of her nose had gone quite white from the strain of deciding. But in the street behind Daniel's house, she stopped and stared at a shop window. It was a Do It Yourself shop full of tools and screws and bits of shelving.

Suddenly she hit her forehead with her hand. 'What an idiot I am, Daniel. What a complete fool! Why *choose* a familiar? Why not *make* one?'

'Oh yes,' said Daniel, his eyes shining. 'A Do It Yourself familiar! The first one in the world!'

And, terribly excited, they hurried back to Heckie's shop. Once she had made up her mind, Heckie wasted no time.

'Do you know what I'm going to make?'

Daniel shook his head.

'A dragon. Yes, honestly. Why not go for the best? A pocket dragon. Well, a bit bigger than that. Sort of between a rolling pin and a turkey in size. About the weight of a Stilton cheese. Oh, I can see him. Slightly fiery round the nostrils, you know, with green scales and golden claws! Let's get the pattern book and have a look.'

She went to the bookcase and got out a book called *Ferocious Dragons and Loathly Worms* and began to turn over the pages. There were pictures of silvery dragons like the ones that ate princesses and were killed by St George, and gloomy, evil-looking dragons with poisonous claws and fiery tongues. But the nicest dragons were the Chinese ones. They had shaggy heads like Tibetan terriers with their hair in topknots and big, bulging eyes and wide mouths chock-full of teeth which gave them a smiling look. Daniel had seen dragons like that painted on kites and liked them very much.

'Can you make a dragon from nothing?' he asked when they had decided that a Chinese dragon was what they wanted.

Heckie looked shocked. 'No, no, dear boy. I'm only a witch, you know. I can change anything into anything else, but I can't make things from nothing. What we'll have to do is find an animal that isn't *happy* any more. An animal that's tired of life – and then I can change it. To mess about with an animal that was enjoying life would be *quite* wrong.'

They went downstairs to the shop to see if there was an animal there that was bored with living, but there wasn't. So they went to the park because Heckie thought she remembered seeing a duck that

28

was no longer glad to be alive and, sure enough, there it was, sitting in a clump of rushes by the pond. It was a white Aylesbury drake; its eyes were filmed, its feathers were limp. The other ducks were swimming and diving and gobbling up bread that the children threw, but not this duck. This duck had turned its face to the wall.

Heckie put out an arm. The duck did not have time even for one 'quack' before it found itself zipped into the tartan shopping basket on wheels and bundled off to the pet shop.

'Can I watch you?' begged Daniel when they had unpacked the animal and set it down on the kitchen floor. 'Can I watch you make a dragon, please?'

'No, dear boy, I'm afraid not. And you wouldn't like it, you know. It's not just my knuckle – a lot of power comes from my feet. Things happen down there that are not suitable for anybody young.' She looked down at her toes and sighed. 'If you come tomorrow after school, the dragon should be ready,' said Heckie, and Daniel had to be content with that.

In the staffroom at Wellbridge Junior School, the deputy head was in a temper. 'I've had another letter from those professors complaining about Daniel's work. They say they'll take him away and send him to a private school if he doesn't do better.'

Miss Jones, who was Daniel's class teacher, put down her cup with a clatter. 'I wish they'd leave him alone. There's nothing wrong with Daniel; he's a thoroughly nice boy and his work's perfectly all right. If they spent a bit more time at home with him

29

instead of nagging about his marks, there'd be some point.'

The deputy head nodded. 'I've gone past that house again and again and there's no one in. He's got a lost look in his eyes sometimes, that child. It's a pretty turn of affairs when the most deprived child in the class is the son of two rich professors.'

But when Miss Jones went to take her class for English, she thought that Daniel looked more cheerful than he had done of late – and indeed Daniel wasn't worrying about how he was going to do in the spelling test or whether he had passed his music exam. He was thinking that in a few hours he would see a dragon made out of an Aylesbury duck, and nobody who thinks that can look unhappy.

Of course, it would happen that on the one day on which Daniel was longing to get away, his parents were both in for tea.

'Well, how did you get on with your spelling test?' asked the Professor Trent who was Daniel's father. He was tall, with greying hair and a big nose.

'I hope you got ten out of ten,' said the Professor Trent who was Daniel's mother. She too was tall, with thick spectacles and a strong chin. When they were both standing looking down at him, Daniel felt a bit like a puppy who has made a puddle on the carpet.

'I got eight out of ten,' said Daniel, hoping that this would be all right, but it wasn't.

'Really?' said Daniel's father. 'And what words did you get wrong?'

Daniel sighed. 'Separate,' he said. 'And mystify.'

Daniel's parents thought this was odd. Daniel's

30

father had been able to spell mystify when he was four years old, and Daniel's mother said that surely when one understood that separate came from the Latin word *separare* there could be no difficulty. 'How many did Sumi get right?' she wanted to know.

'She got them all right. She always does.'

Both professors shook their heads. 'It seems extraordinary, Daniel, that a girl who does not even speak English at home should do so much better than you.'

Daniel said nothing. One day he meant to do something that would surprise his parents and make them proud of him – only what? If the house burnt down he could drag them from the flames (though they were rather large) and if there was a flood he could commandeer a boat and row them to safety. But so far there had been no fire, nor had the streets of Wellbridge turned into rivers, and sometimes Daniel thought that he would never be the kind of boy they wanted.

But when tea was over at last and he slipped out of the house, his face soon lost its pinched, dejected look. He took a deep breath of air and then he began to run.

Heckie seemed pleased to see him, but there was something a little odd in her manner.

'Is he finished? Have you done it?' asked Daniel eagerly.

'Of course,' said Heckie stiffly. 'What I do, I do. It's just . . .'

She led him upstairs and pointed to a dog basket she had brought up from the shop. The new familiar was sitting in it: a Chinese dragon about the size of a dachshund, with a black topknot of hair, big red

31

eyes, fiery-looking nostrils and a pair of wings set close behind his ears.

'Oh!' said Daniel. 'He's beautiful! He's the most beautiful dragon in the world!'

'Yes, he is, isn't he,' said Heckie. 'Most of him, anyway . . .'

Daniel moved closer. The dragon's neck and shoulders were covered in green and golden scales, his pearl-tipped talons gripped the rim of the basket and his teeth were pointed and razor-sharp.

So far so good. It was the back of the dragon that was . . . unexpected.

Heckie cleared her throat. 'You see, I was just in the middle of changing him when the bell rang and it was the postman. You know how exciting it is when the postman rings. It might mean anything.' And Heckie blushed, for she had thought it might mean a letter from her friend Dora to say that she was sorry. 'I left the window open and the pages blew over in the book and . . . well, you see.'

'Yes,' said Daniel.

The front end of Heckie's new familiar was a dragon, but the back end was a worm. It was not an earthworm, it was a Loathly Worm like in the book – but it was a worm. There were twelve segments, each bulgy and carrying a pair of blobby legs, and though the dragon part was green and gold and scaly, the worm part was smooth and pale with faint pink spots.

'What shall I do?' asked Heckie, and Daniel was very touched that she, a witch of such power, should turn to him.

Daniel was usually a shy, uncertain boy, but he

knew exactly what she should do. 'Nothing! Please don't do anything. He's absolutely splendid as he is. I mean, any old witch could have a dragon for a familiar, but there can't be a single witch in the whole wide world who has a *dragworm*!'

Heckie smiled. 'I'm glad you feel like that, dear boy. Because, to tell the truth, it would hurt me now to change him. We'll soon get him trained up. He doesn't talk yet, but he understands quite a lot already.' She patted the dragworm's head and he shot out his forked tongue and licked her hand. 'We're in business, Daniel. You'll see. This time next year there won't be a single wicked person left in the length and breadth of Wellbridge!'

Chapter Six

The Wellbridge Wickedness Hunters met in Heckie's sitting-room the following week.

Heckie had asked all the wizards and witches in the town to join and she had hoped that they might turn out to be a bit like Robin Hood and his Merry Men, but they had not. Mr Gurgle, a wizard who kept a grocer's shop in Market Square, was not at *all* like Robin Hood. He was a small, bald man who spent his time trying to make a cheese that could walk by itself. Not a cheese that could crawl – quite a lot of cheeses can do that – but a cheese that could walk right across a room without help. And Boris Chomsky, the mechanical wizard who serviced the hot air balloons the witches used, wasn't like Robin Hood either. He was a Russian with a long, sad face and wore a woollen muffler which was stained with oil because he worked in a garage.

Next to Boris sat Frieda Fennel, the garden witch who had grown Heckie's carrot. Frieda had green fingers which meant that anything would grow for her, but it was difficult to *stop* it growing. When Frieda scratched her ear or rubbed her neck, little buds or leafy shoots burst out where she had touched herself, so anyone sitting near her had to keep her tidy with garden shears.

And there was Madame Rosalia, who had been

Miss Witch 1965 and didn't let anyone forget it. Like most beauty queens, she was a show-off and was sitting with her chair floating halfway to the ceiling, just to be different. She kept a beauty parlour and always knew exactly what every witch should wear.

'Whiskers are in this year,' she would say, 'and moles are out,' which annoyed Heckie. If you wanted whiskers you wanted whiskers and if you wanted moles you wanted moles. What was in or out had nothing to do with it.

But if the witches and wizards were not quite what Heckie had hoped for, she felt cheered as soon as she looked at the sofa where the three children were sitting very straight with their knees together and their eyes bright as they took in what was going on.

Heckie had known at once that Sumi and Joe could be trusted, and when Daniel, during break at school, had told them who Heckie was, neither of them had been surprised.

'I knew,' said Joe. 'The way that gorilla tried to hold her hand.'

Sumi too had guessed. As she said, if someone has red hair they're not going to have a black moustache – Heckie had to have made up the man in the Boothroyds' garden. But though Joe was excited at once about becoming a Wickedness Hunter and tracking down evil people for Heckie to change, Sumi was not so sure.

'I don't know . . . People have souls, don't they?' she'd said, winding her long hair round her fingers. 'What happens to them when they're turned into animals?'

'Animals have souls too,' said Daniel. 'That bulldog puppy was bursting with soul.'

But Sumi was still troubled. 'I think it could go wrong. I think it could all go horribly wrong.'

But in the end, she'd agreed to join the club, if only to make herself useful. And already she had been useful. The mugs of tea that the witches and wizards were drinking all had tea-bags in them, and the biscuits they were eating came from her parents' shop.

And between the wizards and the children, sat the dragworm in his basket.

Heckie now made a speech. She welcomed everybody and said how pleased she was to see them, and then she told them the kind of person she was looking for.

'What I'm after,' she said, 'isn't someone who's just lost his temper and battered his bank manager to death with a hammer. Battering your bank manager to death with a hammer is not good, of course, but anyone can lose their temper and some bank managers are very annoying. What we're looking for is people who do evil day after day, knowing that they are doing it, and still going on.'

'Like flushers,' interrupted the cheese wizard, getting excited. 'Flushers want changing.'

'What's a flusher?' asked Joe – and Heckie explained that it was a person who flushed unwanted pets down the lavatory. 'Goldfish, newts – even terrapins. What's more, flushers often turn into dumpers,' she said, her eyes flashing. 'People who dump dogs on the motorway when they stop being dear little puppies. And dumpers we definitely want!'

She then became practical. 'You must remember that as soon as a wicked person becomes an animal, he has to be protected and cared for. If I turn an armed robber into a wombat he is not a wicked wombat, he is a *wombat* and has to be taken quickly to the zoo. And I shall need help for that.'

She looked at Chomsky, the mechanical wizard, who nodded and said he had a van which would do.

Madame Rosalia, whose underclothes were showing as she floated in her chair, now said that Heckie was wasting her time. 'Whatever you do there's always more and more wickedness in the world. Look at the newspapers! Every day there's some grandfather starving a child to death in an attic, or a hit and run motorist leaving a boy in the road. There's always been evil in the world and there always will be.'

For a moment, Heckie looked tired and sad. Witches only live for three hundred years and she knew better than anyone how much there was to do. Then she brightened. 'I think you forget,' she said, 'that I don't just have all you dear people to help me. I have my familiar!' She pointed to the drag-worm, still sitting peacefully in his basket. 'With a familiar like that, how can I fail?'

There was a pause. Then from up in the air, there came a titter.

'Come, come, Heckie, you don't think that funny-looking thing is going to be any use?'

'It would certainly be most unwise to expect any-thing from ... er ... *that*,' said the cheese wizard pompously.

'Poor thing, he'd be better dug in for manure,' said the garden witch.

It was exactly at this moment that there was a loud ring at the doorbell of the shop.

'Drat!' said Heckie. 'I put up a notice saying SHOP CLOSED. Why don't they go away?'

But whoever it was didn't go away. There was another loud peal of the bell.

'It's someone with a white Rolls-Royce,' said Joe, who had gone to the window. 'An absolute whopper, and there's a chauffeur driving it.'

Leaning out, the children could see the woman who was ringing the bell so impatiently. She was wearing a fur coat, white like her car, and her hair was piled up into a kind of tower and looked as though it had been sprayed with gold paint.

The bell rang for the third time.

'Oh, blast the woman! I'd better go and see.' Heckie opened the door and the dragworm decided to follow her. This was not so simple. His front end bounded out of the basket quickly enough, helped by the whirring of his little wings. But then he stopped and a frown appeared between his shaggy eyebrows. The worm part of him had twenty-four legs, a pair on each of his bulges, and it was not easy for him to decide which one to start walking with.

The wizards and witches tittered, and the children glared at them.

Then all at once, the legs on the third bulge from the end started to move, which set off all the others, and, suddenly looking very happy, the dragworm bounded and slithered down the stairs.

In the shop, Heckie tucked him up behind one of the food-bins so that no one could see him. Then she opened the door and the woman in the white fur coat swept in. She was carrying a birdcage with a cover which she took off. Inside was a large green and orange parrot.

'Where's Sam?' said the parrot, his head on one side.

'I want you to buy this bird,' said the woman in a bossy voice.

'I'm afraid I don't buy birds from private people. One can never be sure that they are not diseased.'

'This parrot is not diseased,' said the woman huffily, and once again the parrot said: 'Where's Sam?'

'Where *is* Sam?' asked Heckie.

'Sam was his owner. He's gone away and because I am a kind and caring person, I offered to find a home for the parrot. I'll take fifty pounds.'

Heckie was about to say no, but the parrot edged closer on his perch and she saw his eyes. 'I'll give you forty,' she said.

To her surprise, the woman took it and left.

'I'll see you later,' said Heckie to the parrot, and went back to the meeting.

'Now,' she said, when she was back in the sitting-room. 'Is there anything else—'

She broke off. Daniel and Sumi had both leapt to their feet and run towards the door.

'Oh, what has *happened*?' cried Daniel.

The dragworm had managed to get back upstairs but there was something terribly wrong with him. His breath came in rasping gasps, his wings were

39

limp and the hair on his topknot had turned quite white! Worst of all was his wormy end. It had been smooth and pale with gentle pink splodges. Now all the splodges were horribly inflamed, raised up from the skin like boils, and the centre of every one was full of pus.

Up to now, Heckie's familiar had never made a sound, but as they carried him back to his basket, his head fell back and from his poor, sick throat there came a tragic and despairing: '*Quack*!'

Nobody laughed. Even the witches and wizards who had jeered knew that when people are in trouble they often go back to their childhood, crying or calling for their mothers. The dragworm had gone back to *his* early life – the life when he was a duck.

Heckie was beside herself, running backwards and forwards with medicines and blankets, and it was the garden witch who said: 'Wait! I've seen this before. Seen it with Mad Millicent's familiar.' She scratched her head, but Heckie was far too worried to clip off the green shoot that burst out between her eyebrows. 'The fiercest witch in the east, she was, and her familiar with her.'

The cheese wizard nodded. 'That's right. He was a lizard and he'd come on just like that when there was some evil in the place. And Wall-eyed William's familiar too. An eagle, he was – a real brute and he used to come out in great red boils under his feathers. A proper help it was to William.'

'You mean . . .' Heckie looked up and she was blushing. 'Are you saying . . .? Oh, surely not. I'm only an ordinary witch. Surely I couldn't have made one of . . . you know . . . *them*?'

40

The wizards and witches nodded and looked at Heckie with a new respect.

'Made what?' Joe wanted to know.

'A detector! A wickedness detector! A familiar who comes over queer when he meets anyone wicked!' cried Heckie, clapping her hands, and Daniel felt quite cross. How could she look so pleased when the dragworm was suffering? Though actually he was beginning to look a little better: some of the black was returning to his hair and the spots were fading. 'A wickedness detector. Oh my, oh my! So we'll always know for certain whether somebody's evil or not! Well, there's nothing to stop us now!'

'Yes, but who *made* him come out in spots like that?' asked Joe.

Everybody looked at everybody else. In the silence, they could hear the parrot still asking: 'Where's Sam? Where's Sam?'

'Of course!' cried Heckie. 'The woman in the shop. The woman with the white Rolls-Royce. After her, children! Find out everything you can about her. Everything!'

Chapter Seven

It didn't take the children long to trace the owner of the white Rolls-Royce. Her name was Mrs Winneypeg and she was one of the richest women in Wellbridge. She didn't just have a white Rolls-Royce, she had a white BMW and a white Jaguar. She lived alone in a house with seven bedrooms and a private swimming pool and owned seven fur coats, three of them mink.

And she made her money looking after old people.

'But that's a good thing to do, surely?' said Daniel when they had reported back to Heckie. 'So why was the dragworm so ill when he saw her?'

Could the dragworm be wrong? Nobody thought so, but it was odd all the same.

'We'll just go on sniffing round,' said Heckie. 'For one thing, I'd like to know why she sold that parrot.'

For the parrot still said nothing except: 'Where's Sam?' and had to be coaxed to eat.

The way Mrs Winneypeg looked after old people was to run a number of rest homes where they could go when they were too old or ill to look after themselves. They were called the Sundown Homes and it so happened that one of them was at the bottom of Daniel's street. It was made up of three old houses knocked together and from the front it looked nice enough. The brass plate was brightly polished, the paintwork looked new.

But now Daniel slipped in to the alleyway behind the houses, where no one ever went, and here it was very different. The windows were dirty, the dustbins were overflowing, and one could see the wispy grey heads of the old people herded together in a dingy room.

The children began to ask questions in the neighbouring shops and to hang round the home to see if they could find out more, but it seemed that nobody wanted to talk about Mrs Winneypeg and her Sundown Homes. And then, on the third day, when Daniel just 'happened' to be loitering there after school, the door burst open and a nurse in a blue uniform came stumbling down the steps and bumped right into Daniel. She was Irish and very young, and she was crying.

'That place – that awful place!' she sobbed. 'I can't stand it any more. I'm leaving.'

And because Daniel had a listening sort of face and she had to talk to someone, she told him what it was like in the building she'd just left. She told him about the bullying and the disgusting food and the way the old people were sent up to bed at six o'clock to save the heating. She told him about Miss Merrick who so loved flowers and had been told she could have a window-box, and then when she spilled a little bit of earth because her hands were shaky, Mrs Winneypeg had screamed at her and taken the window-box away. She told him about Major Holden who'd fought in two world wars and asked for some boot polish because he liked to keep himself

43

neat even if he couldn't see too well, and who'd been locked in his room for making a fuss.

'She's a fiend, that Mrs Winneypeg – she ought to burn in hell,' said the nurse, mopping her eyes. 'All her homes are like that and the poor old things never get out once she's got hold of them. She takes their pension books and their savings and burns the letters they write, so no one ever knows.'

'Can't the council do anything?' Daniel asked.

The nurse shrugged. 'People have complained, but she's buttered up the councillors for years. I meant to stick it out, but that old chap and his parrot was the last straw. Such a nice bloke – been in the navy all his life and no bother to anyone. He only came because she said he could keep his parrot, and now she's told him it's dead. You should see him – he won't last a month the way he's going. And the parrot isn't dead! I saw the chauffeur put it in the boot of her car. She'll have flogged it or torn its feathers out for a hat.'

'Is his name Sam?' asked Daniel. 'The gentleman with the parrot?'

The nurse blew her nose and looked at Daniel. 'Yes,' she said. 'It is.'

So now they knew why the dragworm had come out in those dreadful boils. Mrs Winneypeg was what is called a Granny Farmer, and there is probably nothing more unpleasant in the world.

But Mrs Winneypeg was about to get a big surprise.

*

A week later, a new resident arrived at the Wellbridge Sundown Home. Miss Smith was ancient and tottery and deaf – and she was very rich. Mrs Winneypeg was waiting to greet her and her greedy eyes lit up when she saw the poor old thing helped out of the taxi by her great-nephew. *She* wasn't going to give any trouble, that was certain! And the nephew and his family were off to Australia, she'd said on the phone, so there'd be no relatives to poke and pry.

'It's very kind of you to let me stay in your lovely home,' quavered Miss Smith – and winked at Daniel. Madame Rosalia might be a show-off, but there was nothing she couldn't do with make-up. Heckie's wrinkles would have fooled anyone; her hair was white; brown blotches covered her skin.

'Not at all. I'm sure you'll be very happy with us,' said Mrs Winneypeg in a plummy voice. 'You've brought some money with you? Cash, I like – it makes less work.'

Miss Smith fumbled in her handbag.

'That'll be fine,' said Mrs Winneypeg, grabbing some notes. 'Now if your dear nephew will just say goodbye, we'll soon make you comfortable.'

An hour later, Heckie was in a small bedroom in which four beds had been shoved so close together that you could hardly move between them. Three wispy-haired ladies in nightdresses sat one on each bed, shivering with cold.

'You shouldn't have come,' said one of them hopelessly. 'It's a dreadful place this.'

'Oh, I expect we can soon get things cheered up,' said Heckie. But she was so angry she could hardly speak. She'd decided not to do anything till she was sure that the home was as bad as the young nurse said. Now she knew that it was worse. She'd seen Major Holden tied to his chair because he liked to wander about and the staff said he got in the way. She'd seen old Sam force-fed with revolting stew because he wouldn't eat since he lost his parrot and Mrs Winneypeg didn't want him to die and bring the doctor to ask awkward questions. She'd seen a woman as thin as a skeleton slip on the bathroom floor and be scolded for carelessness . . .

At eight, a nurse came to turn out the light.

'I'd like a hot-water bottle,' said Heckie. 'I'm cold.'

'A *hot-water bottle*!' said the nurse. 'You must be out of your mind!'

All the kind nurses had left; only the cruel ones could stand working for Mrs Winneypeg and most of them weren't real nurses at all.

At midnight, Heckie got up and stood by the window. Everything was ready; all her helpers knew what to do. Daniel and Sumi were taking it in turns to mind the shop and sit with the dragworm; Joe had 'borrowed' his father's keys to the West Gate of the zoo and would come with Boris in his van to drive whatever it was to safety.

Only what *was* it going to be? Heckie wasn't sure. Nothing *cuddly*, of course. 'I'll just have to see how I feel when the time comes,' she said, and went back to bed.

Breakfast was lumpy porridge and dry bread.

'I want some butter,' said Heckie. 'I've paid good money to be here and I want some butter on my bread.'

After breakfast she said she'd like to go out for a little walk and at eleven she wanted a nice cup of coffee.

By lunchtime it was clear that something would have to be done about Miss Smith and the matron went to ring Mrs Winneypeg.

'She's a troublemaker, Mrs Winneypeg. I don't know what to do with her.'

'Do with her? Do what we always do,' snapped Mrs Winneypeg. 'Undress her, take her teeth out and shut her in her room.'

'Well, I tried . . .' Matron broke off, not really able to explain why it wasn't easy to undress Miss Smith. 'Her teeth don't *take* out,' she complained.

'All right; I'm coming anyway at three o'clock to do the accounts. I'll soon sort her out.'

And Heckie, who had been listening at the door, held up three fingers to Boris, waiting in the street in his parked van, and settled down to wait.

The residents were sitting in a circle in the lounge when the white Rolls-Royce drew up in front of the door. Heckie could see the way they cowered at the sight of it and her chin went up.

'Listen,' she said quickly. 'How many of you can stand up without help? How many of you can walk?'

The circle of faces stared at her blankly.

'Come on,' she said. 'Some of you can, I know. I've seen you.'

Still the poor browbeaten creatures just stared at her. Then slowly, Major Holden's hand went up; then Sam's . . . then those of the ladies who shared Heckie's room – until almost everybody's hand was raised.

'Good,' said Heckie. 'Because I'm going to have a few words with Mrs Winneypeg and I want you to stand quite close in a circle. I need her to come right up to me – I don't want her running away. And I don't want ... anything else running away either. Can you do that?'

The old people nodded. A little colour had come into their faces and Major Holden put up his hand in a salute.

The door opened and Mrs Winneypeg came into the room. She saw all the residents dozing as usual, and she marched straight up to Miss Smith.

'Now then, I hear you've been making trouble,' she said. 'Just exactly what is the matter?'

Heckie rose from her chair. 'Everything is the matter! Just exactly everything. This place is a disgrace. The food is revolting, the staff are unkind and you are a vicious woman!'

Mrs Winneypeg's mouth opened; her chins quivered. 'How dare you! How *dare* you speak to me like that!' She marched towards Heckie which was exactly what Heckie wanted. And the old people had heard and understood. They were doing what Heckie had asked. One by one, with their walking frames and their sticks, they stood in a circle round Heckie and Mrs Winneypeg. They were frail and tottery, but there were a lot of them.

'Well, I do dare. Why can't Major Holden have some boot polish when he's paid you thousands of pounds? Why did you take away Miss Merrick's window-box? And where is Mr Sam's parrot, answer me that?'

'Why you ... you disgusting old woman. I'll have

you put away! I'll have you put in a loony bin. I'll ring the hospital and tell them to come with a strait-jacket.'

This threat had always worked before, but Miss Smith only laughed. 'Try it! Just you try it!'

Mrs Winneypeg blinked because Miss Smith seemed taller somehow and her voice had changed. But she moved forward and grabbed Heckie's arm.

And now Heckie had her. Her own free arm came round Mrs Winneypeg's fat throat. She kicked off her slipper and her toe curled and throbbed with the power that came from it. Mrs Winneypeg was scared now, she wanted to get away, but she was caught in a ring of old people. If she pushed through, someone would probably keel over and die and that meant doctors and people asking questions. And Heckie's grip was tightening. Her knuckle glowed like a ring of flame!

'Sploosh!' spluttered Mrs Winneypeg. 'Shluroop . . . *Oink*!'

And then it was over! At the last minute, Heckie had known exactly what would turn out best. And as they saw what had happened, there appeared on the faces of the old people a look of wonder, and one by one, their wrinkled faces broke into smiles.

But of course no one believed them afterwards. When Mrs Winneypeg had been gone a few days and the police came, and the inspectors from the council, no one believed a bunch of old people when they explained what had happened. Old people have fancies, everyone knows that. But the inspectors were so shocked by what they found in the Sundown Homes that they closed them then and there and moved the residents to council homes where they were properly cared for and had plenty to do. Miss Merrick was given a little bit of garden and Major Holden was put in charge of all the shoe cleaning, not just his own, so that everybody looked smart. And Sam's parrot stopped saying: 'Where's Sam?' and said some other things instead – things it is better not to mention because he'd been at sea with Sam for many years and had picked up some very fruity oaths.

But still no one believed the old ladies and the old gentlemen. Not even when a brand new warthog turned up in the Wellbridge Zoo – a warthog with a greedy snout and blue eyes and a way of banging its back parts furiously against the sides of the cage. Not even then.

Chapter Eight

A new statue had appeared in Kidchester Town Park. It was made of marble and very lifelike. You could almost feel the hair on its moustache and the waxy blobs inside its ears.

The council thought that the statue had been put up by the Lord Mayor and the Lord Mayor thought it had been put up by some ladies who called themselves the Friends of Kidchester and wanted to make their town a beautiful place.

But the statue hadn't been put up by any of these people. It had been dragged there in the middle of the night by the stone witch, Dora Mayberry, who had been Heckie's friend.

Dora had found a nice garden gnome business in Kidchester which was about thirty miles from Wellbridge. She made dwarves and fairies and mermaids for people to put round their garden ponds, and in her spare time she tried to Do Good because that was what she and Heckie said that they would do. When she turned Henry Hartington to marble and put him in the park, she was certainly making the world a better place. She had heard Henry's wife scream night after night while he beat her, and seen his children run out of their house with awful bruises, and when she met him rolling home from

51

the pub, she had simply looked at him in a certain way and that was that.

But she was lonely. She missed Heckie all the time. Dora was shy – she was apt to grunt rather than speak and this made it difficult to make new friends. Far from having a bontebok for a familiar, Dora didn't have a familiar at all. What she did have was a ghost: a miserable, wispy thing which had come with the old wardrobe Dora had bought to hang her clothes in. The ghost was a tree spirit who had stayed in her tree when the woodmen came with their axes, and floated about between the coathangers, begging Dora not to chop down the wardrobe.

'I wonder if I should write to Heckie,' said Dora to herself as she lowered a soya sausage into boiling water for her supper. 'But why doesn't *she* write to me?'

Then she went out to the shed to feed her hat. She too had gathered up the snakes that hissed and slithered on the lawn after the quarrel and brought them with her to her new home. But the hat was really the only pet that Dora had so she was feeding it too much and it was getting fat. The Black Mamba was like a barrel – soon it would be impossible to tie it into a bow.

Oh dear, thought Dora, nothing seems to be going right.

There was plenty to do in Kidchester. She had plans for Dr Franklin who kept twelve dogs in the basement of his laboratory and was doing the most horrible experiments with them. Not experiments to test new medicines, just experiments to test face creams for silly women who were afraid of getting old. Dr Franklin would look nice in granite and she knew exactly where she was going to put him: by the fountain in the shopping centre so that the children could climb on him and the pigeons would have somewhere to sit.

But nothing is much fun if you are lonely, not even Doing Good – and when poor Dora got back to the kitchen, the saucepan had boiled dry and the sausage had exploded in a most unpleasant way.

Should I move to Wellbridge in secret? thought Dora, scraping the sausage into the dustbin. Perhaps if we met by accident, Heckie and I would fall into each other's arms? But if she cut me dead, I couldn't bear it.

And poor Dora stood rubbing her nose, not knowing what to do.

Chapter Nine

Warthogs are not beautiful, with their hairy grey bodies and messy snouts, but the new warthog which had arrived in Wellbridge Zoo was very popular. Lots of people came and watched it snort and snuffle and wallow in its trough, and the way it ignored the other warthog in the cage, barging into him as though he wasn't there, made everybody laugh. Perhaps it was the mysterious way the animal had arrived, sent by an unknown person as a gift to the zoo, that made people so interested. It had turned up in the middle of the night with a label round its neck which said MY NAME IS WINNIE. But whatever the reason, it certainly pulled in the crowds.

The dragworm, meanwhile, settled down happily in Heckie's shop. Everyone made a fuss of him, even the wizards and witches who had sneered, but he was not at all conceited. What he liked best was a quiet life, sleeping in his basket, going for careful walks with enough time to think about which of his legs was which – and having baths. Because of having been a duck, the dragworm loved to be in the water, and he was never happier than when he was sitting in Heckie's bathtub with Sumi washing his hair and Daniel scrubbing his back.

Heckie was still hoping that he would learn to

talk. Familiars often do and it is a great comfort to witches having someone to speak to when they are alone. But though he understood so much of what was said to him, the dragworm didn't open his mouth except to smile or yawn . . . or eat.

The dragworm was very fond of eating and what he ate (because he was, after all, a dragon) were princesses. Not real ones, of course; they would have been too big and anyway there weren't any in Wellbridge, but princesses made out of gingerbread which the children baked for him in Heckie's oven.

And it was a batch of these princesses which led Heckie to a man called Ralph Ticker who must have been about the nastiest person in the world.

Heckie wasn't after Ralph Ticker, she didn't even know he existed; she was after a mugger who had broken the skull of an old lady in a back lane and snatched her handbag. Heckie had decided to turn him into an okapi which is a beautiful animal halfway between a zebra and a giraffe. Wellbridge Zoo didn't have one, and she thought it would be nice if they did, so she spent the evenings tottering through the back alleyways of Wellbridge with a handbag full of money, waiting for the mugger to come, but so far he hadn't.

It was half-term. This was usually a bad time for Daniel. Sumi's aunts and uncles came to visit and she went on outings with her cousins, and Joe spent his time with his father in the zoo. Up to now, Daniel had dreaded the holidays which meant being alone in the tall, gloomy house while his parents went on going to the university.

But now it was Daniel who was the lucky one

55

because he could spend all his time in Heckie's shop. And it was Daniel who went to the market to buy half a dozen eggs, and Daniel who baked the princesses for the dragworm's supper.

He was whistling as he took the baking tray out of the oven and put in the currants for the princesses's eyes and the slithers of glacé cherries for their mouths. They had come out beautifully, with their crowns scarcely wonky at all, and as soon as they were cool enough, he scooped one out and put it on the dragworm's plate.

The dragworm bounded out of his basket; he put his snout down on the plate. Then he lifted his head and gave Daniel a look. And what the look said was: 'What exactly *is* this rubbish?'

Daniel was annoyed. 'They're absolutely fresh. I baked them myself. Now please eat up and don't make a fuss.'

He held the princess up to the dragworm's nose. The dragworm closed his eyes and shuddered. Then he turned his back on Daniel and climbed back into his basket.

It was at this moment that Heckie came back. She was not in a good temper because as she had been hovering in a dark lane, hoping for the mugger, a kind policeman had come and insisted on seeing her home.

'The dragworm's off his food. He won't eat his princess.' Daniel was upset. When your parents have told you for years and years that you're no good, you don't have much confidence, and Daniel was beginning to wonder if he'd done something wrong.

Heckie frowned. 'It doesn't look to me as if he's

sickening for anything. I hope he's not going to turn faddy.'

She broke off a leg and held it under the dragworm's nose. Once again, the dragworm turned away and if he'd been able to speak, there's no doubt that what he would have said was: 'Yuk!'

Daniel now took Heckie into the kitchen and showed her exactly what he had used to bake the gingerbread: the flour, the sugar, the spices, the honey . . .

'And one of these,' he said, holding up the carton which had the words FRESH FARM EGGS stamped on the box. 'But it wasn't rotten. I smelled it carefully.'

There were five eggs left in the carton. Heckie picked up one and carried it to the window. 'Oh dear,' she said. 'Oh dear, oh *dear*!' And then: 'No wonder the poor dear creature wouldn't eat. For a wickedness detector an egg like this would be quite impossible to swallow.'

Daniel was puzzled. 'But surely . . . an egg can't be wicked, can it?'

Heckie was still holding the egg to the light and shaking her head to and fro. 'Not wicked, perhaps. But unhappy . . . full of bad vibes.'

'An *egg*!'

'Why not? An egg is made up of the same things as a person. Everything in nature can suffer – plants . . . seaweed . . . Seaweed can be absolutely *wretched*, you must have seen that.'

So they gave the dragworm some dog biscuits, which he ate, and it was decided that Daniel would

57

go to the market first thing in the morning and ask the stallholder where she got her eggs.

'Because an unhappy egg means an unhappy chicken,' said Heckie, 'and an unhappy chicken we cannot and will not allow.'

The lady who had sold Daniel the fresh farm eggs was helpful. They came, she said, from the Tritlington Poultry Unit, about ten miles north of Wellbridge.

'They weren't bad, I hope?' she said anxiously. 'I've been promised they're not more than two days old.'

Daniel said, no, they weren't bad, not like that.

Two hours later, he got off the local train at Tritlington. It was eleven o'clock in the morning and the little station was almost empty. He asked the way to the poultry unit and was directed down a footpath which ran across two fields, and over the river, to some low, corrugated iron buildings.

'But he won't thank you for going there,' the station-master told Daniel.

'Who won't?' asked Daniel.

'Mr Ticker. The owner. Keeps himself to himself, does Mr Ticker.'

As Daniel made his way down the path, he wondered if he had been wise to come alone. But both Sumi and Joe were helping out at home, and anyway what was the use of being a Wickedness Hunter if you didn't *do* anything?

Mr Ticker's poultry unit was surprisingly large. There were two buildings, each of which looked more like an aircraft hangar or a railway shed than a farm. A high fence surrounded the area and there were notices saying: KEEP OUT and TRESPAS-SERS WILL BE PROSECUTED. Daniel's heart was beating rather fast, but he told himself not to be silly. Mr Ticker was only a chicken farmer; what could he do to him?

Daniel reached the door of the first shed. There was nobody to be seen: the high door was bolted and barred and above it was another notice saying NO ENTRY.

He walked over to the second building. Here the door was open a crack. He slipped inside.

The light was poor and at first, mercifully, Daniel could scarcely see. Only the smell hit him instantly: a truly awful smell of sickness and rottenness and decay.

Then came the sounds: half-strangled cries, desperate squawks . . .

But now his eyes were becoming used to the gloom. He could make out rows and rows of wire cages piled from floor to ceiling on either side of narrow concrete corridors that seemed to stretch away for miles.

And he could see what was inside the cages. Not one chicken, but two, packed so close together that they could hardly turn their heads or move. Unspeak-able things were happening in those cages. In one, a bird had caught its throat in the wire and choked; in another, a chicken driven mad by overcrowding was trying to peck out its neighbour's eyes. There were cages in which one bird lay dead while the other was pressed against its corpse. And yet somehow, unbelievably, the wretched creatures went on laying eggs – large brown eggs which rolled on to the shelf below, ready to be driven to Wellbridge Market and make Ralph Ticker rich.

Daniel was turning back, knowing he'd be sick if he stayed any longer, when he heard voices at the far end of the shed.

'There's another seventeen birds died in the night, Mr Ticker.'

'Well, mince 'em up, feed them to the rest and burn the feathers out at the back.'

'I don't like to, sir. People have been complaining about the smell. If they call the RSPCA . . .'

'They won't.' And then: 'Who's that up there? Why, it's a bloomin' kid!'

Daniel tried to run for the entrance, but it was too late. Mr Ticker pulled down a switch and the building was flooded with light. There was wild clucking from the hens and then the chicken farmer, followed by his assistant, came running up the aisle. Then a hand banged down on Daniel's shoulder and Mr Ticker's red face, with its bulbous nose, was thrust into the boy's.

'What the *devil* are you doing in here?'

'I was . . . just . . . looking.' Mr Ticker was shaking him so hard that Daniel could scarcely get out the words.

'Did you see the notice? Did you see where it says KEEP OUT?' With each question he shook Daniel again. 'You were snooping, weren't you? You were spying. Well, let me tell you, if you say one word about this place to anyone, I'll get you. I'll get your mother too. I've got people everywhere. People who throw acid, people with guns . . . Got it?'

He pushed Daniel forward and the boy stumbled out and ran over the bridge of wooden planks, across the fields ... ran, panting, for the safety of the station.

And Ralph Ticker looked after him with narrowed eyes.

'It's no good, sir,' said the assistant when Daniel was out of sight. 'Even if the kid keeps quiet, they're beginning to talk in the village.'

Ticker said nothing. Twice before, the inspectors of the RSPCA, those snooping Do-Gooders, had closed down his chicken farms. Once in Cornwall, once in Yorkshire – and the second time he'd been fined two hundred pounds. But what was two hundred pounds – chicken feed, thought Ticker, grinning at his own joke. Each time he'd made a whopping profit before they got wise to him.

'Time to move on, Bert,' he said. 'Scotland this time, I think. You know what to do.'

'But, Mr Ticker, there's four thousand chickens here. I can't chop the heads off—'

'Oh, I think you can, Bert. Yes, really I think you can.'

'You've got to do something,' said Daniel, trying not to cry into the 'nice cup of tea' which Heckie had brewed him. 'You've got to turn him into a chicken himself and force him into one of those cages and—'

'Now, Daniel,' said Heckie severely, 'how many times have I told you that the second someone becomes a chicken he is not a wicked chicken, he is a chicken who needs only the best? And anyway, the zoo doesn't want a chicken, what the zoo wants is an okapi. Now drink up and leave everything to me.'

The next day, without saying anything to the children, Heckie called the wizards and witches to a meeting. She had made a map of the Tritlington Poultry Unit from Daniel's description and was feeling important, like Napoleon.

'Now you all understand exactly what you have to do?' she asked.

'I'm to flush him out of the building,' said the cheese wizard gloomily. He was not looking forward at all to changing Mr Ticker into an okapi. He had never seen an okapi and didn't know if he would like it if he did, and he couldn't remember a single spell for flushing anybody out of anything at all.

'And I'm to lure him into the field with my beauty,' said Madame Rosalia, fluttering her false eyelashes which were made of spider's legs.

Heckie frowned. 'I didn't say anything about luring. What I said was, I want him in the field in front of the shed because I shall need space to work in. Boris will take you all down in the van and park it across the drive so that Ticker can't escape in his car. And you, Frieda, must stop him crossing the bridge. If he makes a dash for the station, we're done for.'

'How?' said the garden witch. 'How do I stop him?'

'How? Good heavens, woman, you're a witch. Root him to the ground. Wrap his legs in ivy. Just stop him!'

Frieda scratched her head and Heckie reached

62

irritably for the garden shears. Really, having to deal with witches of such poor quality was hard.

'But what about you?' asked Madame Rosalia. 'How are you going to get there?'

Heckie simpered. 'I shall descend from On High!'

'Eh?'

'I shall float down in one of Boris's hot air balloons,' said Heckie, waving a hand at the mechanical wizard and feeling more like Napoleon than ever. 'And remember, not a word to the children till it's all over. We wizards and witches may be bullet-proof, but not the children.'

Nobody liked the sound of this at all. It was so long since any of them had done any proper magic that they had no idea whether they were bullet-proof or not.

But the cheese wizard had other worries too. 'Do they bite?' he asked, as he shuffled with the others to the door.

'Do what bite?'

'Those okapi things. I just wondered.'

Ralph Ticker was standing by the great hole he'd bulldozed the day before on the waste ground behind the sheds. He was waiting for Bert to come and chop off the heads of the birds and bury them. Once the hole was covered, there'd be nothing to show those snoopy RSPCA people that there'd ever been hens in the place, and he'd be safely away over the border.

Only where was Bert? He was late. Ticker's Porsche was parked in the drive, his case was packed – but he certainly wasn't going to kill four thousand chickens by himself.

What Ralph Ticker didn't know was that Bert had already done a bunk. He was sick of cutting the heads off chickens for peanuts and he was sick of Ticker. While his employer waited by the death pit, Bert was on the pier at Brighton, playing the fruit-machines.

The wizards and witches, meanwhile, were driving down to Tritlington. It was an uncomfortable journey. They had to sit crowded together on the bench seat in the front because the van had been got ready for the okapi, with padding on the walls and lots of straw. Boris, who had an unhappy nature like most Russians, was worried about Heckie's hot air balloon. She had asked for a blue one to match the sky and he'd let her have it before he remembered that that was the one he'd been doing experiments on. Boris had always been sure one could invent a hot air balloon that flew on the hot air talked by politicians, but so far he hadn't managed it – and now he couldn't remember whether he'd put enough fuel back in the machine.

By the time they reached the poultry unit, everyone was feeling ill-tempered and car-sick. As for Mr Gurgle, he wasn't just feeling sick, he was feeling extremely frightened. But he had said he would flush Mr Ticker out of the poultry shed, and flush he would. Trying desperately to remember some useful spells, Mr Gurgle crept towards the door.

'Coo-ee!' he called. 'I see you!'

But he didn't, at first, see anything. He was very short-sighted and the shed was almost dark. Groping his way forward, he felt for his spectacles and put them on – but this was a mistake. Now he *could* see.

Mr Gurgle was not fond of chickens and had thought he didn't mind what happened to them, but he was wrong. As he reeled from cage to cage, his stomach heaved and sweat broke out on his forehead. Stumbling on, his foot hit a zinc bucket with a crack like a pistol shot – and a large black rat, carrying a chewed chicken leg, scurried across his path.

It was too much. Mr Gurgle gave a cry of terror and fainted clean away.

After this, things happened quickly, but not exactly the way Heckie had planned.

Ralph Ticker heard the pistol shot, rushed into the shed – and saw a dead man! A gang fighting it out in his buildings! White with fear, he ran to the entrance, meaning to make a dash for his car. But a van was slewed across the road and in it, a man with a long, cruel face. Ticker doubled back – and straight into the arms of a ghastly gangster's moll!

'Come into the field, you dear man,' leered Madame Rosalia. She fluttered her eyelashes so hard that they came off, and the chicken farmer, seeing what he thought was a Black Widow Spider on his trousers, shrieked and bolted for the bridge.

'You can't come by! Not here you can't!'

Ticker stopped dead. A talking bush. A bush with a leafy top, but two fat pink legs – legs which ended in large green Wellington boots. But if Ticker was terrified of a bush in wellies, he was even more frightened of the gangsters behind him. He pushed the bush violently to one side and set off across the bridge.

The station was ahead now, and safety.

Only what was that thing above him? A hot air balloon – and coming down very fast. Dangerously fast. It was going to land on top of him!

Ticker crouched down on the planks, trying to cover his head with his hands. And then, just as it seemed certain that he would be squashed flat, the balloon veered to one side – and landed with a gigantic splash in the water!

'Ha, ha, ha!' laughed Ticker, forgetting to run. He was the sort of man who loved to see people in trouble.

But even as he leant over and jeered, something was coming up behind him. A bush in boots, which now lifted one leg and kicked him very hard on the backside.

'Whoosh! Phlup! Guggle!' spluttered the chicken farmer as he landed in the deep and icy water.

And then a voice, close by, in the river. A kind voice like a nice nannie's. 'Don't worry,' it said. 'I'll help you. I'll hold you. Just keep calm because I'm swimming right up to you and I'm going to hold you *very tight*!'

The journey back was not a happy one. Mr Gurgle still felt faint and was lying down in the straw they had put down for the okapi. Boris was full of gloom and guilt because of what had happened to the air balloon, and Frieda's left foot was cold.

'All right, that's *enough*,' snapped Heckie. She was soaking wet, but what she was worrying about was what was in Frieda's Wellington boot which she was holding carefully on her lap. She had filled it to the brim with water, but even the best wellies leak a little, and if the poor dear fish that swam inside it should dry out and die before they reached Wellbridge, she would never forgive herself. 'So Frieda's foot is cold, so Rosalia's lost her eyelashes, so you wanted an okapi. I've told you, I can't go struggling about in the water with a kind of giraffe. They're poor swimmers, giraffes – everyone says so.'

'We understand that,' said Madame Rosalia. 'No one's making a fuss because you turned Mr Ticker into a fish. What we don't understand is why you didn't leave him where he was.'

'I told you why,' said Heckie irritably. 'Because the river's polluted. No fish could last in it for more than a couple of days.'

'Well, I can't see that it matters. After what he did to those chickens . . .'

Heckie opened her mouth and shut it again. She was absolutely sick of explaining to people that the second someone was a fish, he was not a wicked fish or a fish who had tortured chickens, he was simply a fish.

Everything had gone well, really. She had phoned the RSPCA and they'd promised to send some men at once to see to the hens, and Ralph Ticker would never harm a living thing again. But it wasn't much fun sharing adventures with these moaners and grumblers. If she'd had her old friend with her, how different it would all have been!

'Oh, where are you, Dora?' sighed Heckie, clutching her watery boot.

Chapter Ten

Dora was sitting on an upturned chamberpot in the back of a swaying furniture lorry. Round her were all the things she had brought from Kidchester: her bed, her kitchen table and chairs, her work bench and her tools.

She had decided to move to the outskirts of Wellbridge, where a nice garden statue business had come up for sale, and she was doing it in secret. She hadn't said a word to Heckie or to anyone she knew. After all, it might be that Heckie was going to be cross with her for ever. On the other hand, if they lived in the same city, even at opposite ends of it, they just could meet by accident and then . . .

The lorry lurched round the corner and Dora clutched the metal jam pan which contained her hat. The hat wasn't well at all – the overfeeding had caused the snakes to start shedding their skins. If she wore it now, people would think she had the most awful dandruff.

'Should I put it on a diet?' wondered poor Dora as the lorry ground up the hill past Wellbridge prison. But what sort of a diet was best for hats? It was Heckie who knew about animals. 'Come to that, I ought to go on a diet myself.'

It was true that Dora, who had never been thin, was now definitely overweight. People who are lonely often eat too much and Dora had really been stuffing herself. Muscles, of course, are important for stonework, but fat is another thing.

Nothing had gone well for the stone witch in Kidchester. She'd managed to do some good all right: Dr Franklin, the one who'd done the awful experiments on dogs, really did look very nice by the fountain in the middle of the shopping centre, and she'd found a comfortable spot for a swindler who'd gone off with the life savings of a lot of poor people. He stood between two pillars in front of the Pensions Office, where the starlings were enjoying him. But Kidchester wasn't pretty like Wellbridge . . .

No, I'm lying, thought Dora. It's because I miss Heckie that I'm moving. It's because I miss my friend.

They bumped over some old tram lines and from the wardrobe, pushed against one wall, there came a worried bleat.

'Don't chop down the wardrobe,' begged the ghost. 'Don't chop—'

'I'm not *going* to chop it down!' said Dora, for the hundredth time. 'It's trees they chop down and *you're not in a tree!*'

They had passed the prison and the football ground. Not much further to go . . .

Well, I've done it now, thought Dora. And even if I don't meet Heckie, I can still do some good here. There must be lots of wicked people left in Wellbridge even after Heckie's finished with the place. But oh, if only I met her. If only we became friends again!

The lorry stopped at the lights. Just a few metres away, facing in the other direction, was a blue van with sealed windows. Inside it sat Heckie, holding the Wellington boot with the fish in it.

Oh, if only Dora was here, she was thinking just at that moment. If only I had her to help me instead of these useless moaners.

Then the lights changed. The vans moved forward – and neither of the witches knew how close to each other they had been.

Chapter Eleven

Daniel never quarrelled with Sumi. She was so gentle and so sensible that he wouldn't have known how to begin. But after Ralph Ticker was changed, they came as close to quarrelling as they had ever done.

'Well, I still don't think it's right,' she said. 'I think it's dangerous changing people into animals and I don't think Heckie should do it.'

They were in her parents' grocery shop, parcelling up black-eyed beans, and Daniel was so cross he let the beans spill from his shovel way past the correct weight.

'I suppose you think it's right to torture four thousand chickens and then plan to murder them in cold blood.'

'No, I don't. You know I don't. But he could have been sent to prison and—'

'He couldn't,' said Daniel angrily. 'The RSPCA kept trying and all he got was a measly fine. And anyway, I don't see that it's so terrible being an unusual fish. Being an ordinary fish might be, but he isn't. People have been coming from all over the country to find out what he is, and I should think it's very exciting.'

This was true. The fish that Heckie had left in a tank by the West Gate of the zoo labelled: ANOTHER

PRESENT FROM A WELL WISHER had really brought the scientists running.

Sumi didn't say any more. She knew how Daniel felt about Heckie, and she knew why. If you had a mother who had written seven books about The Meaning of Meaning and had no time for you, you might well turn to a warm-hearted witch for the love you didn't get at home.

And quite soon they had something more to worry them than whether Ralph Ticker did, or did not, like being an unusual fish.

Although she was so busy Doing Good, Heckie never forgot her pet shop. Since she knew so much about animals, all the rabbits and guinea pigs she sold were healthy, so she made quite a lot of money. At first she had kept this money in her mattress, but she was worried that the mice who lived there would nibble it and this would be bad for them.

'Mice have very tender stomachs,' she told the children. 'Not everyone knows that, but it's true.'

So she went to the bank and signed a lot of papers and after that, every Friday afternoon, she paid in her takings.

Heckie liked going to the bank. She enjoyed chatting with the other shopkeepers and the people in the queue. It made her feel ordinary and that is a thing that witches do not often feel.

On the particular Friday when something unexpected happened at the bank, Heckie found herself standing beside a tall and very distinguished-looking man with a Roman nose, dark eyes set very close together, and a little beard like goats have. He wore a black coat with a fur collar and carried an ivory cane, and Heckie thought she had never seen anyone more handsome. She didn't approve of the fur collar, but there was always the hope that the raccoon it was made of had died in his sleep, and no one is perfect. So she gave him a beaming smile, showing all her large and sticking out teeth, and when he got to the counter, she listened carefully as the clerk said: 'Good morning, Mr Knacksap,' and thought what an unusual name Knacksap was and how well it suited him.

Mr Knacksap wasn't putting money into the bank, he was taking it out, and as she waited, she squinted over his shoulder at his cheque-book and saw that his initial was L. Did that stand for Lucien or Lancelot or Lovelace? Such an elegant man was sure to have an unusual name.

Mr Knacksap took his money and Heckie smiled at him again, but he didn't smile back. Then it was her turn. She had just put her paying-in book down on the counter, when the door burst open and a masked man rushed into the bank, waving a sawn-off shotgun.

'Everybody on the floor!' he shouted to the people in the queue.

Everybody got down at once, even Heckie who had become very excited. She had seen bank robbers on the telly, but never in real life. This one looked a bit thin and she thought he might have a hungry wife and children at home, or perhaps he was going to give the money to the poor like Robin Hood.

'Anyone who moves, gets it,' the robber went on, and strode to the counter. Outside, Heckie could see a van parked alongside the kerb, and a fierce-looking man inside. The getaway car! Really, it was just like the telly!

Mr Knacksap, lying on the floor beside Heckie, did not seem to be excited at all. He looked quite green and his beautiful bowler hat had rolled away. Heckie wanted to comfort him, but she thought it was best to keep quiet till the robber had gone.

'Come on, hand it over. The lot! And hurry!' barked the robber.

Heckie squinted up and saw a little fat cashier run up to the grille with wads of bank-notes, and start pushing them through. 'Don't shoot!' he kept saying, 'Don't shoot!' The other cashiers were huddled together at the back – all except one girl. A very young girl with long blonde hair who looked as though she had only just left school. She was edging her way carefully forward to where the alarm bell was. She had almost reached it . . .

The next second there was a blast from the shotgun, a scream . . . and the blonde girl fell across her desk with blood streaming from her shoulder.

Up to now, Heckie had just been interested. Of course it was wrong to rob banks, but after all if there was one thing banks had plenty of, it was money.

But now she lost her temper. Her eyes narrowed, her knuckle throbbed, she kicked off her shoe. The robber, meanwhile, had turned away from the counter. He felt in his pocket and lobbed a metal canister on to the floor where the people were lying. It was a smoke bomb, and as the choking fumes spread through the room, he made for the door.

At least he started off. But a hand had fastened round his ankle . . . a hand like a steel trap. He raised his gun, ready to shoot . . . but he didn't seem to have arms any more . . . he didn't seem to have . . . anything.

No one else saw. As they groped and struggled to the exit, they thought that the robber had escaped. But Mr Knacksap, lying beside Heckie, had seen. He had seen the robber's shape become dim . . . become wavery . . . shrink almost to nothing. And then re-form in the shape of a small brown mouse which scampered over to the wall panelling – and was gone!

Mr Knacksap's Christian name was not Lancelot or Lucien, it was Lionel, and the raccoon on his collar had not died in its sleep because Mr Knacksap was a furrier. He owned a shop in Market Square where he sold fur coats and he had a workshop in the basement and a store-room where he kept the skins of dead animals ready to be made up into coats or sold to other furriers at a profit.

The shop was called Knacksap and Knacksap, but the first Knacksap, who had been Mr Knacksap's father, was now dead. The old man had been a good craftsman and had made very beautiful coats which ladies had paid good money for, because in those days people did not think it was cruel to kill an animal simply for its skin and there were not so many other ways of keeping warm. But his son, Lionel Knacksap, was not a good craftsman. His coats were badly made, and at the time he took over, people were beginning to ask annoying questions before they bought fur coats. They wanted to know how the animals had been killed – had they suffered at all, and were they rare; because if so they didn't want to wear them.

So Mr Knacksap found himself getting poorer and poorer, and as he was a man who had expensive tastes, he didn't like this at all. In the basement he had kept two ladies who made coats for him. Now he sacked them and started doing business with very dubious people. These were men who came at night and talked to him in the shop with the shutters closed and they wanted him to get skins for them that were no longer allowed to be sold in England: the skins of Sumatran tigers or jaguars from the Amazon – beautiful animals that were almost extinct. They were willing to pay thousands of pounds for pelts like that because there were always vain or ridiculous people who would do anything to lie on a tiger skin or wear a coat like no other in the world. But it wasn't easy to get hold of such skins. Mr Knacksap was finding it very hard to supply his customers and he had been getting into debt.

And then he saw Heckie fasten her hands round the bank robber's ankle and realized that he had been lying next to a very powerful witch. A witch who could change people into animals. But any animal? Mr Knacksap meant to find out.

Chapter Twelve

Heckie was worrying about the mouse. Suppose they set mouse-traps in the bank and it got caught?

'Or killed,' she said, looking desperate. 'Imagine it! An animal I produced, lying dead! I had no time to think, you see, but that's no excuse.'

'I'm sure they don't use traps,' said Daniel. 'I've never seen a mouse-trap in a bank.'

'It'll be perfectly happy behind the panelling, eating the crumbs from the cashier's sandwiches,' said Sumi.

But it was hard to comfort Heckie. Dora had known how to do it; she'd just told Heckie to shut up and not be so daft, but the children couldn't do that, and Heckie went on pacing up and down and saying that if anybody she'd changed into an animal got hurt, she'd never know another moment's happiness again.

'Why don't we take the dragworm for a walk?' said Joe, who was used to dealing with gorillas when they went over the top. 'Then you can go to the bank and *ask* about mouse-traps.'

Heckie thought this was a good idea – she wanted to enquire anyway about the girl who'd been shot in the shoulder. As for the dragworm, he only had to hear the word 'walk' and he was already inside the tartan shopping basket on wheels. It fitted him just like a house with a roof and he was never happier than when he was rattling and bumping through the streets of Wellbridge.

When they had gone, Heckie went to change her batskin robe for something more suitable, but she never got to the bank, for just then the doorbell rang.

Out in the hall, holding a bunch of flowers, stood the tall, distinguished man that Heckie had seen in the bank.

'Forgive me for calling,' he said. 'My name is Knacksap. Lionel Knacksap. May I come in?'

Mr Knacksap was wearing his dark coat with the raccoon collar and his bowler hat, and smelled strongly of a toilet water called Male.

'Yes, please do.' Heckie was quite overcome. 'I was just going to . . . change.'

'You look delightful as you are,' said Mr Knacksap in an oily voice, and handed her the flowers which he had stolen from the garden of an old lady who was blind. 'I came to congratulate you. I saw, you see. I saw what you did in the bank.' And as Heckie frowned: 'But don't worry, Miss . . . er . . . Tenbury-Smith. Your secret is safe with me.'

Heckie now offered him a cup of tea. This time she put in three tea-bags because she had never been alone before with such a handsome gentleman, but Mr Knacksap said that was just how he liked it.

'Tell me,' he said, resting his cup genteelly on his knee. 'Can you turn people into any kind of animal? Or only little things like mice?'

'Oh, yes, pretty well any animal,' said Heckie,

78

looking modest. 'But of course I have to think of what will happen to it afterwards.'

Mr Knacksap's eyes glittered with excitement. 'Could you, for example, could you . . . say . . . turn someone into a tiger? A large tiger?'

Heckie nodded. 'I'd have to make sure they wanted a tiger in the zoo.'

She then went on to tell the furrier of her plans for making Wellbridge a better place. 'I have such wonderful helpers. Wizards and witches – and children. The children in particular! And a most wonderful familiar – a dragworm. He's just out for a walk, but you must meet him. He's a wickedness detector and he can sniff out even the tiniest bit of evil!'

Mr Knacksap didn't like the sound of that at all. 'I'm afraid I'm completely allergic to dragons . . . and . . . er, worms. What I mean is, I can't bear to be in the same room. When I was small, I had asthma, you see; I couldn't get my breath, and the doctors told me that if I went near anything like . . . the thing you have described, I would simply choke to death.'

Heckie was very disappointed. She had set her heart on showing the dragworm to this attractive man. But of course the idea of Lionel Knacksap choking to death was too horrible to think about.

Mr Knacksap, in the meantime, was doing sums in his head. A tiger skin fetched over two thousand pounds. Even after he'd paid someone to kill and skin the beast, there'd be a nice profit. And plenty more where that came from: ocelots, jaguars, lynx . . . All he had to do was butter up this frumpy witch.

'Dear Miss Tenbury-Smith—'

'Heckie. Please call me Heckie.'

Mr Knacksap gulped. 'Dear Heckie – I wonder if you would care to have dinner with me next Saturday? At the Trocadero at eight o'clock?'

'How do I look?' asked Heckie, and Sumi and Daniel said she looked very nice.

This was true. Heckie had gone to Madame Rosalia for advice about what to wear for her night out with the furrier, but she had made it clear that she wanted to be tastefully dressed.

'I may be a witch,' Heckie had said to Madame Rosalia, 'but I am also a woman.'

So she had decided not to wear black whiskers on her chin, or a blue tooth, and just three blackheads – more enlarged pores, really – on the end of her nose. And her dress was tasteful too – a black sheath embroidered all over with small green toads.

'My shoes pinch,' said Heckie, but there was nothing to be done about that. Heckie's Toe of Transformation always hurt when she bought new shoes.

Mr Knacksap had booked a table by the window and ordered a three-course meal. He hated spending money, but he knew that if he was going to get the witch to do what he wanted, he'd have to make a splash for once. The Trocadero was very smart, with gleaming white tablecloths and a man playing sloppy music on the piano, but the dinner didn't get off to a very good start.

The trouble began with a beetle that was crawling

about in the centre of a rose in a cut glass vase on the table. Heckie thought the beetle did not look well and she asked the waiter if he'd mind putting it out in the garden, if possible near a cowpat.

'It's a dung beetle, you see,' she told him, 'so it really cannot be happy on this rose.'

Then the starter came and it was shrimps in mayonnaise.

'Is there anything wrong?' asked Mr Knacksap. 'They look nice and pink to me.'

'Yes,' said Heckie faintly. 'But you see, shrimps aren't meant to be pink. They're meant to be a sort of grey. If they're pink they're dead.'

'Well, we could hardly eat them if they weren't,' said Mr Knacksap, but he had to keep on the right side of Heckie so he sent them back and ordered vegetable soup.

After the shrimps came some meat in a brown sauce and when Heckie saw it, she turned quite pale.

'*Now* what's the matter?' asked Mr Knacksap. 'Those are pheasant breasts done in wine.'

'I know they're pheasant breasts,' said Heckie faintly. 'But you see eating them would be . . . well, like eating a friend.' And as Mr Knacksap frowned at her: 'You must know what I mean. Think of a friend of yours. Any friend.'

Mr Knacksap tried to think of a friend he had had. 'There was a boy called Marvin Minor at my prep school. He used to lend me his roller skates.'

'Well, now you see,' said Heckie. 'Imagine you were served slices of Marvin Minor's chest in wine sauce. How would you feel?'

But even now, Mr Knacksap kept his temper. The

pheasant breasts were taken away and Heckie was given a mushroom omelette instead. And there was no fuss over the pudding. Even Heckie didn't think that caramel custard was like swallowing a friend.

By now they had drunk quite a lot of wine and Mr Knacksap was ready to come to the point.

'I have a favour to ask you,' he said, leaning across the table and fixing Heckie with his piercing eyes. 'A great favour!'

Heckie looked down at the tablecloth and tried to flutter her eyelashes like she had seen Madame Rosalia do. 'Yes?' she said shyly.

'I want you to make a tiger for me. I want you to change the next wicked person you see into a tiger. A male tiger – and large.'

'Well, I will if you like, Lionel,' said Heckie (because she had been told to use his Christian name). 'But are you sure you can manage it? They're tricky things to look after, the big cats.'

'It's not for me personally – I wouldn't ask you anything for myself,' said Mr Knacksap soupily. 'It's for a friend of mine. An aristocrat. A lord.'

'Oh, really?'

Everyone is a bit impressed by lords, and Heckie was no exception.

'Yes. The poor man was left a great castle . . . I don't like to talk about him because he's very shy, but you'd know the name if I told you. But it's in a very bad state – loose tiles on the roof, dry rot, all that kind of thing. So he's started a safari park to bring in the trippers and help him get enough money to do repairs. But what the safari park really needs is a tiger.'

'Well, if you're sure he'd care for it properly.'

'It would live like a prince,' said Mr Knacksap. 'A heated house, a huge enclosure, children to come and photograph it. And my friend would be so happy.'

Heckie stirred her coffee. 'All right, then. Mind you, one can't be absolutely certain with this kind of magic. Sometimes things sort of happen by themselves. There was an animal witch in Germany who kept being overcome by hippopotamuses. Whatever she tried to turn people into, they always came out as hippos.'

Mr Knacksap didn't like the sound of that. No one wore coats made of hippopotamus skins. 'I'm sure that wouldn't happen to you, dear Heckie,' he said. 'You're such a powerful witch. I knew the moment I saw you.'

As soon as he got back to his shop that evening, Mr Knacksap telephoned a man he knew in Manchester. 'Is that you, Ferguson?'

'Yes, it's me.'

'Well, listen; I've got you your tiger skin. A full-grown male.'

'Go on. You're kidding.'

'No, I'm not. I take it the Arkle woman still wants one?'

'You bet she does. She's upped the price to two and a half thousand.'

Gertrude Arkle was married to a chain-store millionaire and had set her heart on a tiger skin to put on her bedroom floor. She wanted to lie on it in silk pyjamas like she had seen film stars do in pictures of the olden days. And the more Mr Arkle told her that she couldn't have one because it was illegal to import them, the more she wanted one.

'All right, then,' said Mr Knacksap. 'I'll give you a call when it's ready.'

Chapter Thirteen

For nearly three weeks after Heckie had dinner with Mr Knacksap at the Trocadero, life went on much as usual. Heckie was still trying to get the dragworm to speak. She told him stories and repeated simple words to him, but though he was always polite and listened to everything she said, it didn't seem as though he was ever going to talk. In other ways, though, he was learning all the time. He could turn the bath tap on now with his front claws, and put in the plug, and he didn't have to think nearly so long about which of his feet was which. Heckie had worried, as the days grew warmer, that he might become unsettled. Chinese dragons usually fly up to heaven in the spring and she would have missed him horribly if he had done so, but he stayed where he was.

Still, things were not quite the same as before and this was because of Mr Knacksap. The furrier never came to the flat because of the dragworm, but the children had seen him in the street and they didn't like what they saw. They thought he looked thoroughly creepy and unreliable and they couldn't understand why Heckie went out with him.

The children weren't the only ones to be worried. The cheese wizard's shop was next door to the furrier's and he knew quite a lot about Mr

Knacksap. Daniel had met him in the street and been asked in to see a Stilton that could walk at least half a metre.

'And it's not maggots, either; it's magic,' said Mr Gurgle, beaming at the cheese as it struggled across the floor. But afterwards he became serious. 'I don't like the way that fellow's paying court to Heckie,' he said. 'He's got a bad name in the trade. Up to his eyebrows in debt – and the way he treated those sewing women who worked for him was a scandal. If she marries him, she'll—'

'Oh, but she couldn't! She *couldn't*!' cried Daniel, looking completely stricken.

'Well, I don't suppose she will. But she's all heart and no head, that witch. Just you keep an eye on her.'

But this was easier said than done. Mr Knacksap was careful always to see Heckie away from the shop. Since he hated spending money, he took her on picnics. Heckie brought the food so it didn't cost him anything, and all he brought was a towel to sit on because he didn't like nature and was fussy about his trousers.

Mr Knacksap realized that it was no good pretending that he wasn't a furrier – after all, his shop was in Market Square for everyone to see. So he told Heckie a lot of lies about the coats he sold.

'That beaver cape in my window was made by a tribe of North American Indians who worship beavers. They sing to them and feed them on pine nuts and take them to sleep with them in their wigwams so that they live for years and years and years. And then when they pass on – the beavers, I mean

86

– the Indians make them into coats so that they won't be forgotten.'

'Oh, Li-Li, that's wonderful,' said Heckie, feasting her eyes on Mr Knacksap as they sat on a rock high above the Wellbridge gas works.

'And the stoats I use come from an organic stoat farm in Sweden. They shave the animals and sew the fur on to canvas so that it looks like a pelt, but it isn't. Only when it's warm, they shave them; no stoat is ever allowed to get chilled.'

So Heckie's last doubts were gone. Not only was Mr Knacksap the handsomest man she had ever seen, but he was kind to animals. But inside, Mr Knacksap was seething. Three weeks and not a sign of a tiger! How long was he supposed to go on buttering up this ridiculous witch?

Sumi had put her three little brothers to bed. She had sung to them and played Three Little Pigs Go To Market with the fat toes of the youngest, and now they were drowsy and quiet.

Down in the shop, her mother was putting the CLOSED sign across the door and her father was emptying the till.

'You're closing early?' she asked in the Punjabi they always spoke when they were alone. It was only eight thirty, and her parents often served customers till late at night.

Her mother nodded. She looked tired and her eyes were swollen.

'Is anything wrong?' Sumi adored her parents and her voice was sharp with anxiety.

'No, no, nothing.' Her mother managed a smile. 'We're just going to have an early night.'

But there was something wrong. Sumi knew from the way her parents went upstairs, walking very close together, their shoulders almost touching. They weren't like the parents of her schoolfriends, kissing and hugging in front of everyone. They were dignified and shy, but tonight they needed to be very close.

Sumi went to bed, but she couldn't sleep. And her mother and father couldn't sleep either. She heard their voices, low and sad, going on and on. After a while she got up and crept to the door. If there was trouble in the family she wanted to know and help.

'Shall we tell Sumi? We'll keep the boys indoors, but she'll have to have protection when she goes to school. I don't want her going out of the house while he's here with his thugs. And we must get metal shutters for the windows.'

'Expensive . . .' Her father sounded worried.

'Expensive? What does that matter? We can borrow. You know what happened to Ved . . . you saw my sister's face when they brought him home, and you talk about expensive!'

Back in her room, Sumi began to shiver. It was a warm night, but she couldn't stop trembling. For she knew what had happened to Ved. She knew what was making her parents so afraid.

Oh, what shall I do? thought Sumi. Whatever shall I do?

Heckie was clearing away her breakfast when Sumi rang the doorbell of the flat. She was pleased to see her – people were always pleased to see Sumi – but worried that she'd be late for school.

'It doesn't matter if I am,' said Sumi – and then Heckie knew that there was something seriously wrong because Sumi really loved school.

'What is it, dear?'

So then Sumi told her. 'A man is coming to Wellbridge; an absolutely terrible man. He's called Max Swinton and he's the leader of something called the White Avengers.'

Heckie frowned. 'Those racist thugs who go round bashing up people?'

'Yes. And it's Swinton that leads them on. He's worse than Hitler. They shout things that don't sound so terrible, like BRITISH FOR THE BRITISH, but by British they only mean people with white skins and they don't care what they do to the . . . others.' She stopped to blow her nose. 'I have this cousin in London. Ved, he's called. He was a violinist – he won a scholarship to music college when he was fifteen. He was coming home alone after a concert when a gang of Swinton's thugs got hold of him. We thought he wouldn't live at first, he was so badly hurt. But he did live. He's alive. Only his hands . . . When they saw the violin, they jumped on his hands. They said wogs shouldn't . . .'

Sumi gulped and groped for her handkerchief, and Heckie put her arms round her and waited till she could go on.

Then she lifted her head and said what she had come to say. 'I told Daniel that I didn't think it was right to turn people into animals, but I've changed my mind. Please, Heckie ... please will you turn Max Swinton into absolutely *anything*.'

Swinton's picture was in the next day's paper. The dragworm wouldn't stay in the same room with it and went to have a bath while Heckie and Daniel studied his face.

'He looks like a pig,' said Daniel.

'No, he doesn't,' said Heckie firmly. 'Pigs may have small eyes, but they are *intelligent* eyes, and if they're fat, it's a firm fatness, not wobbly.'

Swinton was coming to Wellbridge on the following Monday, in a motorcade, to make speeches. The police had broken up Swinton's rallies before; he had even been to prison, but never long enough to keep him and his followers off the streets.

'He's staying at the Queen's Hotel, I see,' said Heckie. 'Didn't you say you had a friend whose mother worked there?'

'Yes, I did. Henry, he's called. He's really nice, and his older brother has just started as a bell-boy. I'm sure he'd help us. Henry's black, I expect he feels just like Sumi does about the Avengers.'

The Queen's Hotel was very grand. It stood on the edge of the park with its pretty flower-beds and statues, and the pond where Heckie had found the duck that didn't want to live. Towers and turrets burst from the roof of the hotel and flags blew in the wind, and there were awnings and waiters rushing about and a whole army of chambermaids.

'So you think Henry can be trusted? That he can keep a secret?'

'Yes, I do.'

'Good. Then I suggest you go and find him straight away and bring him here.'

Mr Knacksap read Heckie's note and his eyes glittered with greed. A tiger at last! He was to arrange for a closed horse box and a driver, and get hold of a wire tunnel of the kind that circus trainers use to lead animals into the ring.

'Because we don't want the poor dear creature getting scared and muddled,' Heckie had written.

Henry's brother was going to meet her in the park at daybreak with the key to Max Swinton's room and a chambermaid's uniform belonging to his mother.

'Then I'll slip into his room with his early morning tea and change him. By great good luck, he's got a downstairs room so you'll be able to park the horse box almost under his window. Remember to have a nice raw steak ready for him. Tigers can get very hungry when they're on the road.'

Oh, yes, the brute would find a steak all right, thought Mr Knacksap. A drugged steak which would knock him out, then a clean shot between the eyes so as to make the smallest possible hole in the pelt – and off to be skinned! Mr Knacksap had even arranged for a man who made pet food to take the carcass!

Two thousand pounds clear! Alone in his shop, the furrier smiled and rubbed his hands.

Heckie was up before it was light, feeling extremely happy. She had enjoyed changing Mrs Winneypeg and the chicken farmer, but in ridding the world of Max Swinton she was doing more good than she had ever done before *and* giving her Li-Li the tiger he wanted so much for his friend!

Daniel was waiting for her at the gates of the park. She had promised he could come just till she met Henry's brother, Clem. But no sooner had Daniel run up to her, than Mr Knacksap came round the corner in his bowler hat and fur-collared coat.

'Lionel! I didn't expect you! Why aren't you with the horse box?'

'I just wanted to see you safely into the hotel, dear,' said the furrier.

But what Mr Knacksap really wanted was to make sure that Heckie didn't change her mind or go all soft. One thing he couldn't be doing with was a hippopotamus.

Daniel wasn't at all pleased to see the furrier, but he had to be polite and together they walked past flower-beds and the pond, and between smooth lawns that were still wet with dew.

Clem had kept his promise. He was waiting by the fountain with the key and the uniform.

'Everything's okay,' he whispered. 'He's in room seventeen like I said.'

Heckie thanked him and they waited while he ran back to the hotel where all the guests still slept. Then they followed him, making their way along a gravel path between neatly clipped hedges.

'Funny, there's a new statue,' said Mr Knacksap, pointing with his cane.

'Yes, there is,' said Daniel.

Heckie had been thinking of the job ahead of her. Now she looked up, stopped, took a step towards the statue . . .

And another . . .

Then she put back her head and screamed.

Daniel reached her first. 'What is it?' he gasped. 'What's the matter?'

But Heckie couldn't speak. She just pointed at the statue with a hand which shook as if she had a dreadful fever.

'It's Dora,' she managed to bring out. 'Dora Mayberry did it. She's betrayed me, she's cheated me! She's done me out of my triumph! This is her work. I'd know it anywhere!'

Daniel went right up to the statue – and then he understood.

It was Max Swinton who stood there, carefully mounted on a marble slab. Max Swinton's mean little eyes, his silly moustache, his fat chin, were all there in stone. His trousers, tight over his straining thighs, his bulging beer belly, the Avenger's badge . . . all were there, for ever and ever, caught in white marble now touched by the first rays of the morning sun.

Chapter Fourteen

The night after she found Max Swinton's statue, Heckie couldn't sleep. She kept thinking how wicked Dora Mayberry had been, snatching the politician from her and doing poor Mr Knacksap out of his tiger. Copying Heckie's hat had been bad enough, but this was far, far worse.

But the more she tried to tell herself how awful Dora had been, the more she kept remembering things from the thirty years that both of them had been at school. The time that Dora had cut her toenails for her because Heckie had hurt her back during chimney landing practice. The way Dora always picked the earwigs out of the Hoover bag when it was her turn to clean the dorm because she knew how it upset Heckie when earwigs were put in the bin. And what a netball player the witch had been!

Was it possible that Dora hadn't meant to upset Heckie? Did she too just think that Max Swinton ought not to be around any longer? And where was Dora? Could she have moved to Wellbridge?

In the morning, as soon as she had fed the animals in the shop and given the dragworm his princess, Heckie went to see Mr Gurgle to ask him if he'd heard anything about the stone witch. The cheese wizard was in a bad mood because his Stilton had developed a limp, but he tried to be helpful.

'I haven't heard anything myself,' he said, 'but Frieda Fennel did say as how a stone-mason's business out in Fetlington has changed hands – that's past the prison, you know. She did say that the quality of work was very high and she was wondering.'

So Heckie went to see the garden witch who was wheeling a single artichoke along in her wheelbarrow, her muscles straining because it was the size of an armchair, and she said, yes, she was almost sure the new owner of the stone-mason's was a witch. There was something about the garden gnomes that was special.

But when Heckie had got the address, she couldn't make up her mind. Suppose Dora was still angry with her? Also, there'd been rather a fuss about Max Swinton since statues, unlike animals, can't run away or be sent to the zoo. Questions were being asked and though no one guessed the truth, there was a lot of puzzlement.

She was still deciding what to do when she met Mr Knacksap for tea at The Copper Kettle.

The furrier had gone off in a rage when he heard that he wasn't getting his tiger, but since then he had done some serious thinking. A witch who could turn people into animals and another witch who could turn people into stone . . . What did that suggest? To Mr Knacksap it suggested riches beyond his dreams, a life of plenty in which he need never work again. The plan he now came up with could only have been worked out by someone half mad with cruelty and greed, but Mr Knacksap was exactly such a man.

So he wrote a little note to Heckie saying he was sorry he had lost his temper, but he'd been so upset at disappointing his friend who was a lord, and inviting Heckie to meet him for tea.

Heckie was terribly pleased to see him and she asked him at once what he thought she should do about Dora Mayberry. 'You see, I do hate to go on quarrelling, but I couldn't bear it if she was unkind to me. What do you think I should do, Li-Li?'

This gave Mr Knacksap just the opening he was looking for. 'I tell you what, my dear,' he said, smiling his gooey smile, 'since you're such a shy and delicate little thing, why don't you let me go? I'll give her your message and tell her you want to be friends and see what she says.'

'Oh, would you, Li-Li? That's so kind of you. So like you. I'll write her a letter and give it to you.'

So Heckie wrote a letter in which she said that while she had been rather cross about Mr Swinton, who was really hers, if Dora really hadn't known what Heckie was going to do, then she was happy to let bygones be bygones. 'Because I have missed you very much, dear Dora,' wrote Heckie, and then she sealed the envelope and gave it to Mr Knacksap to take to her friend.

But what did Mr Knacksap do?

As soon as he was out of sight, he tore the letter into little pieces and threw them away. Not even into a bin because he was a litter lout as well as a creep – just away in the street where the wind blew them all over the place. Then he hailed a taxi and drove to the stone-mason's yard.

Dora Mayberry was in her overalls and Wellington boots, chipping with a chisel at the nose of a Greek hero whom a rich businessman wanted to put in his park. Just as Heckie kept an ordinary pet shop to earn her living in which the rabbits and guinea pigs really were rabbits and guinea pigs and not changed people, so Dora did ordinary stonework for anyone who would pay her and she did it very well. The hero was the kind with a lion skin round his shoulder and a lot of muscles and a club, and Mr Knacksap stood for a while watching before he coughed softly and asked if he was in the presence of Miss Dora Mayberry.

'That's me,' said Dora, nodding, and she wiped her chisel and looked at the handsome man in his dark coat with the raccoon collar and the black hat. 'Come in,' she said, blushing a little because there had been no gentlemen in the Witch Academy and she was very shy.

Mr Knacksap followed her in, his nose twitching with curiosity. So this homely woman could turn a man into stone. Quite a lot of men if need be!

'I've come with a message from a friend of yours. A Miss Hecate Tenbury-Smith.'

'Heckie!' Dora's round little eyes lit up. 'How is she? Tell me about her, please. Oh, I have missed her so!'

For it was true, Dora had not meant to annoy Heckie. Though she had moved back to Wellbridge, hoping to make it up with her friend, she had not dared to go and see her. Suppose Heckie snubbed her? Then she had read about Max Swinton in the paper and become very upset. A man like that shouldn't be allowed to exist, she thought, and when Swinton took a stroll in the park, she'd been ready for him. It had been hard work dragging him to the right spot, mounting him properly, but she'd done it and been proud of her handiwork. In the old days she'd have gone straight to Heckie and shown her what she'd done.

So now she waited eagerly for what Mr Knacksap had to say.

'I'm afraid your friend is absolutely furious with you. In fact you can hardly call Miss Tenbury-Smith your friend. She never wants to see you again.'

'Oh, oh!' Poor Dora put her hand to her mouth and her eyes widened in sorrow and dismay. 'But why? Why?'

'She's very angry with you about Mr Swinton's statue. She was going to change him into a tiger and everything was prepared. But it isn't just that. She feels very bitter about the hat and everything. She sent me to tell you that she never wants to set eyes on you again.'

Poor Dora! She was a solid, well-built woman, but she just seemed to shrink as Mr Knacksap spoke. He went on telling lies for another ten minutes and then he went back to Heckie.

Heckie was waiting for him, her pop eyes bright with hope.

'I'm afraid it's no good, dear,' he said. 'Dora Mayberry never wants to see you again as long as she lives. I won't repeat some of the things she said about you, but they were quite terrible.'

Heckie turned pale with disappointment. She had come down to meet the furrier in the street because the dragworm was at home, and now she leant against a lamp-post, almost as though she might faint.

'Don't be sad, my little prettikins,' said Mr Knacksap, taking her hand. 'Your Li-Li will look after you.'

The horrible man's plan was clear now in his head. He'd been excited at the idea of having one tiger skin to sell, but this . . . If he pulled it off, he'd be the richest furrier in the world!

And he would pull it off. He had one witch in his power. Now he would get the other one too.

And then . . . !

Chapter Fifteen

Mr Knacksap now began to court Heckie seriously. He came to see her on Tuesdays and Thursdays and Saturdays, and on those days Daniel came at tea time to take the dragworm for a walk. He brought her red roses which he stole from the garden of the blind lady, and plain chocolates with hard centres because they were her favourites.

And one afternoon, sitting on the sofa in her cosy flat, he told her that he wanted to change his life.

'I'm tired of living in town among the fumes and the dust,' said Mr Knacksap. 'I want to go and live in the country where the air is clear. In the Lake District, where there are mountains and heather and . . . er . . . lakes. I want to milk cows!' said Mr Knacksap, waving his hand.

'Sheep, dear,' said Heckie. 'It's sheep you have in hill country.'

Mr Knacksap frowned. He did not like to be interrupted and was not quite sure if he wanted to milk sheep.

'Chickens too!' he cried. 'I want to get up at daybreak and look for brown eggs in the straw!'

He fished in the pocket of his jacket and showed Heckie a picture. It was of a pretty whitewashed cottage with a porch, standing in the shelter of a high hill. A stream ran through the garden, with alder trees along its banks, and a dovecote covered in honeysuckle stood by the gate.

'Oh, Li-Li, what a pretty place!'

'It's called Paradise Cottage,' said Mr Knacksap. 'And what I want more than anything in the world is to live there.'

Heckie was silent. When you love somebody it is sad to think that they may go and live a long way away, but she tried to be brave. 'If that's what you want, you must do it, Li-Li. But, oh, I shall miss you.'

Mr Knacksap seized Heckie's hand. 'No, no, dearest Hecate – you don't understand! I want you to come with me. I want us to live there together! I am asking you to marry me!'

In the staffroom of Wellbridge Junior School, they were once again talking about Daniel Trent.

'He's looking thoroughly peaky again,' said the deputy head. 'Just when he seemed so much brighter. I wonder if I ought to have a word with those professors?'

But it wasn't the fault of Daniel's parents that he was unhappy. They did what they had always done. It was Heckie's engagement that had made Daniel so wretched. If she'd just been going to marry Mr Knacksap, it would have been bad enough, but she was going to live miles and miles away in the Lake District. And so soon! Mr Knacksap wanted to have the wedding before the end of the month.

'You'll come and stay with us often and often,' Heckie kept saying, and Daniel always answered: 'Yes, of course I will.' But he knew that he wouldn't.

101

Mr Knacksap didn't like children; anyone could see that.

'I suppose Heckie must be very happy,' said Sumi when the children met at break. 'But she looks awfully tired.'

'She's worried about the dragworm,' said Daniel. 'She can't take him with her because of Mr Knacksap being allergous or whatever he is.'

'Well, I think he's up to something,' said Joe. He was sitting on the coal-bunker eating a banana and looking more like a small ape than ever. 'I believe he's marrying her for a reason. And why can't he ever come and see her on a Monday or a Wednesday or a Friday? What's he doing the other days, do you suppose? I tell you, he's a crook; I just know it.'

But what could the children do?

'If we try and warn her, she'll never believe us,' said Sumi.

'No,' said Daniel thoughtfully. 'She wouldn't believe *us*. But there's someone she'd *have* to believe, isn't there?'

The others looked at him. 'Yes,' said Joe slowly. 'I see what you mean.'

Mr Knacksap opened the door of his shop and stepped into the street. He was carrying a bunch of roses and a box of chocolates, but the roses were white, not red, and the chocolates were not plain ones with hard centres, but milky ones with soft centres.

There were other differences too. When he went to see Heckie, the furrier always wore a dark suit and had his hair parted in the middle. Now he was

102

wearing a white suit and his hair was parted at the side. What was the same, though, was the greedy, furtive look on his face.

He crossed Market Square and made his way down the narrow road which led to the bus station. A Number 33 was waiting to set off for Fetlington, on the north side of the town, and as he rode past the prison and the football ground, the furrier closed his eyes and gloated. In a month he'd be safely in Spain, leading a life of luxury. Fast cars, casinos, beautiful girls to massage his feet and scoop the wax out of his ears as he lay beside the swimming pool!

At Fetlington Green, he got off and walked past a row of shops, then turned down the hill towards a piece of open ground with a barn and workshops. The sound of chipping and hammering came to him across the still air and he smiled his oily smile. She was a real worker, you had to give her that!

'Coo-ee,' called Mr Knacksap, as he opened the gates of the stone-mason's yard. 'It's me!'

The chipping stopped. Dora Mayberry came out of the shed, wiping her hands. 'Lewis!' she said, smiling happily, and bent to sniff the roses. 'Your tea's all ready. I've got those cup cakes you like so much. Come on in and make yourself comfortable.'

When Dora had heard that Heckie was still cross with her, she'd gone to pieces. She fed her hat with any old rubbish and she didn't care what she turned to stone – not just the fish fingers and her potted geranium and the bobble on her bedroom slippers, but the ointment she was supposed to rub on her chest for her cough, so that life in the cottage became quite impossible. Even the ghost in the wardrobe got harder and began to creak like a rusty hinge. It's pretty certain that someone would have come and taken Dora away to a mental hospital before much longer, but one Wednesday afternoon there was a knock at the door and a visitor stood there, carrying a bunch of flowers and a box of chocolates.

After which a new life began for Dora Mayberry. Twice a week, on Wednesdays and Fridays, the tall, dark man who had brought the message from Heckie came to tea. She didn't like to ask him too many questions, but she learnt that he was called Lewis Kingman (she had already noticed the initials L.K. stamped on his wallet) and that he worked in insurance. But he wasn't happy in his work and now, biting into a chocolate cup cake, he told her what he wanted to do with his life.

'You see, dearest Dora, I feel I cannot go on living in town,' he said. 'My lungs are delicate. I need to be in the country. Somewhere open and clean. In a house like this.' And from the pocket of his suit he brought out a picture.

'What a pretty place!' said Dora. 'The dovecote and the trees, and the way the river runs through the garden!'

'It's called Paradise Cottage,' said Mr Knacksap. 'And what I want more than anything else in the world, is to live there with you!'

For a moment he wondered whether to go down on his knees, but Dora wasn't very good at dusting, and anyway there was no need – the silly witch was looking adoringly into his eyes.

'Oh, Lewis!' she said. 'You mean you want to marry me?'

'I do,' said Mr Knacksap.

The next day, he bought two of the cheapest engagement rings he could find and had them engraved with his initials. But it wasn't of the two bamboozled witches that he was thinking as he left the shop. It was of a man in a distant country who was almost as crazy and greedy as he was himself.

Chapter Sixteen

The name of this man was Abdul el Hammed and he was an exceedingly rich sheikh who lived between the Zagros Mountains and the Caspian Sea. The sheikh was rich because his country was full of oil wells, but he was also very old-fashioned – so old-fashioned that he had one hundred and fifty wives, just as Eastern rulers used to do in the olden days. The wives lived in a palace all of their own and the sheikh liked to show them off, all dressed alike in beautiful clothes and fabulous jewellery, so that everyone would be amazed that anyone could have so many women and be so generous.

In the summer, the country in which the sheikh lived was very hot, but in the winter, because there were high mountains near by, it was very cold – and it was then that he liked to dress his one hundred and fifty wives in valuable fur coats. But it is not easy to find a hundred and fifty coats made of priceless skins and all alike. The sheikh had been looking round and had sent messengers to all the furriers in Europe and he had not found what he was looking for.

This sheikh wanted to see every one of his wives dressed in a coat made of snow leopards.

Tigers are beautiful and exciting, so are jaguars and ocelots, and people who like fur coats swear by sable or mink. But in all the world, there is nothing like a coat made of snow leopards.

Snow leopards live in the highest mountains in the world – on the slopes of the Himalayas and the Karakoram, where there are no people, only ice and eagles and the sighing of the wind. They are so graceful and so fearless – and above all so rare – that to look at one is to feel a lump come into your throat. There are so few left now that to shoot or trap one is to risk being sent to prison and only a person with no soul would dream of trying it. To kill one snow leopard and make his skin into a fur coat would be almost impossible. To find three hundred (because at least two leopards are needed for a single coat) . . . well, no one but a mad, rich sheikh would even dream of it.

But the sheikh Abdul el Hammed did dream of it. The more he couldn't have what he wanted, the more he was determined to have it. He had offered a thousand pounds for a snow leopard skin and then fifteen hundred, and at last two thousand and more just for one skin. But there simply weren't any snow leopards to be had. Not even the greediest people were willing to break the law which protected these marvellous and unusual beasts.

And then came the day when Mr Flitchbody, a skin trader who operated in London, but had a network of trappers and hunters all over the world, got a telephone call.

'Hello. Is that you, Flitchbody?' a throaty voice said.

'Yes, Flitchbody speaking. Who is that?'

'It's Knacksap here. Lionel Knacksap from

Wellbridge. Tell me, is that sheikh of yours still after snow leopard pelts?'

'You bet he is. Three hundred, he wants, and he'll sell his soul to get them – and I can't find one.'

'Well, I can,' said Mr Knacksap. 'I can get him the full quantity. If the price is right.'

'The price is two thousand eight hundred per skin and I take ten per cent. But I don't believe you for a moment.'

'Well, you'd better believe me. I've found someone who's been breeding them in secret. I can send you the bodies, but you'll have to get them skinned down in London and no questions asked. Can you fix that?'

'I can fix it. But I still think you're bluffing.'

'Well, I'm not. I'll want the money in cash. Three-quarters of a million in notes, can you do that?'

'If you can get me three hundred snow leopards, there's nothing I can't do.'

'I'll keep you posted,' said Mr Knacksap, and put down the phone.

Chapter Seventeen

Mr Knacksap and Heckie were sitting side by side on Heckie's sofa and being romantic. Mr Knacksap was holding Heckie's hand – the one that didn't have the Knuckle of Power – and they were looking into the gas fire and dreaming dreams.

Or rather, Mr Knacksap was dreaming dreams. Heckie's foot had gone to sleep which sometimes happens when you are being romantic, but she didn't like to say so.

'I was thinking, my dear,' said Mr Knacksap, 'about when we are married and living in our cottage in the hills. Paradise Cottage.'

'Yes, dear?' said Heckie. 'What were you thinking about it?'

'I was thinking how beautiful the mountains are up there. Beautiful, but bare. Terribly bare.'

'Well, yes. Of course there is the heather, isn't there?' said Heckie. 'That's very pretty when it flowers.'

'But it only flowers in August. I would like to be able to look up at the hills and see them covered with something really wonderful. With animals that are happy in high places and that are graceful and lovely and a joy to gaze at all the year round. Heather is all right for ladies,' said Mr Knacksap, 'but gentlemen like something a little stronger.'

'What sort of something?' Heckie wanted to know.

Mr Knacksap let go of her hand and turned to look into her eyes. 'I am going to tell you a secret, Hecate,' he said. 'Something I've not told anyone in my life. Always, I've had the same dream. That I wake in the morning and I look up – and there, on the mountain-side above me, are the loveliest and most impressive animals in the world.'

Heckie was very interested. 'Really, dear? And what are they?'

Mr Knacksap blew his nose. Then he said: 'Snow leopards.'

'Snow leopards?' Heckie was very surprised. 'But, dearest, you don't find snow leopards in the Lake District. They're not English things at all. You find them in the Himalayas.'

'I know, dearest,' said Mr Knacksap. 'So far you don't find them in England. But you *could*.' He seized both her hands. 'You could make my dream come true,' he said, rolling his eyes. 'You, my dearest, sweetest witch, could fill the hillside with snow leopards. You could grant me my greatest wish! Every morning I would lift up my eyes and there they would be! They're the most valuable . . . I mean, the most beautiful creatures in the world. Their pelts . . . I mean, their fur, is the deepest, the palest; their tails are thick and long. They have golden eyes and every day as I ate my porridge and kippers, which you would cook for me, I would see them roaming free and lovely over the hills. If I could do that, I think I would be the happiest man in the world.'

110

He looked sideways under his sinister eyebrows at Heckie who was looking very worried indeed.

'But, dearest, a whole hillside of snow leopards . . . I don't see how I could do that. And I'm afraid they'd eat the sheep.'

'Oh, but once the snow leopards came, it would become an animal reserve, that's certain. And think of the tourist trade, and the work it would bring to the unemployed.'

'I could make one or two leopards for you; I'm sure to meet one or two really wicked people before we get married. But a whole hillside – I don't see how I could possibly do that. How many do you want?'

'Three hundred!' said Mr Knacksap firmly. 'At least.'

Heckie leapt to her feet. 'Three hundred! My dearest Li-Li, that's quite impossible. There probably aren't three hundred wicked people in Britain, let alone Wellbridge!'

'Yes, there are, my treasure. There are three hundred wicked people right here in this town. Very wicked people. Murderers and terrorists and embezzlers and thugs. People who shouldn't be eating their heads off at the government's expense. People who'd be much happier roaming the hills as free and graceful leopards for me to look at when I ate my kippers.'

'But where?' asked Heckie. 'What do you mean?'

'In the prison, of course. In Wellbridge prison not a mile from here.'

He leant back, well pleased with himself, and waited for Heckie to tell him how clever he was.

111

'You mean you want me to turn all the prisoners into leopards?' asked Heckie, looking stunned.

'I do,' said the furrier smugly.

The witch shook her head. 'I'm sorry, Li-Li, but I can't do that.'

Mr Knacksap was absolutely furious. How *dare* she go against his wishes? 'Can't! What do you mean, you can't?' he said, and turned away so that she wouldn't see him grinding his teeth.

Heckie sighed. 'You see, people get sent to prison for all sorts of things. There's no way I could be sure that all of them are wicked. If someone had bopped his mother-in-law with a meat cleaver, he mightn't be really bad. It would depend—'

'Everybody in Wellbridge jail is bad,' hissed the furrier. 'It's a high security prison. That means that anyone who gets out will certainly strike again. And anyway, I'd have thought you'd want to make your Li-Li happy. I'd have thought—'

'I do want to make you happy,' said Heckie. 'I want to *terribly*. But one has to do what is *right* and changing people who are not wicked is Not Right.'

It was at this moment that the doorbell rang and Daniel and Joe came in, carefully carrying a large, round box covered in brown paper.

'We took this from the delivery boy,' said Joe. 'It's addressed to both of you. I expect it's a wedding present.'

He handed the box to the furrier who took it and simpered. If people were sending silver or valuable glass, he'd have to be sure of getting it to his place so that he could sell it before he bolted for Spain.

'But where's the dragworm?' asked Heckie,

looking at Daniel. 'I thought you were taking him out.'

'I was,' said Daniel. 'But I met Sumi and she wanted to take him for a bit.'

Heckie nodded and smiled at Mr Knacksap who was eagerly undoing the parcel. Perhaps it was a soup tureen, thought the furrier – that could fetch a couple of hundred. Or an antique clock . . . But as he tore off the wrappings, his look of greed turned to one of puzzlement. For there seemed to be holes in the cardboard box and surely neither soup tureens nor clocks needed to breathe?

'Ugh! It's a monster! A horrible diseased THING full of boils. Get rid of it! Get it out! Shoo!'

The boys stood very still and looked at Heckie. Now at last she would see! It had been very hard to bring Heckie's familiar into the room, knowing what would happen to him, but the children would have done anything to save the witch.

'It's the dragworm, Heckie,' said Daniel quietly.

Too late, Mr Knacksap realized his mistake. He began to cough and splutter and totter round the room. 'Oh, help! My asthma! I'm choking! I can't breathe!'

But for once, Heckie didn't rush to the furrier's side. She had gathered up the dragworm, so shocked by what she saw that at first she couldn't speak.

Her familiar had been in a bad way when he was close to Mrs Winneypeg, but it was nothing to the state he was in now. The hair on his topknot wasn't just white, it was as brittle as that of a ninety-year-old. Some of his scales had actually flaked off, his eyes were filmed over. As for his other end – the most hardened sick nurse would have shed tears when she saw the dragworm's tail.

'Oh, you poor, poor love; you poor thing!' cried Heckie – and as she stroked his head, there came from his throat that ghostly, faint, heartbreaking: 'Quack!'

'I don't understand it,' said Heckie. 'What has happened? What made him come on like that?'

It was Joe who spoke. 'He did. Mr Knacksap did. That's why we brought the dragworm, so that you could see what kind of a person—'

'Stop it! That's enough!' Heckie's pop eyes snapped with temper. 'How *dare* you speak like that about the man I'm going to marry?'

But she looked at Mr Knacksap in a very puzzled way.

The furrier, though, had recovered himself. Still pretending to cough and wheeze, he drew himself up to his full height and pointed at the boys.

'You lying, evil children! How dare you tell poor Heckie such untruths? As though I didn't see you. I saw you quite distinctly taking this poor, sensitive creature right up to the prison gate and along the prison walls. Quite distinctly, I saw you, and I thought then how foolish it was to risk him like that.'

'We didn't!' said Daniel and Joe together. 'Honestly we didn't! We wouldn't do a silly thing like that.'

'In the tartan shopping basket,' Mr Knacksap went on. 'I saw you not half an hour ago.' He turned to Heckie. 'Now will you believe me? Now will you believe me when I tell you how evil those prisoners are?'

Heckie looked desperately from the furrier to the boys and back again. She was a sensible witch, but no one can be in love and stay sensible for long.

'Oh, Daniel . . . Joe . . . that was foolish of you. Run along now and I'll put him in the bath. He'll soon be better.'

So the children left, wretched and defeated, having made the dragworm ill for nothing. And that night, Heckie phoned the furrier.

'All right, Lionel,' she said wearily. 'I'll do what you ask. You shall have your leopards.'

To the stone witch, Mr Knacksap didn't say anything about snow leopards. What he spoke to Dora about was his Cousin Alfred.

'What's happened to my poor dear cousin is the one thing that is spoiling my happiness,' he said, dabbing his eyes with his handkerchief.

'What has happened to him?' asked Dora Mayberry.

'He is in prison,' said Mr Knacksap, and sighed. 'Here in Wellbridge. That sweet, sensitive soul eating his heart out among all those ruffians.'

'Oh, Lewis, that's so sad. How did it happen?'

'It wasn't Alfred's fault, I promise you. He was led astray by bad people. If only you could have seen him as a little boy. We were such friends. He used to build sandcastles for me, and whenever his mummy bought him a lollipop, he would let me have a lick. Look at his photograph – isn't that an innocent face?'

Dora took the picture and said, yes it was, and fancy him having ringlets! (The picture was actually of a child actor who had played Little Lord Fauntleroy in a film.)

'What is he in prison for?' she asked.

'He stole the purse out of an old lady's handbag. The wicked people he fell in with made him do it.' He dabbed at his eyes again and sniffed. 'If only I could get him out of prison, I would send him to a wonderful mind doctor that I know of. Then he'd soon be well again and never do anything bad any more.'

'But how could you, Lewis? How could you get him out?'

This time, Mr Knacksap did go down on his knees. After all, soon he would be able to buy dozens of pairs of new trousers, hundreds of them . . .

'With you to help me, dearest Dora, I could do it. If you could turn the prison guards to stone, just for one night, I could get him out.'

Dora thought for a while and then she said that if it was only his Cousin Alfred he was going to get out, and if she could turn the guards back into people the next day, she didn't mind. 'I couldn't leave them stone, of course, because they aren't wicked. Not so far as I know. But for a night it shouldn't hurt.'

'Oh, my dearest, dearest Dora,' said Mr Knacksap, 'you've made me so happy! I just couldn't face sitting over my porridge and kippers in Paradise Cottage, knowing that poor dear Alfred was lying in a cold stone cell.'

Then he went back to town and put up a big

116

FOR SALE notice outside his shop. Everything was ready – and there was nothing between him and three-quarters of a million pounds.

Chapter Eighteen

Mr Knacksap's plan was simple. He would take Dora to the prison as soon as it was dark and when she'd turned the guards to stone, he'd send her packing. Then two of his accomplices, Nat and Billy, would drive the vans into the prison – they were huge ones, hired from a circus, and would take the leopards comfortably enough. Nat knew about electronics too; there'd be no trouble with the alarm system with him around.

When they'd taken over the prison, he'd go and fetch Heckie and let her in by a side door so that she wouldn't see the stone guards, and bring the prisoners to her one by one – and when she'd changed them into leopards, she'd be sent packing too.

And then the following morning both witches would meet on the station platform to catch the 10.55 to the Lake District! It was this part of the plan that always made Mr Knacksap titter out loud when he thought of it. For he had told both witches to wait for him at the Windermere Hotel. He had told both of them that he would marry them in a little grey church by the edge of the water. Both of them thought they were going to live happily ever after with him in Paradise Cottage!

If only he could have been there to see them

scratch each other's eyes out! But by that time the leopards would be dead and skinned, and he'd be on the way to Spain!

As for how to kill three hundred leopards without marking their pelts, Mr Knacksap had got that sorted out too. About five miles to the east of Wellbridge, there was a derelict stately home called Hankley Hall. No one went there – it was said to be haunted – but some of the rooms were still in good repair. The ballroom, in particular, had windows that fitted well and a wooden gallery that ran round the top. The man he'd hired to do the actual killing said it was a doddle. You just lobbed a canister down from the gallery and waited.

When you wanted to kill someone and leave no mark, Sid had said, there was nothing like plain, old-fashioned gas.

Farewell parties are often sad, and Heckie's was sadder than most.

She gave it on her last day before leaving Wellbridge, and she gave it in the afternoon because in the evening she had to go and change the prisoners. Heckie had told no one of Mr Knacksap's plan – not even her helpers – but they could see that she looked tired and strained, and not really like a bride.

The furrier couldn't be at the party, but almost all her friends were there and had brought presents. Sumi's parents had sent a huge tin of biscuits with a picture of Buckingham Palace on the lid, Joe had made some book-ends, and the cheese wizard brought a round Dutch cheese.

'It can't do much,' he explained. 'Just a few centimetres. But if you're going to eat it, it won't matter.'

Madame Rosalia gave her a make-up bag full of useful things: pimples, blotches, pockmarks and a tuft of hair for joining her eyebrows together; and the garden witch brought a cauliflower which got stuck in the door and had to be cut free with a hatchet.

But the best present – really an amazing present – came from Boris Chomsky, and it was nothing less than a hot air balloon which really did fly on the hot air talked by politicians!

Boris had been very upset by what happened at the Tritlington Poultry Unit and he began to work much harder at his invention. He got out all his books of spells and studied late into the night. Then he went up to the Houses of Parliament with his tape recorder hidden under his greatcoat and started to record the speeches that the members made. He took down the waffle that the Minister for Health talked about it being people's own fault if they got ill, and the piffle that the Minister for Employment talked about there really being lots of lovely jobs for everyone if only they weren't too lazy to look, and the garbage that the MPs shouted at each other during Question Time.

Then he went back to his garage and boiled things in crucibles and burnt them in thuribles – and at last the day came when he put a tape of the Chancellor's speech at the Lord Mayor's Banquet into one of the fuel converters, and the balloon rose up so quickly that it hit the roof.

So now they all trooped across the road and round

the corner to Boris's garage and admired Heckie's balloon (which was grey because it rains a lot in the Lake District) and the other balloons which he had converted so that they could be used by any wizard or witch who wanted them.

But when Heckie had thanked him again and again, and taken her guests back to the party, her face grew very sad and her eyes went more and more often to the door to look for the one person who hadn't come.

'I'm sure he'll be along soon,' said Sumi, who always seemed to know what was troubling people. 'I expect the professors have made him do some extra piano practice.'

But the clock struck five, and then six, and Heckie had to face the fact that the boy she loved as though he was her son had not even troubled to say goodbye.

Chapter Nineteen

The prison crouched on its hill, surrounded by warehouses and factories. Even by day it was a grim building, but at night, rearing out of the mist, it looked deeply sinister.

Dora and Mr Knacksap walked up to the main gate just as the clock was striking eleven. There was no one about; they could hear the echo of their own footsteps. Dora wasn't so much nervous as shy, and she was carrying a powerful electric torch because stone magic depends on being able to see the victim's eyes.

'I'm sure you're going to do splendidly, dear,' said Mr Knacksap in his oily voice – and pressed the big brass bell.

They could hear it shrilling and then a uniformed guard came out, carrying a gun.

'My friend is feeling faint,' said Mr Knacksap. 'I wonder if you could help?'

'This isn't a bloomin' hospital,' said the guard. 'It's a pris—'

And then he didn't say anything more.

It was almost too easy. If Mr Knacksap hadn't been so ignorant, he'd have realized how honoured he was to see such a powerful witch at work. A second guard appeared, wanting to know what was going on, and then he too fell silent. Mr Knacksap pushed Dora through the crack in the gate and into the guardroom where two more men were playing cards – and in an instant even the playing cards they were holding turned to stone.

Within half an hour, the prison was full of statues. Statues of the warders in charge of each corridor, one caught as he peered into the spy-hole of a cell . . . A statue of the chief warder, sitting in his office – a statue with ear-phones because he'd been listening to the radio to make the long night pass more quickly. There was a statue of a patrol man, still shouting at his dog, and a most graceful one of the dog itself, an Alsatian whom Dora had looked at just before it sprang at her throat.

'Well, that seems to be it,' said Mr Knacksap when they had walked up and down the corridors and the winding iron stairs without anybody challenging them. 'Now you just go home and make sure you're on that train, otherwise you won't be ready for your Lewis when he comes.'

Dora had hoped he might ask her to stay till he had found his Cousin Alfred. She was curious to see what a little boy with ringlets, who'd let Lewis have a lick of his lollipop, looked like after his time in prison. But the furrier took her firmly to the gate. He didn't even say thank you, or hail a taxi, or give her a kiss.

But Dora was a humble witch. She turned up her collar and trudged out into the night.

'Oh, Li-Li, not that one! Please! He looks so young.'

An hour had passed and Heckie sat in a small cloakroom off the prison yard, facing her first prisoner. She had kicked off her shoe and her Toe of Transformation felt icy on the bare tiles.

'Surely he can't have done anything terrible?' Heckie went on.

The furrier leant forward. 'He strangled a little girl in cold blood,' he hissed – and the prisoner looked up, puzzled. They couldn't be talking about him, surely? He was doing three years for house-breaking.

But Heckie had believed Mr Knacksap. She leant forward and touched the young man with her knuckle – and then even the horrible Mr Knacksap gasped in wonder.

There are no words that can describe the beauty of a snow leopard. Their coats are a misty grey with black rosettes that are clouded by the depth of the rich fur. Their golden eyes stare out of a face that belongs on shields or banners, it is so grave and mythical – and when they move, their long, thick tails curve and coil and circle in a never-ending dance.

Mr Knacksap had retreated behind a chair, his hand in the pocket of his coat where he kept a gun, but Heckie knew her job. She had made the leopard as sleepy as the prisoner had been. The great cat yawned slowly and delicately. Then it loped off, out of the door, through the wire tunnel, and up the ramp to the first lorry which had SIMPSON'S CIRCUS painted on its side.

Everything was going the way Mr Knacksap had planned. The prisoners had been woken and told they were going to be moved to a new jail with better food and more space, and they shuffled out of their cells, half-asleep, giving no trouble. Nat, who brought them to Heckie, didn't need the sub-machine gun he'd insisted on carrying.

And how Heckie worked! She turned one prisoner and then two and three and four . . . Sometimes she stopped when a particularly innocent-looking prisoner was brought to her, but always Mr Knacksap would bend over her and hiss some frightful lie into her ear and she would go on with her job.

When she had changed over fifty prisoners, she swayed and her head fell forward. Mr Knacksap had no idea what he was asking her to do. Turning one person into an animal can leave a witch completely exhausted. Turning three hundred . . . well, witches have died from over-straining themselves like that. But the furrier knew exactly how to get round her.

'Dearest Hecate,' he said with his gooey smile, 'if you knew how happy you are making me!'

That did it, of course. Heckie lifted her head, blew on her throbbing knuckle and got to work again. And by one in the morning, her task was done.

But if Heckie had hoped that Mr Knacksap would thank her or give her a kiss or order a taxi, she, like Dora, had hoped in vain. As the door of the lorry slammed on the last of the leopards, Heckie let herself out of a side door and half limped, half staggered, home.

But though she fell straight into bed, Heckie couldn't sleep. Her Toe of Transformation ached and stabbed every time she moved, and when her knuckle caught on the sheet, she flinched with pain.

After an hour, she got up and fetched the dragworm and packed him carefully in his tartan shopping basket. What she had decided to do probably wouldn't work out, but it was her only chance, for familiars never thrive except with witches, and powerful ones at that. It wasn't as though she was asking anything for herself. Heckie knew that Dora wanted nothing more to do with *her* – but could anybody turn away something so appealing and unusual as the dragworm?

Dora, too, was overtired and couldn't sleep, and after a while she gave up trying and put on her boiler suit and went downstairs.

The wardrobe was lying flat in the van that Dora had hired to take her furniture to be stored. Everything else had already gone to the warehouse to wait till Dora knew what she would need in Paradise Cottage. Only the wardrobe was left and as Dora approached, the wood spirit floated out and gave her a shy and wavery smile.

Dora had not wanted a ghost at all, and when the spirit first started floating about among her coathangers, she had been quite annoyed. But gradually she had become fond of it. It still didn't say much except 'Don't chop down the wardrobe,' but in its own way the thing was affectionate. Dora would have liked to take the wardrobe with her to Paradise Cottage, but Lewis did not care for ghosts. The first time he had come to tea and the spirit had called down from the bedroom, Lewis had leapt from the sofa and dropped his cup cake on the floor.

Dora had found some people to buy the stonemason's business, but suppose they got annoyed with the poor spirit? Suppose in a fit of anger they *did* chop down the wardrobe. Dora would never forgive herself.

Could her friend really refuse to take in this doleful ghost? It wasn't as though Dora was asking anything for herself. She knew Heckie never wanted to see *her* again. But could Heckie, who had never turned away a stray in her life, refuse to give a home to this poor sad thing?

And Dora climbed into the cab and drove up the hill towards the town.

Chapter Twenty

The cheese wizard went to bed early. Serving in his shop by day and doing magic on his cheeses at night made Mr Gurgle very tired. But on the night of Heckie's farewell party, he was woken in the small hours by an odd tapping noise. Tap, tap, tap, it went, and then stopped again, and just as he was dropping off, it began once more.

'Oh, bother!' said Mr Gurgle, and got out of bed and put on his slippers. The tapping seemed to be coming from right below him, from the cellar. Could his prize cheese be learning to tap dance? Sometimes people who couldn't walk very well got on better when they tried to move to music.

But when he got down to the cellar, the Stilton lay quietly on its shelf, looking as fast asleep as only a cheese can do.

The wizard scratched his head. Had he imagined the tapping? No, there it was again. Sounding louder, sounding really frantic. But it wasn't in his cellar, it was in the cellar next door. Which was very strange . . . Because the shop next door belonged to the furrier, Mr Knacksap, who had gone away to get ready for his wedding to Heckie. Mr Knacksap's shop should have been empty.

Another burst of tapping . . . Mr Gurgle went up to the dividing wall and tapped in turn, and the tapping became louder. Something or someone was trapped in there. The wizard slipped on his coat and went outside. The front of the furrier's shop was locked – the back too. But there was a grating across the top of the cellar steps, out in the back yard. He fetched a stepladder and climbed over the wall, wobbling a little, for he was holding a torch in one hand.

The grating was ancient and rusty, but though Mr Gurgle was weedy, he was also obstinate. He tugged and he tugged and at last it came away and he could make his way carefully down the cellar steps.

At the bottom, curled in a heap, lay a boy. Blood had hardened on his forehead and his face; there was more blood on his hands where he had pounded the rough stone wall.

It was only when he tried to speak, muttering words that made no sense at all, that the wizard recognized Daniel.

Everyone had been worried about Heckie's engagement to the furrier, but as the day of the wedding grew closer, Daniel became quite frantic. Though he knew that Heckie was a powerful witch, he couldn't rid himself of the feeling that some frightful harm would come to her through Mr Knacksap.

He had bought Heckie a present: a tea-making machine which dropped exactly the right number of bags into the pot. He was actually wrapping it up when he decided not to go to the party. Instead, he made his way to the furrier's shop in Market Square. Perhaps even now he could still get proof of the furrier's treachery.

Over the FOR SALE notice, another notice had been plastered, saying SOLD. The beaver cape had been taken from the window. But, to Daniel's surprise, the door of the shop was ajar. Mr Knacksap's cleaning lady, in a very nasty temper, was just leaving.

'If you want him, you'd better come in and wait,' she said. 'I'm not hanging around any longer. If he doesn't want to give me a bit of a farewell tip like any decent gentleman would, then good riddance to him.'

She left, and Daniel slipped in to the furrier's office. It was stripped and bare. Beside the desk stood three leather suitcases with gaudy labels.

L. KNACKSAP, HOTEL SPLENDISSIMA, ALICANTE, SPAIN, read Daniel.

Spain? Why Spain? thought Daniel. Surely it was beside Lake Windermere that the furrier was going to marry Heckie?

At that moment he heard the sound of a key turning in the lock. Mr Knacksap coming back for his luggage! There was a cupboard in the corner for coats and overalls. Daniel slipped inside, his heart pounding, and closed the door.

Mr Knacksap was whistling jauntily as he sat down at his desk. Then he picked up the telephone. 'Flitchbody? It's Knacksap here. I just wanted to make sure you've got everything sorted. The bodies should be with you by six this morning. Three hundred snow leopards. They'll be dead and without a scratch on them – we're going to use gas. All you've got to do is get them skinned.'

'Where are you going to gas them for heaven's sake?'

'Hankley Hall – it's about five miles from Wellbridge. Don't worry, it's a doddle.'

'I still don't know where you think you can get them from.'

'Well, if I told you I'd found a witch who can turn people into leopards, you wouldn't believe me. So just take it I've found someone who breeds them in secret and thinks I'm going to let them loose on the hills. And remember, Flitchbody, I want the money in cash or I'll blow the lot to kingdom come.'

He put down the phone.

Oh, God, thought Daniel. What does it mean? What shall I do?

Then something awful happened. His foot slipped and bumped against one of Mr Knacksap's walking sticks, propped in the corner of the cupboard. Daniel lunged, trying desperately to catch it – and missed. There was a frightful clatter. Then slowly . . . very slowly . . . the cupboard was opened by an unseen hand.

Heckie pulled the dragworm through the lamplit streets of Wellbridge, past Sumi's shop, past Boris's garage. Everything was shuttered; everyone slept. It was a long way to Fetlington, but the night was fresh and cool.

She was turning into Market Square when she saw, coming towards her, a furniture lorry which stopped suddenly with a squeal of brakes. Then a dumpy lady in a boiler suit got down from the cab.

It couldn't be . . . But it was!

131

'Dora!' said Heckie – and waited for her friend to snub her and turn away.

'Heckie!' said Dora – and waited for her friend to shout rude things at her.

There was a pause while both witches looked at each other. Then:

'Oh, Dora, I have missed you,' said Heckie.

'Oh, Heckie, I have missed *you*,' said Dora.

And then they were hugging each other and talking both at once, explaining how miserable they had been and promising that they would never, never quarrel with each other again.

All this took a little while, but then Heckie said: 'Why are you moving furniture at this time of night?'

'Well, actually . . . I was coming to see you. I was going to have a last try at being friends and I wanted to ask you if you'd take my wardrobe. It's haunted, you see, and I'm getting married and my fiancé doesn't like ghosts.'

'But of course I'll take it. Only it's so funny, Dora, because *I* was coming to see you! I wanted to have a last try at being friends and I wanted to ask you if you'd take my familiar because I'm getting married and my fiancé doesn't like dragworms!'

So then they both laughed so much they nearly fell over and said wasn't it amazing that both of them were going to get married, and then Dora opened the wardrobe and the thing came out looking white and vague and blinking worriedly – and as Dora had known she would, Heckie took to it at once.

And then Heckie unzipped the dragworm's basket and of course it was love at first sight. 'Oh, Heckie, you were always so clever with animals! The way the back of him is so different from the front and yet somehow he's all of a piece!'

So now their worries were over and they could settle down to a good gossip.

'Wouldn't it be wonderful if we could visit each other every week like proper married ladies?' said Heckie.

'Oh, wouldn't it!' said Dora. 'But I'm going to live in the Lake District.'

Heckie gave a shriek of delight. 'But so am I! So am I going to live in the Lake District! Isn't it absolutely splendid! We'll be able to swap recipes and have tupperware parties and—'

She never finished her sentence. The door of the cheese wizard's shop burst open and Mr Gurgle came running across the square, still in his bedroom slippers, and as white as a sheet.

'Thank goodness!' he said, grabbing Heckie's arm. 'I thought I heard you. It's the boy . . . Daniel. I found him trussed up in Knacksap's cellar. He's been hit on the head and he's got brain fever, I think. He keeps talking about leopards. Three hundred snow leopards going to be gassed at Hankley Hall!'

Daniel lay on Mr Gurgle's sofa. He had lost so much blood that the room was going round and round, but when he saw Heckie, he made a desperate effort to speak.

'Leopards,' he said again. 'Three hundred . . . at Hankley Hall . . . killed.' And struggling to make her understand what he had heard: 'Flitchbody . . .' he began – and then fell back against the cushions.

Heckie felt his head with careful fingers. 'He must

go to hospital at once and his parents be told. Get an ambulance, Gurgle. When he's safe you can rally the others, but the boy comes first.' She turned to Dora. 'I did it,' said Heckie, and she looked like a corpse. 'I made the leopards out of the prisoners, for Li-Li to turn loose on the hills. This Flitchbody must have got wind of Li-Li's plans and kidnapped them!'

'Oh, but that's terrible, Heckie. You see one of them must be Lewis's Cousin Alfred! He went to the prison to free him. Lewis will never forgive me if Cousin Alfred gets gassed and skinned.'

'Perhaps it's not too late,' said Heckie – and both witches ran like the wind for the lorry.

Chapter Twenty-One

It had been a splendid place once – a long, low building with towers and turrets and an avenue of lime trees. There was a statue garden with queer griffins and heraldic beasts carved in stone, and a lake and a maze – a really frightening maze, the kind with high yew hedges that could trap you for hours and hours.

But now the hall was empty and partly ruined. The people who owned Hankley couldn't afford to keep it up and then it was found that an underground river was making the back of the house sink into the ground, so nobody would buy it.

The ballroom, though, was in the front and it looked almost as it had done a hundred years ago. There were patches of damp on the ceiling and the plaster had flaked off, but the beautiful floor was still there, and the carved gallery. And now, with candles flickering in the holders and graceful shadows moving across the windows, it might have seemed as though the grand people who had danced there had come back to haunt the place in which they had once been happy.

But the creatures who moved between the pillars wore no ball gowns and carried no fans – and when they turned and wove their patterns on the floor, it was on four legs, not on two.

*

The leopards had been quiet when Heckie made them, but now it was different. The men who brought them had handled them roughly, prodding and poking with long-handled forks to send them faster down the wire tunnels and into the room. The big cats had smelled the fear in the men; their eyes glinted and they lashed each other with their tails.

A door opened high up in the gallery and a man dressed in black leather came out. His gas-mask hung by a strap round his neck and he carried a zinc-lined box which he lowered carefully on to the floor.

Sid would do anything for money. It didn't matter to him what he killed. Only the week before he'd shot two dozen horses between the eyes so that they could be sent off to be eaten. He never asked questions either. How Mr Knacksap had got hold of three hundred leopards was none of his business. All the same, as he looked down on the moving, frosty sea of beasts, he felt shivers go up and down his spine.

I wish I hadn't take it on, thought Sid.

Which was silly ... He'd clear a thousand just for an hour's work and nothing could go wrong. The windows were sealed up; the men who drove the lorries would drag the brutes back into the vans. They had masks too. There'd be no trouble.

Better get on with it. He fitted the rubber tight over his face. Now, with his black leather suit, he looked like someone from another planet. Then he bent down and began to prise open the box.

'Stop! Stop!' A wild-haired woman had burst through the door and was running between the leopards who, strangely, parted to let her pass. 'Stop at once, Flitchbody! Those aren't leopards, they're people!'

'And one of them is Cousin Alfred,' yelled a second woman, small and dumpy, in a boiler suit.

Sid straightened up. He could knock off these two loonies along with the leopards, but killing people was more of a nuisance than killing animals. There were apt to be questions asked.

'Get out of here!' he shouted, his voice muffled by the mask. 'Get out or you're for it!'

Neither of the witches moved. Heckie couldn't touch the assassin with her knuckle because there were no steps from the floor of the ballroom to the gallery. Dora couldn't look at him out of her small round eyes because he wore a mask.

They were powerless.

Sid picked up the canister of gas. The women would just have to die too. Nat and Billy could throw them in the lake afterwards.

A large leopard, scenting danger, lifted its head and roared. And high in the rafters, a family of bats fluttered out and circled the room.

The witches had always understood each other without words. Heckie knew what Dora was going to do and it hurt her, but she knew it had to be done.

'Ouch! Ow! Ooh!'

The shriek of pain came from Sid, hopping on one leg. Something as hard as a bullet had crashed down on his foot – a creepy, gargoyle thing with claws and wings made of stone. And now another one – a bat-shaped bullet hurtling down from the ceiling, missing him by inches. This wasn't ordinary danger, this was something no one could endure!

Sid put down the canister and fled.

He didn't get far. Almost at once he ran into someone who was very angry. Someone whose voice made both witches prick up their ears.

'It's Li-Li,' cried Heckie. 'It's Li-Li telling off the horrible man who's been trying to kill the leopards!'

'It's Lewis,' cried Dora at the same time. 'He's come to save his Cousin Alfred!'

Mr Knacksap appeared on the gallery. He had snatched Sid's gas-mask and was heaving with temper. No one could be trusted these days. He'd have to do the job himself.

'Li-Li!' shouted Heckie. 'Thank goodness you've come!'

'Lewis!' cried Dora. 'You're just in time!'

The witches looked at each other.

'What did you call him?' asked Heckie.

'Lewis. He's my Lewis. The man I'm going to marry. What did *you* call him?'

'Li-Li. He's my Lionel. The man *I'm* going to marry.'

Then at last the scales dropped from the witches' eyes and they understood that they had been tricked and double-crossed and cheated.

And in those moments, Knacksap fixed on Sid's mask, lobbed the canister of gas high into the room – and ran.

Chapter Twenty-Two

'Right? Is everybody ready?' said Boris Chomsky. He climbed into the basket of the black air balloon, and Sumi and the garden witch moved over to make room for him.

'Just checking the ammunition,' said Mr Gurgle importantly, from the second balloon. His balloon was grey, but it only lacked a couple of hours till dawn so it wouldn't show up too much. Joe sat beside him, and Madame Rosalia, whom no one would have recognized as Miss Witch 1965. She wore no make-up, her hair was tousled. For the past half hour she had crouched on the floor of Boris's garage, muttering the spells she'd learnt at school and thought she had forgotten. Spells to raise the wind – and the right wind. A westerly, to take them as fast as they could go to Hankley Hall.

Daniel's parents might not be able to show him much affection, but when their son was still not at home at one in the morning, the professors were frantic. They called the police, but they also went to Sumi's house, and to Joe's, to see if he was with his friends. And Sumi and Joe, running round to Heckie's in case Daniel was with the witch, had met Mr Gurgle rallying the Wickedness Hunters.

'Ammunition on board,' called Mr Gurgle. 'Ready for take-off!'

Boris put a tape of the Minister for Education saying schoolchildren needed more exams into the fuel adaptor – and the black balloon shot into the air.

Mr Gurgle inserted a cassette of the Minister for Trade saying that dumping nuclear waste was good for the fish – and the grey balloon shot upwards also.

Madame Rosalia had done her work well. The wind was keen and exactly where they wanted. Blowing them to the east and Hankley Hall!

Mr Knacksap was running, running . . . stumbling along gravel paths, blundering between trees. He'd thrown off the gas-mask and the branches stung his face.

Gas-proof witches! Who would have believed it? He'd been certain that the witches had died along with the leopards when he threw the canister – but just now he'd heard them calling to each other down by the lake.

Oh, Lord, don't let them get me, prayed the furrier. Don't let me become a louse. Don't let me become a statue. And please, please don't let me become the statue of a louse!

If he could just find somewhere to hide till the witches gave up and went home. Then he could haul the leopards away – Nat and Billy should be waiting at the bottom of the drive for a signal.

But where? Where could he be safe from the women he had cheated?

Panting, gasping, almost at the end of his tether, Mr Knacksap staggered on, past fountains, down a flight of steps, tripping over roots . . .

And then he saw in front of him a mass of high, dark hedges. Of course, the Hankley Maze! The first streaks of light had appeared in the east, but he'd be safe in there – no one would find him. If he was lost, so would the witches be if they tried to follow him. All he needed to do was wait till he heard them driving away, and then he'd get out all right. One just had to turn always to the left or to the right, it was perfectly easy.

Only what was that? Good heavens, WHAT WAS THAT? A thing high up in the sky. A blob . . . an Unidentified Flying Object. No, two of them. Two UFOs . . .

'It's the Martians!' screamed Mr Knacksap, weaving frantically between the hedges.

'There he is, down in the maze,' said Joe. 'We need to lose some height.'

Boris nodded and turned down the sound. In both balloons the taped gabble died to a whisper and the balloons dropped quietly to hang over the hedges of yew.

'Ready with the ammunition?'

The garden witch nodded and heaved the first of the missiles on to the edge of the basket, where Sumi steadied it and let it go.

'No! No! Don't do it!' yelled the furrier.

But the unspeakable THING was already hurtling towards him – gigantic, hideous, deformed . . . to fall not a foot away from him, spattering him with ghastly misshapen bits of itself. And now a second one – not a death-dealing cauliflower this time, but an artichoke whose spiky leaves drew blood as they gashed his cheek.

141

'Spare me! Spare me!' implored Knacksap – and a stick of celery the size of a tree caught him a glancing blow on the shoulder.

The furrier was on his knees now, gabbling and praying. But there was a fresh horror to come! From the second of the UFOs came a new menace: a rain of deadly weapons, round ones like landmines, which splattered to the ground beside him, releasing an unbearable, poisonous stink!

'No, not that one,' begged Mr Gurgle, up in the balloon. 'I'm teaching that one to skip.'

'Can't be helped,' said Joe tersely. He heaved the round, red cheese on to the rim of the basket, took aim – and fired.

This time he scored a bull's-eye. The furrier screamed once and rolled over. He was still lying on the ground, twitching, when the witches ran into the maze.

Chapter Twenty-Three

'Have some soup,' begged Dora Mayberry, putting the tray down beside Heckie's bed. 'Please, dear. Just try a spoonful.'

'I couldn't,' said Heckie in a failing voice. 'It would choke me.'

For two weeks now she had been lying in bed in her flat above the pet shop, refusing to eat and getting paler and weaker with every day that passed.

'My heart is broken,' Heckie had explained at the beginning.

'Well, my heart is broken too,' Dora had said – but of course it had always been agreed between them that Heckie was the sensitive one and felt things more.

Dora had moved in with Heckie because her own business was sold, and she cooked for Heckie and looked after the shop and baked the dragworm's princesses, but nothing could make Heckie take any interest in life. Sumi came with nice things from her parents' shop, and Joe, and of course Daniel as soon as he was well enough. Daniel had left hospital after a few days and his parents had been so relieved that they actually took time off to make a fuss of him. But even Daniel couldn't stop Heckie lying back on her pillows and talking about death, although it was his bravery that had prevented a terrible disaster.

For the leopards had not been gassed. There was something that Mr Knacksap had forgotten if he ever knew it – and that was that Dora Mayberry had been the netball champion of the Academy.

This plump and humble witch had leapt high over a crouching leopard, caught the canister, and run – as she used to run down the pitch – to throw it safely into the lake.

The rest of that strange, exhausting night had been spent driving the leopards back to the prison, changing them back to people, and undoing the stone magic on the guards. Everyone had helped. Nat and Billy had fled, along with Sid, so it was Boris and Mr Gurgle who drove the circus vans, and the other Wickedness Hunters stood guard outside the prison till the job was done. Since the prisoners couldn't remember how they had got into the exercise yard, and the guards couldn't remember anything at all, nobody could punish anybody else, and soon the prisoners were back in their cells and quite glad to catch up on their sleep.

So everyone should now have been happy, but instead they were completely miserable – and this was because of Heckie.

When she first realized that it was Mr Knacksap who had half-killed Daniel and tried to murder three hundred people in cold blood, Heckie had felt nothing except anger and rage. But as the days passed she couldn't help remembering the chocolates with hard centres, and the red roses, and the careful way the furrier had brushed the crumbs off his trousers as they picnicked above the gas works – and she felt so sad that really there seemed no point in staying alive.

And while Heckie faded away, the power of her magic grew weaker too and very strange things happened in the zoo. The warthog had to be taken out of her cage and sent to the veterinary hospital because an odd fleshy bulge, just like a human leg, had appeared on her back end, and the unusual fish began to gasp and come up for air. The others tried to keep news of these things from Heckie, but they were all very worried indeed.

'I really think I ought to call the doctor,' said Dora now, taking away the tray with Heckie's untasted soup.'

'There's nothing he can do,' said Heckie dramatically. 'I'm better off dead.'

So poor Dora shuffled off and Heckie lay back on the pillow and thought about her ruined life and what she wanted put on her tombstone. She had decided on: HERE LIES HECATE TENBURY-SMITH WHO MEANT WELL BUT GOT EVERY-THING WRONG, when she heard a voice somewhere in the room.

'Quite honestly,' it said, 'I think this has gone on long enough.'

Heckie opened her eyes. All her visitors had gone. Dora was in the kitchen. Then she looked down, and there was the dragworm sitting in his basket and looking peeved.

'But you can't speak!' she said, amazed.

'I never said I *couldn't*,' said the dragworm. 'I *didn't* because there's too much conversation in the world already. Babble, babble all day long. But to see you going on like this just turns me right off. And all for a man who, to say the least, is thoroughly vulgar. Furthermore, I have no wish to turn back into a duck. Being a duck was the most boring thing that ever happened to me.'

'But surely—'

The dragworm rose from the basket and slithered over to the bed. 'There,' he said, lifting his tail. 'On the fifth bulge from the end. *Feathers*.'

'Oh, *dear*!'

'And more to come, I shouldn't wonder. Everything's going to pieces. I wouldn't be surprised if that mouse you made in the bank hasn't got himself a machine-gun by now. So I suggest you pull yourself together and forget that creep. The smell of his toilet water . . .'

Heckie had propped herself on one elbow. 'You didn't like it?'

'*Like* it? You must be joking!'

'Perhaps it was a little strong,' Heckie agreed. 'But I don't really know what to do with my life any more. I feel such a failure.'

'Well, for a start you can eat something. As for me, I could do with a change. What's with this Paradise Cottage there was all that fuss about?'

Chapter Twenty-Four

There is nothing like country air for mending broken hearts, and it was not long before Heckie and Dora realized that marriage would not have suited them. However hard gentlemen try, they always seem to snore in bed, their underclothes need washing and they throw their socks on to the floor.

And Paradise Cottage was exactly the kind of home the witches had dreamt of. Mr Knacksap had cut the picture out of a house agent's catalogue and when Heckie and Dora went up to the Lake District to enquire, they found that it was still for sale. So they bought it with the money from both their businesses and settled down to be proper country ladies.

Heckie did not often turn people into animals now; she liked to Do Good more quietly, healing the wounded sheep she sometimes met on her walks, or comforting a cow that was having trouble with its calf. Dora, too, preferred just to help with the stonework of the church, adding noses to chipped statues or building up the missing toes on tombstones. Country people are used to seeing strange creatures and they could take the dragworm out without having to zip him in to his basket, and he and the spirit in the wardrobe had become firm friends.

But though they were so happy in the country, the witches had been looking forward for weeks to

Daniel's first visit, and they had planned a special surprise. He arrived on a beautiful frosty afternoon at the little station beside the lake, but they were not there to meet him. Instead, they sent a friendly taxi driver who took Daniel up the steep winding lane and left him at the garden gate. The front door of the cottage was open, but when Daniel knocked there was at first no answer. He could see two bats hanging upside down on the umbrella stand – the bats that had fallen on Sid in the ballroom, which they had changed back and adopted – but no sign of the witches.

'Is anybody there?' he called.

There was the sound of rustling and whispering, and then Heckie's voice.

'This way, Daniel. We're in here!'

Daniel pushed open the door of the dining-room. The table was set for a party, with candles burning in silver holders, and a bright fire danced in the grate.

But it was the witches themselves who really caught Daniel's attention.

Both of them wore their hats – the hats they had quarrelled about so stupidly a year ago. The snakes were bigger now – the Black Mamba had grown enough to tie in a double bow which hung enchantingly over Heckie's eyes and nestled on Dora's serious forehead. The Ribbon Snakes on the crown shimmered and flickered and the King Snakes, with their brilliant red bands, caught the fire from the lamp.

'We wanted to surprise you,' said Heckie, holding out her arms.

'You look beautiful,' said Daniel. 'Absolutely *beautiful*!' and went forward to hug them both.

But that was not the end of it. When Daniel took his place at the table, he found a small tank beside his plate – and inside it, a hat of his own!

'We made it for you,' said Heckie. 'It's more of a cap, really, like sportsmen wear.'

'We do hope that you will like it,' put in Dora. 'The colours are suitable for gentlemen, we feel.'

There was a time when Daniel would have been worried about putting his hand into a tank of writhing snakes and placing them on his head – but that time was past. And when he went over to the mirror, he could not stop smiling, for really he had never worn anything that suited him so well. The witches had used young green pythons which brought out the colour of Daniel's eyes, and in the place where fishermen sometimes stuck feathered flies, the bright head of a cobra flickered and swayed.

With everyone so smart, it couldn't help being a lovely party. The food was delicious and the tea, of course, was perfect because of Daniel's present – the machine that dropped exactly the right number of tea-bags into the pot. But when they had eaten, and Daniel had given them the messages from Joe and Sumi, who were coming to stay at Easter, the witches put down their cups and sighed.

'Tell us, dear,' said Heckie. 'How is . . . *he*?'

'Yes, how *is* . . . he?' asked Dora.

'Well, I haven't seen him myself because they don't let children into the prison,' said Daniel. 'But Sumi's mother goes sometimes. She says he doesn't like the food, but the other prisoners don't bully him or

149

anything. And they're teaching him to sew mailbags which must be useful, I suppose?'

For Mr Knacksap had not ended up as a statue or a louse. The witches had planned to do dreadful things to him, but when they found him in the maze, felled by cheese, they had looked at each other and left him where he was. They had both loved him truly and though they knew what an evil man he was, they could not bring themselves to use their magic powers against him.

So they had dropped a note in at the police station, and when the police reached him with their tracker dogs, they had taken him straight to the police station and charged him with attacking Daniel. And when they began to ask questions, they found a lot more things that he had done: bouncing cheques, cheating on his income tax, embezzling – and now he was Prisoner Number 301 in Wellbridge jail.

The rest of the evening passed in a flash and then it was bedtime.

'Am I sleeping in the room with the wardrobe?' Daniel asked hopefully.

'Of course, dear,' said Heckie.

When he had brushed his teeth and put on his pyjamas and placed the tank with his hat in it on a chair where he could see it first thing in the morning, Daniel opened the window and drank in the cool, fresh country air. He was much happier now in the tall, grey house in Wellbridge. His parents had not forgotten the shock of finding their son in hospital with his head in bandages. They nagged him less and tried to spend more time with him, and he knew that, in their own way, they loved him. But home for him would always be where Heckie was, and as he burrowed down between the sheets, he sighed with contentment because there were days and days of the holidays still to come.

He was just closing his eyes when he heard the wood spirit's reedy little voice.

'Don't chop—' it began.

And then the dragworm, firm and strict, like an uncle. 'Now that's enough. I don't want to hear another word about chopping. Go to sleep.'

'Will you tell me a story, then?'

'Oh, all right.'

There was a rustle while the spirit settled itself among the coathangers.

'Once upon a time,' began the dragworm, 'there was a fierce and mighty dragon.'

'Like you?' asked the wood spirit.

'Like me,' agreed the dragworm. 'In the spring this dragon flew up to heaven and in the autumn he plunged down into the sea, but in the winter he lived in a crystal cave high on a bare and lonely rock . . .'

It was a beautiful story with everything in it that a story should have: knights in armour and princesses and noble deeds. But long before everyone lived happily ever after, Daniel was asleep.

Dial A Ghost

I set my foot upon my enemies

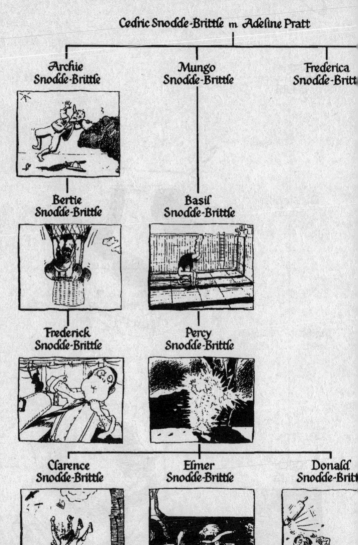

The Snodde-Brittle

Cedric Snodde-Brittle m Adeline Pratt

Archie Snodde-Brittle

Mungo Snodde-Brittle

Frederica Snodde-Britt

Bertie Snodde-Brittle

Basil Snodde-Brittle

Frederick Snodde-Brittle

Percy Snodde-Brittle

Clarence Snodde-Brittle

Elmer Snodde-Brittle

Donald Snodde-Britt

# of Heston Hall

James
changed name to
Smith

Rollo
Snodde-Brittle

Christopher
Smith

Leonard
Snodde-Brittle

Fulton
Snodde-Brittle

Frieda
Snodde-Brittle

Thomas ᵐ Madeline
Smith   Renaud

Oliver
Smith

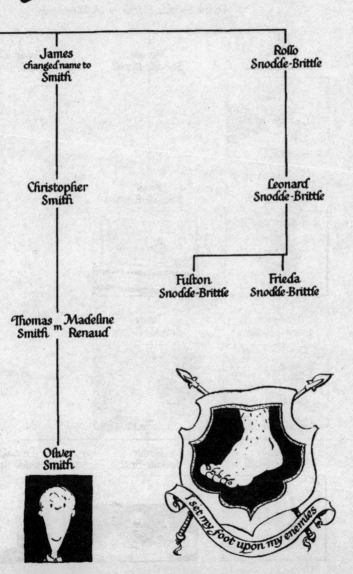

I set my foot upon my enemies

Chapter One

The Wilkinson family became ghosts quite suddenly during the Second World War when a bomb fell on their house.

The house was called Resthaven after the hotel where Mr and Mrs Wilkinson had spent their honeymoon, and you couldn't have found a nicer place to live. It had bow windows and a blue front door and stained glass in the bathroom, and a garden with a bird table and a lily pond. Mrs Wilkinson kept everything spotless and her husband, Mr Wilkinson, was a dentist who went to town every day to fill people's teeth, and they had a son called Eric who was thirteen when the bomb fell. He was a Boy Scout and had just started having spots and falling in love with girls who sneered at him.

Also living in the house were Mrs Wilkinson's mother, who was a fierce old lady with a dangerous umbrella, and Mrs Wilkinson's sister Trixie, a pale, fluttery person to whom bad things were always happening.

The family had been getting ready to go to the air raid shelter at the bottom of the garden and they were collecting the things they needed. Grandma took her umbrella and her gas mask case which did not hold her gas mask but a bottle labelled POISON which she meant to drink if there was an invasion rather than fall into enemy hands. Mrs

1

Wilkinson gathered up her knitting and unhooked the budgie's cage, and Eric took a book called *Scouting for Boys* and the letter he was writing to a girl called Cynthia Harbottle.

In the hall they met Mr Wilkinson, who had just come in and was changing into his khaki uniform. He belonged to the Home Guard, a brave band of part-time soldiers who practised crawling through the undergrowth and shooting things when they had finished work.

'Hurry up everyone,' he said. 'The planes are getting closer.'

But just then they remembered that poor Trixie was still in her upstairs bedroom wrapped in a flag. The flag was her costume for a show the Women's Institute was putting on for the gallant soldiers, and Trixie had been chosen to be The Spirit of Britain and come on in a Union Jack.

'I'll just go and fetch her,' said Mrs Wilkinson, who knew that Trixie had not been at all happy with the way she looked and might be too shy to come down and join them.

She began to climb the stairs . . . and then the bomb fell and that was that.

Of course it was a shock realizing that they had suddenly become ghosts.

'Fancy me a spook!' said Grandma, shaking her head.

Still, there they were – a bit pale and shimmery, of course, but not looking so different from the way they had before. Grandma always wore her best hat to the shelter, the one with the bunch of cherries trimmed with lover's knots, and the whiskers on her chin stuck out like daggers in the moonlight. Eric was in his Scout uniform with the woggle and the badge to show he was a Pathfinder, and his spectacles were still on his nose. Only the budgie didn't look too good. He had lost his tail feathers and seemed to have become rather a *small* bird.

'Oh, Henry, what shall we do now?' asked Mrs Wilkinson. The top half of her husband was dressed like a soldier in a tin hat which he had draped with leaves so as to make him look like a bush, but the bottom half was dressed like a dentist and Mrs Wilkinson, who loved him very much, glided close to him and looked up into his face.

'We shall do what we did before, Maud,' said Mr Wilkinson. 'Live decent lives and serve our country.'

'At least we're all together,' said Grandma.

But then a terrible silence fell and as the spectres looked at each other their ectoplasm turned as white as snow.

'Where is Trixie?' faltered Mrs Wilkinson. 'Where is my dear sister?'

Where indeed? They searched what was left of the house, they searched the garden, they called and called, but there was no sign of a shy spook with spectacles dressed in nothing but a flag.

For poor Maud Wilkinson this was an awful blow. She cried, she moaned, she wrung her hands. 'I promised Mother I would look after her,' she wailed. 'I've always looked after Trixie.'

This was true. Maud and Trixie's mother had run a stage dancing school and ever since they were little, Maud had helped her nervy sister to be a Sugar Puff or Baby Swan or Dandelion.

But there was nothing to be done. Why some

3

people become ghosts and others don't is a mystery that no one has ever solved.

The next years passed uneventfully. The war ended but nobody came to rebuild their house and the Wilkinsons lived in it much as they did before. It was completely ruined but they could remember where all the rooms were, and in a way being a ghost is simple; you don't feel the cold or have to go to school, and they soon got the hang of passing through walls and vanishing. Having Mr Wilkinson to explain things to them was a great help of course.

'You have to remember,' he said, 'that while people are made of muscle and skin and bone, ghosts are made of ectoplasm. But that does not mean,' he went on sternly, 'that we can allow ourselves to become feeble and woozy and faint. Ectoplasm can be strengthened just the way that muscles can.'

But however busy they were doing knee bends and press-ups and learning to move things by the power of their will, they never forgot poor Trixie. Every single evening as the sun went down they went into the garden and called her. They called her from the north, they called her from the south and the east and the west but the sad, goose-pimpled spook never appeared.

Then, when they had been phantoms for about fifteen years, something unexpected happened. They found the ghost of a lost child.

They were out for an early morning glide in the fields near their house when they saw a white shape lying in the grass, under the shelter of a hedge.

'Goodness, do you think it's a passed-on sheep?' asked Mrs Wilkinson.

But when they got closer they saw that it was not the ghost of a sheep that lay there. It was the ghost of a little girl. She wore an old-fashioned nightdress with a ribbon round the neck and one embroidered slipper, and though she was fast asleep, the string of a rubber sponge bag was clasped in her hand.

'She must be a ghost from olden times,' said Mrs Wilkinson excitedly. 'Look at the stitching on that nightdress! You don't get sewing like that nowadays.'

'She looks wet,' said Grandma.

This was true. Drops of water glistened in her long, tousled hair and her one bare foot looked damp.

'Perhaps she drowned?' suggested Eric.

Mr Wilkinson opened the sponge bag. Inside it was a toothbrush, a tin of tooth powder with a picture of Queen Victoria on the lid – and a fish. It was a wild fish, not the kind that lives in tanks, but it too was a ghost and could tell them nothing.

'It must have floated into the sponge bag when she was in the water,' said Mr Wilkinson.

But the thing to do now was to wake the child, and this was difficult. She didn't seem to be just asleep; she seemed to be in a coma.

In the end it was the budgie who did it by saying 'Open wide' in his high squawking voice. He had learnt to say this when his cage hung in the dentist's surgery because it was what Mr Wilkinson said to his patients when they sat down in the dentist's chair.

'Oh the sweet thing!' cried Mrs Wilkinson, as the child stirred and stretched. 'Isn't she a darling! I'm sure she's lost and if she is, she must come and make her home with us, mustn't she, Henry? We must adopt her!' She bent over the child. 'What's your name, dear? Can you remember what you're called?'

The girl's eyes were open now, but she was still not properly awake. 'Adopt . . . her,' she repeated. And then in a stronger voice, 'Adopta.'

'Adopta,' repeated Mrs Wilkinson. 'That's an odd name – but very pretty.'

So that was what she came to be called, though they often called her Addie for short. She never remembered anything about her past life and Mr Wilkinson, who knew things, said she had had concussion, which is a blow on the head that makes you forget your past. Mr and Mrs Wilkinson never pretended to be her parents (she was told to call them Uncle Henry and Aunt Maud), but she hadn't been with them for more than a few weeks before they felt that she was the daughter they had always longed for – and the greatest comfort in the troubled times that now began.

Because life now became very difficult. Their house was rebuilt and the people who moved in were the kind that couldn't see ghosts. They thought nothing of putting a plate of scrambled eggs down on Grandma's head, or running the Hoover through Eric when he wanted to be quiet and think about why Cynthia Harbottle didn't love him.

And when they left, another set of people moved in who *could* see ghosts, and that was even worse. Every time any of the Wilkinsons appeared they shrieked and screamed and fainted, which was terribly hurtful.

'I could understand it if we were headless,' said Aunt Maud. 'I'd *expect* to be screamed at if I was headless.'

'Or bloodstained,' agreed Grandma. 'But we have always kept ourselves decent and the children too.'

Then the new people stopped screaming and started talking about getting the ghosts exorcized, and after that there was nothing for it. They left their beloved Resthaven and went away to find another home.

Chapter Two

The Wilkinsons went to London thinking there would be a lot of empty houses there, but this was a mistake. No place was more bombed in the war and it was absolutely packed with ghosts. Ghosts in swimming baths and ghosts in schools, ghosts whooping about in bus stations, ghosts in factories and offices or playing about with computers. And older ghosts too, from a bygone age: knights in armour wandering round Indian takeaways, wailing nuns in toy shops, and all of them looking completely flaked out and muddled.

In the end the Wilkinsons found a shopping arcade which didn't seem too crowded. It had all sorts of shops in it: shoe shops and grocer's shops and sweet shops and a bunion shop which puzzled Adopta.

'Can you *buy* bunions, Aunt Maud?' she asked, looking at the big wooden foot in the window with a leather bunion nailed to one toe.

'No, dear. Bunions are nasty bumps that people get on the side of their toes. But you can buy things to make bunions better, like sticking plaster and ointments.'

But the bunion shop was already haunted by a frail ghost called Mr Hofmann, a German professor who had made himself quite ill by looking at the bowls for spitting into, and the rubber tubes, and the wall charts showing what could go wrong with people's livers – which was plenty.

So they went to live in a knicker shop.

Adopta called it the Knicker Shop but of course no one can make a living just by selling knickers. It sold pyjamas and swimsuits and nightdresses and vests, but none of them were at all like the pyjamas and swimsuits and vests the Wilkinsons were used to.

'In my days knickers were long and decent, with elastic at the knee and pockets to keep your hankie in,' grumbled Grandma. 'And those bikinis! I was twenty-five before I saw my first tummy button, and look at those hussies in the fitting rooms. Shameless, I call it.'

'It's the children I'm bothered about,' said Aunt Maud. 'They shouldn't be seeing such things.'

And really some of the clothes sold in that shop were *not* nice! – suspender belts that were just a row of frills, and see-through slips and transparent boxes full of briefs.

'Brief whats?' snorted Grandma.

Still they really tried to settle down and make a life for themselves. Adopta was put to sleep in the office, where she wouldn't be among pantalettes and tights with rude names, and Uncle Henry stayed among the socks because there is a limit to how silly you can get with socks. They hung the budgie's cage on the rack beside the Wonderbras and told themselves that they were lucky to have a roof over their heads at all.

But they were not happy. The shopping arcade was stuffy, the people wandering up and down it looked greedy and bored. They missed the garden at Resthaven and the green fields, and although they

9

went out and called Trixie every night, they couldn't help wondering whether a shy person dressed in a flag would dare to appear in such a crowded place even if she heard them.

Aunt Maud did everything she could to make the knicker shop into a proper home. She arranged cobwebs on the ceiling and brought in dead thistles from the graveyard and rubbed mould into the walls, but the lady who sold the knickers was a demon with the floor polisher. She was another one who couldn't see ghosts and, though they slept all day and tried to keep out of her way, she was forever barging through them or spinning the poor budgie round as she twiddled the Wonderbras on their stand. Grandma was getting bothered about Mr Hofmann in the bunion shop who was coming up with more and more diseases – and Eric had started counting his spots again and writing awful poetry to Cynthia Harbottle.

'But Eric, we've been ghosts for years and years!' his mother would cry. 'Cynthia'd be a fat old lady by now.'

But this only hurt Eric who said that to him she would always be young, and he would glide off to the greetings card shop to see if he could find anything to rhyme with Cynthia, or Harbottle, or both.

'Oh, Henry, do you think we shall ever have a proper home again?' poor Maud would cry. And her husband would pat her back and tell her to be patient, and never let on that when he was pretending to go to the dental hospital to study new ways of filling teeth, he was really house hunting, and had found nothing at all.

But Aunt Maud's worst worry was about Adopta. Addie was becoming a street ghost. She often stayed

10

out all night and she was picking up bad habits and mixing with completely the wrong sort of ghost: ghosts who had been having a bath when their house caught fire and hadn't had time to put on any clothes; the ghosts of rat-catchers and vulgar people who swore and drank in pubs.

And she was bringing in the most unsuitable pets.

Addie had always been crazy about animals. She liked living animals, but of course for a ghost to drag living animals about is silly, and the ones that held her heart were the creatures that had passed on and become ghosts and didn't quite understand what had happened to them. But it was one thing to fill the garden at Resthaven with phantom hedgehogs and rabbits and moles, and quite another to keep a run-over alley cat or a battered pigeon among the satin pyjamas and the leotards.

'Please, dear, no more strays,' begged Aunt Maud. 'After all, you have the budgie and your dear fish.'

But though she wouldn't have hurt Aunt Maud for the world, Addie couldn't help feeling that a bird who said nothing but 'Open wide' and 'My name is Billie' wasn't very interesting. Nor was her fish much fun. He stayed in the sponge bag and did absolutely nothing, and though Adopta didn't blame him, she longed for an exciting pet. Something unusual.

So she began to haunt London Zoo, and it was on the way back from there one winter's night that she saw something that was to change all their lives.

She had had her eye on a duck-billed platypus which had not looked at all well the day before. Its brown fur looked limp and dull, its eyes were filmed over and its big flat beak seemed to be covered in some kind of mould. Of course she knew that even

11

if it died the duck-bill would not necessarily become a ghost – animals are the same as people: some become ghosts and some don't. Even so, as she glided towards its cage, Adopta was full of hope. She imagined taking it to bed with her, holding it in her arms. No one had such an unusual pet, and though Aunt Maud would make a fuss at the beginning, she was far too kind to turn it out into the street.

But a great disappointment awaited her. The silly keeper must have given the duck-bill some medicine because it looked much better. In fact it looked fine; it was lumbering round the cage like a two-year-old and eating a worm.

Perhaps it was because she was so sad about her lost pet that she took a wrong turning on the way home to the knicker shop. The street she was gliding down was not the one she went down usually. She was just about to turn back when she saw a sign above a tall grey house. It was picked out in blue electric light bulbs and what it said was:

ADOPTA GHOST

Addie braked hard and stared at it. She was utterly amazed. 'But that is extraordinary,' she said. 'That is *my* name. I'm called Adopta and I'm a ghost.'

She floated up to the roof and stared at the letters. 'Is it my house?' she wondered. 'Is it a house for me?'

But that didn't seem very likely. Could there be *two* Adopta Ghosts in the world? Was this the home of a very grand spook with a green skin and hollow eyes; a queenly spook with trailing dresses ordering everyone about? But when she peered through the windows she saw that the rooms looked rather dull

12

– offices with files and a desk and a telephone. A queenly spook with green ectoplasm would never live in a place like that.

Very much excited, Addie hurried home.

'Aunt Maud, you must come at *once*,' she said. 'I've seen the most amazing thing!'

'Addie, it's your bedtime; it's nearly eight in the morning. They'll be opening the shop in half an hour.'

'Please,' begged Adopta. 'I just know this is important!'

So Maud came and landed on the ledge beneath the notice, and when she had done so she was quite as excited as the child had been.

'My dear, it doesn't say "Adopta Ghost". Look carefully and you'll see a space between the middle letters. It says "Adopt a Ghost". And I really believe it's an agency to find homes for people like us. Look, there's a notice: *Ghosts wanting to be re-housed should register between midnight and three a.m. on Tuesdays, Thursdays or Saturdays.*'

She turned to the child and hugged her. 'Oh, Addie, I do believe our troubles are over. There is someone who cares about us – someone who really and truly cares!'

13

Chapter Three

Aunt Maud was right. There *was* someone who cared about ghosts and who cared about them very much. Two people to be exact: Miss Pringle, who was small and twittery with round blue eyes, and Mrs Mannering, who was big and bossy and wore jackets with huge shoulder pads and had a booming voice.

The two ladies had met at an evening class for witches. They were interested in unusual ways of living and thought they might have had Special Powers, which would have been nice. But they hadn't enjoyed the classes at all. They were held in a basement near Paddington Station and the other people there had wanted to do things that Miss Pringle and Mrs Mannering could not possibly approve of, like doing anticlockwise dances dressed in nothing but their underclothes and sticking pins into puppets which had taken some poor person a long time to make.

All the same, the classes must have done some good because afterwards both the ladies found that they were much better than they had been before at seeing ghosts.

They had always been able to see ghosts in a vague and shimmery way but now they saw them as clearly as if they had been ordinary people – and they did not like what they saw.

There were ghosts eating their hearts out in

cinemas and bottle factories; there were headless warriors in all-night garages, and bloodstained brides who rode round and round the Underground because they had nowhere to sleep.

And it was then they got the idea for the agency. For after all if people can adopt whales and trees in rain forests – if schoolchildren can adopt London buses and crocodiles in the zoo – why not ghosts? Only they would have to be proper adoptions, not just sending money. Ghosts after all are not whales or crocodiles; they can fit perfectly well into the right sort of house.

'There might be people who would be only too happy to have a ghost or two in their stately home to attract tourists,' said Miss Pringle.

'And they'd be splendid for keeping off burglars,' said Mrs Mannering.

So they decided to start an agency and call it *Dial A Ghost*. Miss Pringle had some money and was glad to spend it in such a useful way. She was a very kind person but a little vague, and it was Mrs Mannering who knew what to do about furnishing the office and getting filing cabinets and putting out leaflets. It was she too who arranged for separate doors, one saying *Ghosts* and one saying *People*, and printed the notice explaining that they would see ghosts on Tuesdays, Thursdays and Saturdays, and people who wanted to adopt them on the other days.

But it was kind, dithery Miss Pringle who engaged the office boy. He was called Ted and she gave him the job because he looked hungry and his parents were out of work. He was a nice boy, but there was something he hadn't told the ladies – and this 'something' turned out to be important.

*

After the agency had been going for a few months Miss Pringle and Mrs Mannering began to specialize. Miss Pringle dealt with the gentle, peaceful ghosts – the sad ladies who had been left at the altar on their wedding days and jumped off cliffs, and the cold, white little children who had fallen off roofs in their boarding schools, and so on. And Mrs Mannering coped with the fierce ones – the ones that were livid and revolting and rattled their chains.

And every evening when they had finished work, the two ladies went to the Dirty Duck and ordered a port and lemon and told each other how their day had gone.

'I had such a delightful family in just now,' said Miss Pringle. 'The Wilkinsons. I just must fix them up with somewhere to go, and quickly.'

'I think I saw them. Not bloodstained at all, as I recall?' said Mrs Mannering.

'No, not at all. You could say ordinary, but in the best sense of the word. They told me such interesting things about the war. Mrs Wilkinson used to queue for three hours just for one banana, and the old lady once held down an enemy parachutist with her umbrella till the police came to take him away. And there is such a dear little girl – she wasn't born a Wilkinson, they found her lost and abandoned. She could be anyone – a princess even.'

'It shouldn't be difficult to find them a home if they're so nice.'

'No. Except that there are five of them; I don't seem to have anyone on my books who'll take as many as that. They've had such trouble in their lives – there was a sister . . .' She told the sad story of Trixie and the flag. 'And Mrs Wilkinson is so worried

16

about her son. Apparently he was really clever – the top of his class and a patrol leader in the Scouts – and then he got mixed up with this dreadful girl who cadged chewing gum from the American soldiers and sneered at him. It seems to me so wrong, Dorothy, that a family who gave their lives for their country should have to haunt a knicker shop.' She looked across at her friend and saw that Mrs Mannering was looking very tired. 'My dear, how selfish of me! You had the Shriekers in, didn't you? I saw Ted going to hide in the lavatory – and the poor geranium is still completely black.'

'Yes.' Mrs Mannering was a big, strong woman but she sat with her shoulders hunched and she had hardly tasted her drink. 'I really don't know what to do, Nellie. They're so rude and noisy and ungrateful. If it wasn't for the way they carry on about children, I might find them a place – after all they're nobly born, and people like that.'

'We can't have them hurting children, that's true,' said Miss Pringle. 'I wonder what made them the way they are? I gather even the sight of a healthy child drives them quite mad?'

Mrs Mannering nodded. 'There's nothing they wouldn't do to children: slash their faces, strangle them in their bedclothes, set fire to them.' She sighed. 'I'm not mealy-mouthed, Nellie, you know that. If someone comes to me with his head under his arm and says "Find me a home", I'll say "Fair enough". I've fixed up spooks that played chopsticks with their toe bones; I've fixed up moaners and I've fixed up dribblers – but I won't take any risks with children. I really think we'll have to cross the Shriekers off our books.'

17

Miss Pringle shuddered. 'I wouldn't like to make an enemy of the Shriekers.'

'No.' Even Mrs Mannering, tough as she was, didn't like the idea of that. 'Well, we'll give it a bit longer. Perhaps something will turn up.'

The Shriekers were a most appalling set of spooks. They weren't just violent and cruel and fiendish; they were snobbish as well. Nothing on earth would have made the Shriekers haunt anything as humble as a knicker shop. They lived in a frozen meat store on the other side of the city.

It was a dreadful place, but the Shriekers didn't mind the strings of sausages that fastened themselves round their throats as they glided about, or the tubs of greasy white lard, or the sides of cut-up animals hanging from hooks in the ceiling. They were so filthy and loathsome themselves that they hardly noticed the stench or the cold or the slime on the floor.

Once it had not been so. When they were alive, the Shriekers had been rather a grand couple. Their names were Sir Pelham and Lady Sabrina de Bone and they lived in a fortified tower beside a lake. Sir Pelham rode to hounds and shot pheasants, and Sabrina wore fine clothes and gave dinner parties and kept a house full of servants. In fact they were so important that Queen Victoria once came to stay with them on her way to Scotland.

But when they had been married for about ten years, the de Bones had a Great Sorrow and this had driven them mad. No one knew what their sorrow was; they never spoke about it, and the grief and guilt of it had turned inwards and made them wilder and crazier with every year that passed. Even before they became ghosts people had been terrified of the de Bones, and now the sight of them sent the strongest man running for cover. Sir Pelham still wore the jodphurs and hunting jacket he had worn when he broke his neck, but they were covered with filth and gore and he carried a long-thonged whip with which he slashed at everything that crossed his path. His forehead had been bashed in by a horse's hoof so that it was just a mass of splintered bone; his left ear hung by a thread, and through the rent in his trousers you could see his scarred and vicious knees.

His wife was even worse. Sabrina's dress was so bloodstained that you couldn't see the fabric underneath, and hatred had worn away two of her toes and her nose, which was nothing but a nibbled stump. She had picked up a phantom python on her travels and wore it slung round her neck so that the evil-smelling eggs it laid broke and dribbled down inside her vest. Worst of all were her long fingernails, from which bits of skin and hair stuck out because of the tearing and scratching she did all day.

Not only were the Shriekers hateful to look at, but they were the most foul-mouthed couple you could imagine. You could hear them shouting abuse at each other from the moment they woke up to the moment they went to bed.

'Do you call that blood!' Sabrina would shriek when her husband dripped some gore on to the ground. 'Why that isn't even tomato ketchup! I could put that on my fish fingers and not even notice it, you slime-grub!'

'Don't you dare call me names, you maggot-ridden cow-pat,' Sir Pelham would yell back. 'What have *you* done today, I'd like to know? You were going to strangle the butcher's boy before lunch and there isn't a mark on him. And your python looks perfectly ridiculous. You've tied it in a granny knot. Pythons should be tied in a *reef* knot, everyone knows that.'

The only time the Shriekers were cheerful was when they were working out something awful to do to children. When they had thought of some new way of harming a child, Sabrina would open one of the containers and take out a pig's trotter to put in her hair, and string a row of pork chops together to make a belt for her husband, and they would do a stately dance in the dark, cold hall so that one could see how proud and grand they had once been.

But it never lasted long. Soon they'd tear everything off again and bombard each other with pieces of liver and start screaming for more horror and more blood.

The Shriekers had a servant, a miserable, grey, jelly-like creature; a ghoul whom they had found asleep in a graveyard with a rope round his neck. He slept behind a waste bin and every so often they would kick him awake and tell him to cook something and he would totter about muttering, 'Sizzle' or 'Roast' or 'Burn' and swipe vaguely at the sausages with a frying pan. But the cold had almost done for him – ghouls are not suitable for freezing – and the thought of doing their own housework made the Shriekers absolutely furious with the kind ladies of the adoption agency.

'Those human blisters,' yelled Sir Pelham, 'those suppurating boils!'

'I bet they're lying in their beds snoring while we rot in this hell-hole,' shouted Sabrina.

But the Shriekers were wrong. At that very

moment, though it was late at night, Miss Pringle and Mrs Mannering were putting one hundred leaflets into brown envelopes and sticking on one hundred stamps. The leaflets were addressed to the owners of grand houses and stately homes all over Britain, and offered ghosts of every kind suitable for adoption straight away.

And two days later, one of those leaflets dropped on to the dusty, marble floor of Helton Hall.

Chapter Four

Helton Hall was a large, grand and rather gloomy house in the north of England. It was built of grey stone and had a grey slate roof, and grey stone statues of gods and goddesses with chipped and snooty-looking faces lined the terrace. Helton had thirteen bedrooms, and stables, and outhouses, and a lake in which a farmer had once drowned himself. At the end of the long grey gravel drive was a large iron gate with spikes on it, the kind you could have stuck people's heads on in the olden days, and on top of the pillars sat two carved griffons with evil-looking eyes and vicious beaks.

Helton had belonged for hundreds of years to a family by the name of Snodde-Brittle. They owned not just the house but most of the village and a farm and they were very proud of their name, though you might think that a name like Snodde-Brittle was nothing to be cocky about. Their family motto was 'I Set My Foot Upon My Enemies', and if any Snodde-Brittle tried to marry someone who was common and didn't speak 'nicely' they were banished from Helton Hall.

But then things began to go wrong for the Snodde-Brittles. Old Archie Snodde-Brittle, who liked to hunt big game, was run through by a rhinoceros. Then his son Bertie Snodde-Brittle took up hot air ballooning and was shot down by a mad woman who thought he was a space invader, and Bertie's son Frederick was strangled by his tie. (He had been chasing a housemaid in the laundry room and his tie had got caught in the mangle.)

Helton then passed to a cousin of Bertie's who was not very bright and dived into a swimming pool without noticing that it was not filled with water, and the cousin's son was struck by lightning when he went to shelter under the only tree for miles around which was sticking straight up into the air.

Fortunately the cousin's son had had time to marry and have children, but the luck of the Snodde-Brittles was still out. The eldest son fell over a cliff while robbing an eagle's nest in Scotland; the next one overtook an oil tanker on a blind bend, and the youngest was hit on the head with a rolling pin by an old lady he was trying to turn out of her cottage on the estate.

That was the end of that particular batch of Brittles and the lawyers now had to search the family tree to find out who should inherit next. It looked as though it would be a man called Fulton Snodde-Brittle, who was the grandson of Archie's youngest brother Rollo. Fulton had watched eagerly as the ruling Snodde-Brittles were struck by lightning and dived into empty swimming pools and had their heads bashed in by fierce old ladies. But just as he was getting ready to come to Helton, a most exciting discovery was made.

It seemed that Archie had had another brother called James who was older than Rollo. James had quarrelled with his family and changed his name and gone to live abroad, but it now turned out that James's great-grandson was still alive. He was an orphan, not more than ten years old, and had spent most of his life in a children's home in London.

The name of this boy was Oliver Smith and there was no doubt at all that he was the true and rightful owner of Helton Hall.

The news soon spread all over Helton Village.

'It's like a fairy story!' said the blacksmith's wife.

'Imagine his little face when they tell him!' said the lady in the post office.

Even the family lawyer, Mr Norman, and the bank manager who was a trustee for the estate, were amazed.

'It's really extraordinary,' said the bank manager. 'A child brought up in an orphanage. One wonders how he will be able to cope. I suppose there's no doubt about who he is?'

'None at all. I've checked all his papers. We'll have to appoint a guardian, of course.' The lawyer sighed. It was going to make a lot of work, putting a child into Helton Hall.

The Lexington Children's Home was in a shabby part of London, beside a railway line and a factory which made parts for washing machines and fridges. The building was grimy, and the beds the children slept in were old bunk beds bought from the army years and years ago. Instead of soft carpets on the floor there were hard tiles, some of them chipped; the chairs were rickety and the only telly was so old that you couldn't really tell whether the pictures were meant to be black and white or in colour.

But there was something odd about the Home and it was this: the children who lived there didn't want to be adopted.

When there was talk of someone coming to foster a child and take it away, the children slunk off to

24

various hiding places, or they pretended to be ill, and the naughty ones lay down on the floor and drummed their heels. People from outside couldn't understand this, but it was perfectly simple really. The Home might be shabby and poor, but it was a happy place; it was their place. It was where they belonged.

The children came from all sorts of backgrounds, but there was something a little bit wrong with most of them and perhaps that made them kinder to each other than if they'd been big and blustering and tough. Harry stammered so badly you could hardly tell what he was saying and Trevor had lost a hand in the accident which killed his parents. Nonie still wet her bed though she was nearly ten, and Tabitha couldn't help stealing; things just got into her locker and wouldn't come out.

And Oliver, who thought he was called Oliver Smith, suffered from asthma; he'd had it since his parents died when he was three years old. The doctor said he'd probably grow out of it, but it could be scary, not being able to catch one's breath.

Most of the time though Oliver was fine. There were things in the Lexington Children's Home that made up for all the shabbiness and the rattling of the trains and the smell from the factory chimneys. Behind the house was a piece of ground where every single child that wanted to could have a little garden. Matron had saved a three-legged mongrel from a road smash – a brave and intelligent dog who lived with them – and they kept bantam hens which did not lay eggs very often but sometimes. Trevor had a guinea pig and Nonie had a rabbit and Durga had a minah bird which she had taught to sing a rude song in Urdu.

Best of all, the children had each other. You never had to be alone in the Home. At night in the bunk beds there were stories told and plans hatched, and if Matron couldn't come to a crying child there was usually someone who got in beside the child who was miserable and made them laugh.

To Oliver the other children were his brothers and sisters; Matron – if she couldn't come near to being his mother – was kind and fair. There was no dog like Sparky, racing round on her three legs, no conkers like the ones they shook down from the old tree on the embankment – and when the mustard and cress came up on his patch of garden and he could make sandwiches for everyone for tea, he was as pleased as if he'd won first prize at the Chelsea Flower Show.

So you can imagine how he felt on the day that Matron led him into her office and told him that he was not Oliver Smith but Oliver Snodde-Brittle and the new owner of Helton Hall.

Though she spoke slowly and carefully, Oliver at first thought that she must be joking – except that she wasn't a person who teased people and if this was a joke it was a very cruel one.

'It will be a fine chance for you, Oliver,' she said. 'In a place like that you'll be able to help people and do so much good.'

She tried to smile at the little boy staring at her in horror out of his large dark eyes. He did not look very much like the master of a stately home, with his stick-like arms and legs and his soft fawn hair.

'You mean I have to go miles and miles away and live by myself?'

'You won't be by yourself for long. Some cousins

26

are coming to fetch you and help you settle in. Think of it, Oliver – you'll be in the country and able to have all the animals you want. Ponies . . . a dog . . .'

'I don't want any dog but Sparky. I don't want to go away. Please don't make me go. *Please!*'

Matron took him in her arms. She had never told children that it was sissy to cry – sometimes one cried and that was the end of it – and now as she smoothed back his hair, she felt his tears run down her hand.

As a matter of fact she didn't feel too good herself. She made it a rule not to have favourites but she loved this boy; he was imaginative and kind and funny and she was going to miss him horribly.

And she wasn't the only one. There was going to be a nasty fuss when Oliver's friends heard he was leaving. A very nasty fuss indeed.

The cousins who were coming to fetch Oliver were called Fulton and Frieda Snodde-Brittle. Fulton was the headmaster of a boys' prep school in Yorkshire and Frieda was his sister and they had sent a letter to the lawyer, Mr Norman, offering to take charge of him.

'Our school will be shut for the Easter holidays,' Fulton had written, 'and we shall be happy to help him settle in. It must be rather a shock for the poor little fellow. As you know we are used to boys; the pupils in our care are just like our own children and we shall know how to make him comfortable.'

'I must say that's very kind,' said Mr Norman, showing the letter to the bank manager. 'I was going to go and fetch Oliver myself but I'm very busy. And really I didn't know what was going to be done with the child in that barrack of a place. It's been shut up for months and the servants are very old.'

'You haven't heard from Colonel Mersham?' asked the bank manager.

Mr Norman shook his head. The man they had chosen to be Oliver's guardian was an explorer and away in Costa Rica looking for a rare breed of golden toad.

'He's due back at the end of the summer, but in the meantime this offer of Fulton's is most convenient.'

'Yes. I must say he's been very decent when you think that if it wasn't for Oliver, Fulton himself would be master of Helton Hall.'

Which just shows how simple-minded lawyers and bank managers can sometimes get.

Because Fulton wasn't kind at all; he was evil, and so was his sister Frieda. The school that they ran was called Sunnydell, but no place could have been less sunny. The children were beaten, the food was uneatable and the classrooms were freezing. The sweets the parents sent were confiscated, and the letters the boys wrote home to say how miserable they were never got posted.

But you can only run a school like that for so long. The inspectors were getting wise to the Snodde-Brittles, and so were the parents. At first they had liked the idea of their boys being toughened up, but gradually more and more children were taken away, and as the school got smaller and smaller the Snodde-Brittles got poorer and poorer.

So when they heard that the last owner of Helton had had his head bashed in by a fierce old lady, their joy knew no bounds.

'I'm the new master of Helton!' yelled Fulton.

'And I'm the new mistress!' shouted Frieda.

'We'll Set Our Foot Upon Our Enemies!' shouted Fulton.

'Both our feet!'

And then came the letter from the lawyer saying that Oliver had been found and that he and not Fulton was the rightful owner of Helton.

For two days the Snodde-Brittles nearly choked themselves with rage. They prowled the corridors muttering and cursing; they practised every kind of cruelty on the pupils, twisting their arms, shutting them in cupboards; they shook their fists at the heavens.

Then Fulton calmed down. 'Now listen, Frieda, there must be something we can do about this boy.'

'Kill him, do you mean?' asked Frieda uneasily.

'No, no. Not directly. The police would get on to that; they've got all sorts of scientific equipment these days. But there'll be something. We've just got to show that he's unfit to take over . . . that he's mad or ill. There's bound to be bad blood in him somewhere. Now listen; we've got to pretend to be his friends . . . his loving relations,' said Fulton with a leer. 'We've got to show everyone that we're on his side – and then . . .'

'And then what?'

'I don't know yet. But I will soon. Just leave it to me.'

So they wrote to the lawyer and two weeks later they were on their way to London.

'What a shabby house,' said Frieda disgustedly as the taxi drew up in front of the Home. 'The curtains are

29

patched and the plaster is peeling. Really, I don't know what the council is doing to allow such a place.'

Both the Snodde-Brittles were dressed in black; both were tall and bony, and both had moustaches. Fulton's moustache was there on purpose – a dung-coloured growth on his upper lip. Frieda's was there by mistake.

'One could hardly expect anything else in this part of London,' said Fulton, not giving the taxi driver his tip and sneering at an old lady shuffling to the corner shop in her slippers. 'It is given over to beggars and the Poor. People who are shiftless and don't work.'

The door was opened by a cheerful girl in a pink overall which Frieda disapproved of: maids should wear uniform and call her 'Madam'. She also disapproved of the rich smell of frying chips, the sound of laughter from the garden and the children's paintings tacked to the walls of the corridor.

'Matron will be along in a minute,' said the girl, and showed them into an office with two sagging armchairs and a large desk almost completely covered in photographs of children who had been in the Home throughout the years.

'It's quite extraordinary that a true Snodde-Brittle should have been living in a place such as this,' said Frieda.

'If the brat *is* a true Snodde-Brittle,' said Fulton, biting his moustache.

Matron came in. She wore a woollen skirt and a hand-knitted cardigan, and clinging to her hand was a small boy.

'Good heavens!' said Frieda rudely. 'Is *that* the child?'

'Yes, this is Oliver,' said Matron quietly, giving his hand a squeeze.

'I do not see even a trace of the Snodde-Brittles in this boy,' said Fulton, frowning.

This was true. The Snodde-Brittles were tall and long-faced with bulging eyes and mouthfuls of enormous teeth.

'His mother was French,' said Matron. 'We think that Oliver takes after her.'

'Ha!' Fulton was disgusted. Foreign blood! Then remembering that he was posing as Oliver's friend, he leaned towards him and said: 'Well now, boy, you will have heard of your good fortune?'

'Yes.'

Oliver's voice was almost a whisper. His troubled eyes were turned to Matron.

'You don't seem to realize how lucky you are. Children all over the world would give anything to be in your shoes.'

Oliver raised his head, suddenly looking cheerful. 'If there are children all over the world who want to live there, can't I give it to them – Helton Hall, I mean – and stay here?'

'Stay here?' said Fulton.

'Stay *here*?' said Frieda.

The Snodde-Brittles were flabbergasted. They couldn't believe their ears.

'Oliver, you must try out your new life,' said Matron. 'We'll write you lots and lots of letters, and as soon as you're settled, some of the children will be able to come and stay.'

The Snodde-Brittles looked at each other. Long before common and scruffy children were allowed to come and stay at Helton, Oliver should be safely out of the way.

'We have to catch the three-twenty from King's Cross,' said Frieda.

Matron nodded. 'Go and get your things, dear,' she said to Oliver. 'And tell the others that they can come and see you off.'

When the boy had gone she turned to the Snodde-Brittles. 'You will find Oliver a willing and intelligent child,' she said, 'but he's delicate. When he's upset or if he gets some kind of shock, he has asthma attacks and finds trouble in breathing. I've put in his inhaler and exact instructions about what to do, and of course you'll have a doctor up there. But the main thing is to keep him on an even keel, and happy. Then he's fine.'

The Snodde-Brittles exchanged glances.

'Really?' said Fulton, licking his lips. 'You mean it could be dangerous for him to have a shock? Really dangerous?'

'It could be,' said Matron. 'But if you're careful everything will be fine. We've never had any trouble here.'

In the taxi on the way to the station Fulton was silent, thinking hard. A shock could be dangerous, could it? But what sort of a shock?

Frieda sat with a grim face, thinking of the ridiculous fuss there had been when Oliver left. Children swarming all over him, stuffing things into his pockets; a three-legged mongrel who should have been shot, jumping up and down – and all of them running after the taxi and waving like lunatics.

Between Fulton and Frieda sat Oliver, holding his presents carefully on his lap. A torch from Trevor, a box of crayons from Nonie . . . they must have saved up all their pocket money. There was a huge 'good luck' card too, signed by everyone in the home. Even Sparky had added her pawmark in splodgy ink.

The taxi was crawling, caught in a jam. Now it stopped for traffic lights ahead. Looking out of the window, Fulton saw a number of signs on a tall grey house.

Adopt A Ghost, said one . . . and *Dial A Ghost*, said another.

Dial a ghost? Now where had he seen those words before? Of course, on the leaflet he'd picked off the mat at Helton when he went ahead to give orders to the servants. 'Every kind of ghost,' the leaflet had offered . . .

Fulton bared his yellow teeth in the nearest he ever came to a smile, and his eyes glittered.

He knew now what he was going to do.

Chapter Five

No sooner had Oliver's taxi disappeared down a side street than two nuns, looking like kind and intelligent penguins in their black and white habits, made their way up the steps of the agency. It was one of the days when people came to ask for ghosts, not ghosts for people, and as soon as she saw them Miss Pringle felt that something good was going to happen.

Mother Margaret, who was the head of the convent, came to the point at once.

'We have been very lucky,' she said, 'and our order has just moved into new buildings. Very beautiful buildings with a cloister and a refectory, and a little chapel where we shall be able to pray without the rain coming on to our heads from the broken roof.'

'God has been very good to us,' said Sister Phyllida.

'So we wanted to share our good fortune,' said Mother Margaret.

'You see, our old abbey buildings are still standing. It was too expensive to pull them down and we thought we might offer a home to a suitable family. They would be quite undisturbed. We shouldn't trouble them – and of course we would expect them not to trouble us.'

Miss Pringle was becoming very excited.

'You know, I think I have just the family for you. The nicest ghosts you could possibly ask for.'

'I know you will understand that we need ghosts

who are not too noisy. Sadness wouldn't worry us,' said Mother Margaret, 'or cold kisses from blood-stained lips. We would completely understand about sadness and cold kisses. Someone headless would be all right too, as long as they didn't frighten the goats. We keep goats, you know.'

'And bees,' said Sister Phyllida eagerly. 'It's quite a little paradise we have at Larchford Abbey. Our rose garden—'

'Yes, the bees are important. We ourselves would not be disturbed too much by screams and that kind of thing, but bees are very sensitive. So we would ask you to be very choosy.'

'Indeed, yes – I think you couldn't help being pleased with the Wilkinsons. You wouldn't mind a very old lady? She has rather a fierce umbrella but she is an excellent person and in no way shrivelled or withered – or at any rate no more than is usual at her age.'

'Being shrivelled or withered would be no problem at all,' said Mother Margaret with her kind smile. 'We are used to nursing old people and have great respect for them.'

'Then there is Mr Wilkinson – he was a dentist, a most upstanding man, and his wife is one of the nicest people you could imagine. She has done wonders trying to make the knicker shop into a home.'

Miss Pringle blushed, wondering if she should have said the word 'knickers' in front of nuns, but they did not mind in the least.

'They sound just the sort of people we want,' said Mother Margaret. 'And I may say that the accommodation we offer must be what any ghost would want. A ruined cellar – rat-infested of course. A

35

roofless chapel overgrown with weeds and the haunt of large white owls. A tumbledown refectory with a fireplace open to the roof . . .'

'And such a pretty bell tower,' put in Sister Phyllida, 'full of tangled ropes and iron rings and trap doors. A child would love to play there.' She looked wistfully at Miss Pringle. 'There don't happen to be any children?'

'But there are, there are! Eric is a teenager and a bit wrapped up in himself – but there's a delightful little girl – she's not a real Wilkinson, they found her lost and abandoned, but they quite think of her as their own. She's rather strong-willed and very fond of animals but—'

Miss Pringle paused, wondering if she should warn the nuns about Addie's passion for unusual pets. But the nuns just said that it was natural for children to grow up with animals, and it was arranged that the family should come to Larchford Abbey in three weeks' time.

'Friday the 13th seems a nice date,' said Mother Margaret, looking at her diary. 'Ghosts would like to come on a date like that, I feel sure.'

'Yes indeed,' said Miss Pringle, quite overjoyed at the news she was going to give the Wilkinsons. 'Now if you would just be kind enough to fill in this form . . .'

That night in the Dirty Duck the ladies had not one port and lemon, but two.

'If only we could get your Shriekers placed as happily,' said Miss Pringle.

Mrs Mannering sighed. 'I don't know what's going to become of them, Nellie. They're wrecking the meat store, and that servant of theirs has climbed into one of the containers and passed out cold. I keep wondering what would happen if someone came for a tray of hamburgers and found a completely frozen ghoul.'

Miss Pringle made sympathetic tutting noises. 'We must just go on hoping, dear,' she said. 'Perhaps getting the Wilkinsons fixed up will turn our luck.'

Chapter Six

'Is this really mine? All of it?' asked Oliver.

'Yes, it is,' said Fulton grimly. 'I hope you're impressed.'

But Oliver was not impressed; he was appalled. They had driven through a spiked iron gate along a gravel drive and now stood at the bottom of a flight of steps on either side of which were statues. To the left of Oliver was a lion being stepped on by a man who was beating him on the head with a club. On the right was an even bulgier man wearing a sort of nappy and strangling a snake. The windows of the tall grey building stared like a row of dead eyes; pointless towers and battlements sprouted from the roof, and the front door was studded with nails.

Almost worse than the gloomy building and the statues of animals being bullied by bulging men was the icy wind sighing and soughing in from the sea. Tall trees bent their branches; rooks flew upwards shrieking. Everything at Helton looked grey and miserable and cold.

Oliver shivered and wondered again if there was some way he could give the place away. Perhaps he should ask his guardian? Colonel Mersham sounded sensible, trying to save the lemurs in the rain forest and looking for golden toads; but he wasn't going to be back for months.

The door now opened from the inside and Oliver

found himself in a stone hall which was full of things for killing people. Crossed pikes, a blunderbuss, a row of rusty swords fastened to the wall . . . A stuffed leopard snarled from a glass case and beside it stood the butler and the housekeeper waiting to greet him.

Oliver thought he had never seen two people who looked so old. The housekeeper, Miss Match, had a grey bun of hair and a pink hearing aid stuck lopsidedly to one ear. The butler, Mr Tusker, was bent almost double with rheumatism. As he shook their dry leathery hands Oliver was shocked that they should be working as servants; they should have had servants working for them.

'Dinner is ready in the dining room, sir,' said Miss Match to Fulton. She had been told to take her orders from him and she was too ancient and tired to be curious about the little boy who now owned Helton Hall.

Oliver followed them down a long corridor hung with portraits of the Snodde-Brittles in heavy golden frames. They passed through a shuttered billiard room . . . a library with rows of leather-bound books locked up behind an iron grille . . . and reached the dining room where Oliver's first meal at Helton Hall was waiting.

It was a meal he never forgot. Cousin Fulton and Cousin Frieda made him sit at the head of the table and his feet, hanging down from the high carved chair, didn't even touch the ground. The table was the size of a skating rink, the room was freezing cold – and beside his plate were more knives and forks than Oliver had ever seen in his life.

'Start from the outside in,' Matron had told them when they went for a treat to the Holiday Inn and had a proper banquet. So he picked up the round spoon and ate the soup, and then Mr Tusker shuffled away and came back with a very red-looking bird and some potatoes and cabbage. Oliver ate the vegetables and took two mouthfuls of the bird, which was full of round dark pellets and tasted of blood. Then he put down his knife and fork.

'Have you finished, sir?' asked the butler.

'Yes, thank you,' said Oliver.

'What's the matter, boy?' said Fulton. 'There's nothing wrong with the meat, is there?'

'No, I expect it's fine, but I don't eat meat. I'm a vegetarian.'

'A vegetarian?' said Fulton, his eyes bulging.

'A *vegetarian*?' echoed Frieda.

'A lot of us were in the Home. About half. It was after we saw a film about a slaughterhouse.'

No one said anything after that. It was as though Oliver had said he was a wife-beater or had the plague.

But if the meal was bad, going to bed was much, much worse.

'You're to sleep in the master bedroom,' said Frieda. 'It's up in the tower, quite on its own. Nobody will bother you there.'

'I don't mind being bothered,' said Oliver in a small voice. 'Couldn't I sleep a bit closer to other people?'

'Certainly not,' said Fulton, for it was part of his plan to keep Oliver as lonely and as far away from help as possible. 'The owner of Helton has always slept in the tower.'

So Oliver followed Cousin Frieda up a wooden staircase, through the Long Gallery with its faceless statues and rusty suits of armour, along a corridor lined with grinning African masks... up another flight of steps – a curving stone one this time, lit only by narrow slits in the walls – down a second corridor hung with snarling heads of shot animals... and reached at last a heavy oaken door.

The room in which he found himself was huge; the single light in its heavy shade scarcely reached the corners. Three full-length tapestries hung on the wall. One showed a man stuck full of arrows; one was of a deer having its throat cut, and the third was a battle scene in which rearing horses brought their hoofs down on screaming men. An oak chest shaped like a coffin stood by the window, and the bed was a four-poster hung with dusty velvet curtains and the words 'I Set My Foot Upon My Enemies' carved into the wood.

'The bathroom's through there,' said Frieda, opening a door beside the wardrobe. 'I'll leave you to unpack and put yourself to bed.'

Oliver listened to her steps dying away and followed her in his mind along the corridor with the stuffed heads, down the curving stone stairs, across the Long Gallery... He had never in his life felt so alone.

The bathroom was a room for giants. All the cupboards were too high for him, and the only way he could reach the lavatory chain was to stand on the seat. In the bathtub, scrubbing himself with a long-handled brush which hurt his skin, Oliver tried hard not to think about the Home. Bath-time had been one of the best times of the day; they'd blown bubbles and told silly jokes and afterwards there was cocoa and a story from Matron. They were reading *The Lion, the Witch and the Wardrobe.*

The only way to get into bed was to run fast across the blood-red carpet and leap in under the covers. But it didn't help much. He could still hear the stealthy tap-tap of the tassel of the blind against the window – and surely there was *something* in that big brown wardrobe . . . the way it creaked even when there was no one near.

The sound of footsteps returned. At the thought that someone had come back to say goodnight to him, Oliver brightened and sat up in bed. Perhaps they did care at Helton; perhaps he wasn't quite alone.

Cousin Frieda entered the room.

'Well, you're all settled, I see.' She moved to the bed and looked down at the inhaler which Oliver had put on the night table beside him. 'You won't want that,' she said briskly. 'I'll put it in the bathroom cabinet.'

'Oh no, please.' Oliver was frightened now. 'I always have it by my bed. Sometimes I need it in the night.'

'Well, it won't be far away,' said Frieda. She took it off to the bathroom and put it in the high medicine cupboard, far out of Oliver's reach. 'Now I know you're not one of those silly children who ask for night lights,' she said, and her bony fingers moved towards the switch.

She was halfway out of the door when Oliver's choked voice came out of the darkness. 'Cousin Frieda,' he said. 'There aren't . . . are there any ghosts here? Does Helton have ghosts?'

Frieda smiled. Standing there in the shadows in her black dress, she might have been a phantom herself.

'Really, Oliver,' she said. 'What a silly question! Of *course* there are ghosts in a house as old as this.'

Then she shut the door and left him alone in the dark.

Fulton was in the drawing room, smoking a cigar.

'It'll work, Fulton, you're right,' said Frieda. 'He's scared already – in a week or two he'll be ready.'

Fulton nodded. 'I've had another look at the leaflet and there shouldn't be any trouble about getting what we want. "Spooks of every kind," it says. I'll ring up in the morning to make an appointment. I'll go down in a few days and book some that'll do the trick. Then when the boy's properly softened up, we'll move them in.'

'You hadn't thought of us being in the house when . . . you know. Not that I'm frightened in the least, but . . .'

'No, no. When the time's right we'll go away and leave him quite alone. I tell you, Frieda, our troubles are over. Helton is as good as ours!'

Chapter Seven

Three days later Fulton walked into the *Dial A Ghost* agency. He had put on a blond wig and gave his name as Mr Boyd because he didn't want anyone to know what he was doing to Oliver.

Mrs Mannering smiled at him. 'What can I do for you, Mr Boyd?' she asked.

'Actually, it's more what I can do for you,' he said. 'Which is to offer a home to some ghosts. But not any ghosts. I want fearful ghosts; frightful and dangerous ghosts. Ghosts that can turn people's limbs to jelly.'

Mrs Mannering leant forward eagerly. Was it possible that she could get rid of the Shriekers at last?

'You see, I think that people nowadays want a bit of danger,' Fulton said. 'They want a thrill. They don't want things to be boring and tame.'

'No, no, of course not. You are so *right*!' cried Mrs Mannering. 'If only more people thought like you!'

'Now, I'm the manager of this big house in the north of England. It's been empty for a long time and now the owners want to open it to the public. They want to charge money for letting people go round the place.'

'Yes, I see. It's sad the way these stately home owners have fallen on hard times.'

'Only of course there's a lot of competition in this

business. At Lingley they've got lions and at Abbeyford they've got a funfair and at Tavenham they've got a boating lake. Well, there's nothing like that at the place I'm talking about. So I thought if we got some proper ghosts we could advertise it as The Most Haunted House In Britain or Spook Abbey or some such thing. That should pull in the crowds.'

'It should indeed,' agreed Mrs Mannering. 'Only I have to ask . . . what would you offer the ghosts – and what would you expect from them?'

'What would we *offer* them? My dear Mrs Mannering, we'd offer them accommodation like no ghosts in Britain could boast of. Thirteen bedrooms with wall hangings. Corridors with howling draughts and hidden doors. Suits of armour to swoop out of . . . and a master bedroom with a coffin chest which they could have entirely to themselves. As for what we'd expect – well, some really high-class haunting. Something that would make people faint and scream and come back for more.'

Mrs Mannering was getting more and more excited. 'My dear Mr Boyd, I have exactly the ghosts for you! Sir Pelham and Lady Sabrina de Bone. They come of a very good family as you can gather and would be absolutely at home in such a setting.'

'They're the real thing, are they? You know . . . icy hands, strangling people, rappings, smotherings?'

'Yes indeed. All that and more. Pythons, bloodstains, nose stumps . . . I promise you won't be disappointed. There's a servant too who I believe is very fiendish, but he's in cold storage at the moment so I haven't seen him. There's only one thing – the de Bones really hate children. Especially children asleep in their beds. Of course if the house is empty at night that wouldn't be a problem. But I would be worried about any children going round the house with their parents.'

'We would certainly have to be careful about that,' said Fulton smarmily. 'I tell you what, we could put up a notice saying "This guided tour is not suitable for children under twelve". Like in the cinema. We might even build a playground so that the children are kept out of the way.'

'That sounds fine,' said Mrs Mannering. 'Quite excellent. Now tell me, how soon would you like them to come?'

Fulton was silent, thinking. Oliver was already going under, but he needed a bit longer to get properly softened up. 'How about Friday the 13th,' he said. His lips parted over his yellow teeth and Mrs Mannering realized he was smiling. 'But I have to make it quite clear that I won't take anything namby-pamby. You know, spooks wringing their hands and feeling guilty because they stole tuppence from the Poor Box or were nasty to their mummy. I need ghosts with gumption; I need evil and darkness and sin.'

'You will get them, Mr Boyd, I promise you,' said Mrs Mannering.

As soon as her visitor had gone, Mrs Mannering hurried across the corridor and hugged her friend. 'You were right, Nellie, our luck has turned! I've found a place for the Shriekers!'

'Oh my dear, what wonderful news! When are they leaving?'

'Friday the 13th – the same day as the Wilkinsons!'

The following morning they each wrote out the adoption papers, and made careful maps for both sets of ghosts and instructions about what to do when they got there. They put the Wilkinsons' maps into a green folder and the Shriekers' maps into a red folder and placed them in the filing cabinet, ready for the day when the ghosts should leave.

'Now be sure and look after these very carefully,' they told Ted the office boy.

And Ted said he would. He was a nice boy and a hard worker, but he had not told the ladies that he was colour-blind.

This didn't mean that he couldn't see *any* colours. He could see yellow and blue and violet perfectly well. But for a person who is colour-blind there is absolutely no difference between green and red.

Oliver had been ten days at Helton and no one would have recognized him as the cheerful, busy child he had been in the Home. He was pale, his dark eyes had rings under them; he jumped at sudden noises.

He knew he had to be grateful to Cousin Fulton and Cousin Frieda who had come to stay with him even though the boys at their school needed them so much, and he knew that people couldn't help how they looked.

But he couldn't feel comfortable with them and there was no one else to talk to. The servants were so old and deaf that it was a wonder they didn't drop down dead every time they picked up a duster, and the people who worked outside weren't friendly at all. The gardener hurried away whenever he saw Oliver, and the people from the village scarcely spoke to him.

Oliver did not know that Fulton had told them to do this.

47

'The boy's delicate,' he told everyone. 'He's got to be kept absolutely quiet.'

So Oliver spent most of the day alone, which was exactly what Fulton had planned. He wandered down the long corridors being sneered at by the Snodde-Brittle ancestors in their heavy frames. He sat in the library turning over the pages of dusty books with no pictures in them, or tried to pick out tunes on the piano in the dark drawing room with its shrouded windows and enormous chairs.

If the inside of Helton was gloomy and dank, the outside was hardly any better. The weather was windy and grey, and the garden seemed to grow mostly stones: stone statues, stone benches covered in rook droppings, stone fountains with cracked rims. The lake was a black, silent hole and something bad had happened there.

'A stupid farmer drowned himself,' said Frieda.

'Oh!' Oliver looked down into the water, wondering what it was like to lie there in all that blackness. 'Is he still there?'

'I expect so,' said Frieda. 'It was his own fault. He had the cheek to fall in love with a Snodde-Brittle.'

'Didn't she want him?' Oliver asked.

'*Want* him? A Snodde-Brittle *want* a common farmer! Don't be stupid, boy.'

Something bad had happened on the hill behind the house as well. Two hikers had been caught in a blizzard and frozen to death.

'They were townies,' said Fulton. 'Not properly dressed.'

'I'm a townie too,' said Oliver. 'I come from a town.'

But he could see that it was the fault of the hikers, like it was the fault of the farmer for falling in love.

What made everything so much worse for Oliver was knowing that all his friends in the Home had forgotten him.

'We'll write to you at *once*,' Nonie had promised. 'Even before you get there we'll start.'

Everybody had said they would write straight away, and Matron too.

But they hadn't. Every day he waited for a letter and every day there was nothing at all. Oliver had written the very first morning, trying not to sound miserable and drawing them a picture of the hall. Since then he'd written three more letters and he hadn't had a single one back, not even a postcard.

'Are you *sure*, Cousin Fulton?' Oliver said each day as Fulton returned from the post office, shaking his head.

'Quite sure,' Fulton would say. 'There was nothing for you. Nothing at all.'

And Oliver said no more. How could a boy brought up to trust people as he had been, look into the black heart of a man like Fulton? How could he guess that the letters he wrote to his friends were torn up before they ever reached the post office, and that the letters that came for him – lots of letters and postcards and a little packet from Matron – were destroyed by Fulton on the way back to the Hall.

Even thinking that Fulton might have made a mistake and not looked properly made Oliver feel guilty, because his cousin was trying so hard to be kind. Every evening, for example, Fulton would take him into the drawing room and turn out the overhead light and tell him ghost stories.

'You like ghost stories, I'm sure,' Fulton would say, making Oliver sit beside him on the sofa. 'All the boys in my school love a good creepy story and I bet you do too.'

Then he would start. There was the story of the eyeless phantom that tapped each night on the window pane asking to be let in, and when the window was opened, he seized the person and sank his teeth into their flesh. There was the story of the wailing nun who plucked off people's bedclothes and strangled them as they slept, and the story of the skeleton who came to look for his own skull.

'And do you know where he found it?' Fulton would say, bringing his face close up to Oliver's. 'In an old coffin chest exactly like the one in your room!'

Then he would pat Oliver on the head and Frieda would come and say, 'Bedtime, Oliver!' – and the little boy would go alone through the Long Gallery with its faceless marble statues, along the corridor lined with grinning masks, up the cold stone staircase, past the bared teeth of shot animals – and reach, at last, his room.

Oliver did not cry; he did not run back and beg to be allowed to stay downstairs. But as he lay in the cave he had made for himself under the bedclothes, he thought he wouldn't mind too much if it was soon over; if they came quickly, the ghosts that were going to get him. If he was frightened to death he could go and lie quietly under the ground in the churchyard. He had seen the graves and the tombstones covered with moss and it had looked peaceful there.

And for a child to think like that is not a good idea at all.

Chapter Eight

In the knicker shop, the Wilkinsons were having a
party. It was the day before they were due to leave
for their new home in the country and they had
invited their friends to say goodbye. Mr Hofmann
had come from the bunion shop, sniffing a little
because he was going to lose Grandma, and a lovely
Swedish phantom called Pernilla, with luminous hair
and gentle eyes, had drifted in from the music store.
There was a jogger who had jogged once too often,
and various children Addie had picked up: the son of
a rat-catcher who came with a dozen of his father's
phantom rats, and a pickpocket called Jake who knew
everything there was to know about living off the
land.

It was a good party. Though the ghosts were sad
to see such a nice family leave the district, they tried
hard not to begrudge the Wilkinsons their good luck.

'Aaah . . . imagine . . . to breathe again the fresh
clear air,' sighed Pernilla, who was dreadfully home-
sick for the pine forests of her native land.

'And living with nuns,' said the jogger, who had
been a curate before he dropped dead of a heart
attack on the A12. 'Such good people!'

Aunt Maud was everywhere, filling glasses with her
nightshade cordial, making people feel comfortable.

'If only you could all come with us,' she sighed.

'Maybe you can,' said Adopta. 'If the nuns are so kind, maybe they'll make room for you all!'

She had filled Grandma's gas mask case with the ghosts of beetles and woodlice which she meant to re-settle in the country and was so excited that she found it impossible to keep still.

Everyone had been very well behaved up to then, but perhaps Aunt Maud's drinks were stronger than she realized because Eric, who was usually so quiet, suddenly said, 'No more knickers!' and sent a box of mini-briefs tumbling to the floor.

'No more Tootsies and Footsies and Bootsies,' shouted Grandma, who had been particularly annoyed at the silly names that people nowadays gave to socks, thwacking at the display stand with her umbrella.

'And down with tummy buttons,' yelled Adopta, and a pile of polka-dot bikinis tumbled from their shelves.

At first Aunt Maud and Uncle Henry tried to stop them, but it was no use. The relief of getting away from all that underwear was just too great, and soon even Mr Hofmann, who could hardly glide, was thumping a see-through nightdress with his crutch, while Pernilla zoomed to the ceiling with a box of body stockings which she draped like streamers round the lamp.

But when the clock struck eleven, they quietened down. Mr Hofmann was led away by Grandma, the jogger jogged back to the A12, the rat-catcher's son called to his rats – and the host and hostess, as is the way with parties, were left to clean up the mess.

There was only one more thing to do. Sober and

solemn now, the Wilkinsons filed out into the street and called to Trixie.

'We love you, Trixie,' they said, bowing to the north.

'We need you, Trixie,' they said, bowing to the east and the west and the south.

'And we shall never forget you,' they promised.

Of course if Trixie had come just then it would have been a miracle, but she didn't. So they went back to pack and cover the budgie's cage, while Uncle Henry made his way to the *Dial A Ghost* agency and the office of Miss Pringle.

The folder with all their instructions and the maps was exactly where she had said it would be, on the window sill beside the potted geranium. Uncle Henry took it and passed it backwards and forwards across his chest so as to cover it with ectoplasm and make it invisible.

And an hour later, the Wilkinsons were on their way.

The Shriekers did not have a farewell party. To have a party you need friends and the Shriekers didn't have any. All the same, in their dark and nasty way they were excited.

'A place that's fit for us at last,' said Sabrina. 'Statues . . . suits of armour . . . a tower!'

Mrs Mannering had come herself to tell the Shriekers about Helton Hall, which was noble of her because the frozen meat store had not been a nice place even before the de Bones came, and now it was unspeakable. Sides of beef lay sprawled on the floor where they had tried to drink blood from them;

sheep's kidneys and gobbets of fat squelched underfoot.

'Perhaps there'll be some children we can scare to death,' said Sir Pelham, and the hatred in his eyes was terrible to see.

'A little girl I can scratch with my fingernails,' gloated Sabrina. 'Long, deep scratches right to the bone.'

'A little boy I can squeeze and squeeze till he turns blue and chokes.'

But now it was time to thaw out the ghoul and get ready to leave. They had tipped him out of his container the night before but he was still rigid, and while Sir Pelham beat him with his riding crop, Sabrina jerked the rope round his neck and screamed her orders. 'You're to get up, you pullulating blob. You're to get up and cook something and clean something and pack something and hurry!'

While the poor ghoul tottered about muttering, 'Fry! Sizzle! Sweep!' Sabrina made herself beautiful for the journey. She squeezed the juice from a pig's gall bladder and dabbed it behind her ears; she smeared her dress with lard to give a shine to the bloodstains, and she unknotted the python from her neck and fed him a dead mouse.

Meanwhile Sir Pelham glided to the *Dial A Ghost* agency and through the window of Mrs Mannering's office. The folder with the maps in it was just where Mrs Mannering had promised. It even had 'de Bone' on it in Ted's rather wiggly handwriting.

And as midnight struck, the de Bones too, dragging their wretched servant by his rope, set off for their new life.

*

54

Oliver had woken with the feeling that he just couldn't go on. He would have run back to the Home, but the letter he wrote to Matron begging her to let him return had gone unanswered like all his other letters.

So there was nowhere to go. He got up wearily and dressed and began the long journey down to the dining room where Fulton and Frieda were waiting.

'We have a nice surprise for you, Oliver,' said Frieda. 'You've been looking a bit pale lately so we've asked Mr Tusker to drive you to the sea. He's going to York tonight to visit his sick sister, so this is your last chance to see something of the countryside.'

Oliver felt guilty, of course. He'd thought how creepy Frieda and Fulton were and here they were planning a treat. The idea of seeing the sea cheered him up. They'd gone to the seaside a few times from the Home. There'd been donkey rides and ice cream and he and Trevor and Nonie had made the best sandcastle on the beach.

But when doddery Mr Tusker stopped the car beside the dunes, Oliver realized he'd been silly again. The sea at Helton wasn't at all like that. The butler wouldn't even get out but shut all the windows and unfolded his newspaper. Then he handed Oliver a packet of sandwiches and said, 'Don't come back till four. We're to stay out till then.'

So Oliver trudged off across the tussocky grass and tumbled down on to the shore. The wind hit him so hard he could scarcely stand upright; the waves slapped and pounded and thumped; dark clouds raced across the sky. The tide was high, so there were no rock pools, and as he fought his way up the beach he was almost blinded by flying sand. After a while he gave up the struggle and climbed into a hollow between two dunes, where he ate his sandwiches. Then he dug a deep hole and lay down in it and fell asleep.

It was teatime when they got back to Helton. Mr Tusker drove off to the station and Oliver made his way to the dining room. A glass of milk and some biscuits were laid out on the table, but there was no sign of Fulton and Frieda. Instead, beside his plate, there was a note.

'Dear Oliver,' he read. 'I'm afraid we have had to go away for a few days. The boys in our school have been unhappy without us and there has been some trouble which we have to put right. I know you will not mind being alone. After all, the master of Helton Hall has got to get used to being by himself. Miss Match has left your supper on the kitchen table; it is her day off and she is going to spend the night in the village, but there is plenty of food in the larder. We will be back as soon as possible . . . Your affectionate Cousin Fulton.'

Oliver looked up, straight into the sinister marble face of the god Pan crouching on top of a clock. It was true then. In all the thirty rooms of Helton, he was the only living soul.

I won't panic, he told himself. I'll manage. He drank his milk and went outside. It was less frightening out of doors, but no more cheerful. He walked round the dark lake with its drowned farmer, through the grove of weeping ash trees, up the hill where the two hikers had died . . .

The cold drove him in at seven, and he went to fetch his supper. The kitchens were down in the basement. He made his way through the maze of dank

56

stone corridors, sure that at every corner something was waiting to pounce . . . past a pantry where dead birds hung by their legs . . . past an iron boiler chuntering like an evil giant . . .

The kitchen was huge, with a scrubbed wooden table. On the table was a tray with a salad, slices of bread and butter, a glass of lemonade. He ate it there, and when he had finished, carried his empty dishes to the sink. It was then that he noticed the calendar hanging on the wall. It was a pretty calendar with views of the countryside, and the day's date ringed by Miss Match.

Friday the 13th. The unluckiest day of the year! The day that ghosts and ghouls and vampires like best of all!

At that moment Oliver knew that it would happen this very night – the thing he waited for every time he crawled into the great bed and pulled the covers over his head. It might be the flesh-eating phantom at the window, it might be the wailing nun who strangled people with their sheets, or the skeleton looking for his skull – but one of them would come.

And when they did so, he would die.

Chapter Nine

The Wilkinsons travelled by train.

The 1 a.m. from King's Cross goes direct to York, where you must be sure to leave the train, said the instructions in the folder.

So the Wilkinsons, who were all invisible of course, settled themselves down and had a very pleasant journey. The one o'clock was a sleeper, the kind with cubicles and bunk beds, and people were already lying in them, but the ghosts were used to mucking in. Grandma stretched out on the luggage rack, Addie and Eric lay down on the floor, and Uncle Henry and Aunt Maud took the budgie to the deserted dining car.

Travelling by train is always enjoyable, and when you don't have to pay fares there is an extra glow, but Uncle Henry, as the train raced through the night, was troubled. He was so sure that Miss Pringle had said the nuns lived in the West Country, and there was no doubt that York was in the north. Several times he checked the instructions in the folder but what they said was perfectly clear.

'I must be getting forgetful,' he said worriedly. 'It's a good job I'm not a dentist any more. I'd be pulling out the wrong teeth.'

At York they got out, stretching their limbs in the cold dawn, and made their way to the station buffet.

Your next train, which leaves from Platform Three,

is the 11.40 for Rothwick. You must, however, get out at Freshford Junction, which is the fifth station after York.

'Well, nothing could be plainer than that,' said Henry. 'And yet I was sure Miss Pringle said that the nuns lived in the west. I remember her mentioning the gentle climate.'

'It certainly isn't very gentle here,' said Aunt Maud, for a fierce draught was whistling in at the door of the refreshment room.

They decided to say nothing to the others for fear of worrying them and, punctual to the minute, the 11.40 drew up at Platform Three.

The next part of the journey was slow and the scenery wild and beautiful. They travelled through heather-clad hills and valleys with brown rushing rivers and little copses of wind-tossed trees. Both the children, as they looked out of the window, were lost in dreams. Eric imagined himself camping alone by a stream, his tent perfectly pitched, his kettle hissing over the fire which he had lit with a single match as Scouts have learnt to do. He would be whittling a stick with his lethal knife and there she would be, Cynthia Harbottle herself, stumbling into his camp, soaked to the skin and terrified.

'Eric,' she would say, 'Eric, I am lost, save me, help me and I promise I will never look at an American soldier again.'

Addie's dreams were different. She was watching the hillsides covered with shaggy, black-faced sheep. Surely in a place where there were so many of these animals, just one would pass on and become a ghost? She had always wanted a phantom sheep; she was absolutely sure she could train it to sit, or even to fetch a ball she threw for it. Sheep were much cleverer than people realized. They had to be or Jesus would not have preached about them so much.

Grandma's thoughts were in the past. She was worried about Mr Hofmann in the bunion shop. He was such a clever man, a German professor who had been a teacher in the university before he fell into the canal from thinking about poetry instead of looking where he was going. But he was not very strong-minded. Every time he woke and saw a picture of a stomach he got a tummy ache and every time he saw an enamel bowl, he wanted to cough into it, and he was working himself into a dreadful pother.

'I shouldn't have left him,' thought Grandma.

At Freshford Junction the last part of their journey began.

You must now take the bus to Troughton-in-the-Wold, which leaves from the first stand opposite the station. Go to the terminus at the Horse and Hounds, cross the road, and make your way along the lane which leads uphill between clumps of firs.

Once again, everything went like clockwork. They found the lane and glided along it in the fading light. Then suddenly their way was blocked.

Uncle Henry opened the folder once more.

After two kilometres you will find yourself in front of a high gate with a pair of griffons on the pillars. When you reach that, your journey is over.

'This is it then,' he said. 'No doubt about it. This is the place.'

It was a shock. Their new home was not at all what they expected. Jagged battlements glowed black against a crimson sunset, writhing statues led up to the great front door – and the griffons' claws rested on a shield with the words 'I Set My Foot Upon my Enemies' carved into the stone.

Grandma was the first to speak.

'I won't curtsy,' she said. 'Let's get that clear. It may be grand but I won't curtsy to nobody.'

She had been very poor when she was young and forced to go and work as a housemaid in a big house, and it had made her very cross with anyone who was a snob and ordered people about.

'No, of course not, Grandma,' said Maud. 'Who ever heard of a curtsying ghost?' But she herself was very troubled. 'Henry, are you sure it's us they want? I mean . . . shouldn't we be more . . . you know . . . skeletal and headless? Won't they expect hollow rappings and muffled moans . . . and that sort of thing?'

'You can moan through my muffler, Ma,' said Eric. But he was only trying for a joke. The little scarves that Scouts wear round their necks are not at all suitable for moaning through.

The only person who wasn't in the least put out was Adopta.

'I can't see what the fuss is about,' she said. 'It's just a house with roofs and windows like any other' – and as she spoke Aunt Maud wondered yet again what Addie's life had been before she came to them.

But Uncle Henry now read out the last of the instructions.

You are asked to wait till midnight and then go to the master bedroom in the East Tower and begin your haunting. Good luck and best wishes for your new life.

'Come on then,' said Addie. 'What are we waiting for?' And before they could stop her, she had swooped up the gravel drive and zoomed into the house.

*

61

Oliver did not think he would be able to sleep, but he did sleep – a restless, twitchy sleep filled with hideous dreams.

Then suddenly he was awake. The clock in the tower was striking the hour, but there was no need to count. He knew it was midnight. He knew by the frantic beating of his heart, by the shivers of terror running up and down his spine, and by the clamminess of his skin.

He tried to sit up, and felt the familiar tightening of his chest. He was going to have an asthma attack – and he reached out for the inhaler before he realized it was gone.

And then, as he was struggling for air, he saw it. A hand! A pale hand coming through the wardrobe door, its fingers searching and turning . . . The hand was attached to an arm in a white sleeve: a wan and lightless limb, sinister and ghastly.

The wailing nun? The murdered bride?

The other arm was coming through the fly-stained mirror now – and dangling from it on a kind of string was something round and horrible and loose.

Its head. The phantom was carrying its head.

Knowing that his end had come gave Oliver a sudden spurt of strength. Managing to draw air through his lungs, he sat bolt upright and switched on the light. 'Come out of there,' he called, 'and show yourself.'

The figure did as it was told. If it was a nun or a bride it was a very small one, and it seemed to be dressed for bed.

'Who are you?' asked Oliver, between the chattering of his teeth.

The ghost came forward. 'I'm Adopta Wilkinson,'

she said. 'There's no problem about *that*. But who are you, because you're certainly not a nun.'

Oliver stared at her. She seemed to be about his own age, with a lot of hair and sticking-out ears. 'Why should I be a nun?' he asked. 'It's you who are supposed to be a nun. And headless.'

'Do I *look* headless?' she asked, sounding cross.

'No. I thought . . . your sponge bag was your head.'

The ghost thought this was funny. 'Would you like to see what's inside?' she asked.

Oliver nodded and she unpacked her tooth-cleaning things. Then she took out the fish and put it down on the counterpane, where it lay looking peaceful, but not at all energetic. 'I tried to find a friend for it when we were living in the knicker shop. I haunted every fishmonger in London – you know how there are always rows and rows of dead fish on the slabs – but not one of them had become a ghost to keep him company. Not a single one.'

'He doesn't look unhappy,' said Oliver.

'No.' Addie repacked her bag. 'But I don't understand; we were supposed to come to a convent and this can't possibly be a convent. Nuns don't have little boys and they wouldn't have those awful rude words carved everywhere.' She pointed to the head of the bed and the words 'I Set My Foot Upon My Enemies' carved into the wood.

'No – that's the motto of the Snodde-Brittles,' said Oliver.

'They sound awful. I bet the feet they set upon their enemies have yellow toes with hair on them and bunions.'

Oliver began to explain about Helton, but he was

interrupted by the most extraordinary sound: a gurgling, guggling sort of noise ending in a hiccup.

'Good heavens, what's that?'

'Don't worry, it's only Aunt Maud. She's practising wailing woefully or moaning muffledly, you can't be sure. She's terribly worried, you see, about not being dreadful enough for you. All of them are. Shall I tell them it's all right?'

'Yes, please do. And Adopta, could you just make it clear that muffled moans are not at all big with me?'

So one by one the Wilkinsons came and Addie introduced them. As soon as she saw Oliver all the nonsense about being horrible went straight out of Aunt Maud's head and she glided over to the bed and gave him a big hug. Being hugged by a ghost who cares about you is a most wonderful feeling, like resting inside a slightly bouncy cloud. Not since he had left the Home had Oliver been so comfortable.

'Well, this is a big room for a small boy,' said Aunt Maud. 'And I can't see the point of all those nasty people hanging on the wall, but never mind – we'll soon have you shipshape.'

Grandma then came down from the curtain rail where she had been hovering.

'I said I wouldn't curtsy,' she said, 'and I mean it. But the dust up there's shocking and if you find me a nice feather mop in the morning, I'll give it a good going over.'

Eric had been standing by the door. Going to new places always made him shy and brought out his old worries about his spots and being unhappily in love, but now he came forward and gave the Scout salute, and then the budgie fluttered his wings and said

'Open wide', and 'My name is Billie', and even 'Ottle' which was the nearest he could get to saying Cynthia Harbottle, this not being an easy thing for budgerigars to say.

But Uncle Henry now took charge. 'I think we should make ourselves known to your parents. It would be polite and they might have orders for us.'

'I don't have any parents,' said Oliver. 'I'm an orphan. I lived in a Home till three weeks ago and they brought me here. I'm . . . I'm actually . . . I mean, I seem to *own* this place,' he said, and blushed because it really embarrassed him, having this huge house when so many people had nowhere to live.

The ghosts stared at him in amazement. This small boy who had welcomed them so warmly was the owner of Helton Hall!

'Well, in that case we had better speak to your guardian or whoever is in charge of you.'

'There's no one here, Uncle Henry.' Calling this manly ghost 'uncle' made him feel less alone in the world. 'I've got some cousins but they're away, and so are the servants. There's no one here at all except me.'

Aunt Maud couldn't believe her ears. 'You mean you're all alone in this great barrack of a house?'

Oliver nodded. 'Actually,' he said, 'I was a bit frightened before you came. But now . . .' He looked up and gave her the most trusting and delightful smile.

'Well that's it then, isn't it?' said Grandma. 'We wanted something to do and we've got it.' She gave Oliver a prod with her umbrella. 'I can tell you this, little sprogget, while there's a spook called Wilkinson left on this planet, you aren't going to be alone again.'

*

An hour later, the ghosts were settled for sleep. Grandma was in the coffin chest, Eric was curled up on top of the wardrobe, and Uncle Henry and Aunt Maud lay side by side on the hearthrug.

As for Addie, she'd made it perfectly clear where *she* was going to spend the night.

'That bed is far too big for you,' she said to Oliver. 'We'll lie head to feet and if you snore I'll kick you.'

It was when she came back from cleaning her teeth that Oliver noticed a dark patch on her arm where the sleeve of her nightdress had rolled back.

'Have you hurt yourself?' he asked.

She shook her head. 'You mean that mark on my ectoplasm? It's a birthmark. I've always had it.'

'Goodness! They have them in fairy stories and then people come and say: "You must be my long-lost daughter the Princess of So-and-So!"'

Addie was not pleased. 'No one had better try any of that stuff on me. I'm a Wilkinson and that's the end of it.'

Her eyes began to close, but she forced them open. 'Oliver, when we came here we passed a farm right close to your grounds. Does that belong to Helton too?'

'Yes.'

'Well, look . . . if . . . just *if* there happened to be a sheep who'd passed on . . . you'd let me have it, wouldn't you?'

'Of course I would. You shouldn't even *ask*,' said Oliver. 'And anyway—'

But at that moment Aunt Maud's cross voice came from the hearthrug. 'Will you two stop talking at *once* and go to sleep.'

Oliver smiled. Matron had sounded just like that

when they were fooling around in the dormitory. Feeling wonderfully safe, he closed his eyes and, for the first time since he'd come to Helton, he fell into a deep and dreamless sleep.

Chapter Ten

The nuns of Larchford Abbey were very excited. It was the morning of Saturday the 14th and they knew that their ghosts had come. The owls had screeched horribly, the field mice had scuttled for shelter, and the bell in the ruined chapel had given a single, death-like clang. Moreover when they woke at dawn they saw that a strange, chill vapour hung over the old buildings which they had offered to their guests.

'Oh, it is a real adventure, having proper spooks!' Mother Margaret said.

'Yes, indeed. What is better than being able to share our lovely home with others,' said Sister Phyllida.

Larchford Abbey was certainly a most beautiful place. Set in a green valley with a little burbling stream, it was surrounded by gardens and orchards. Bees flew up from the hives; the apple trees were coming into blossom; a herd of pedigree goats gambolled in the meadow.

'I wonder if we shouldn't just go and see if they have settled in all right,' said Mother Margaret in her kind and caring way. 'We wouldn't bother them of course, but there may be some little thing they would like to make them comfortable.'

'Yes indeed,' said Sister Phyllida, who had been a nurse before she became a nun and was very practical and sensible. 'The first few days in a new place are so important.'

They waited till the evening and then made their way over the wooden bridge towards the ruined part of the abbey.

'We must remember that this is their breakfast time; they will only just have woken up. Sometimes people are not very friendly first thing in the morning.'

'Oh dear, I hope they're not in bed,' said Mother Margaret. She remembered that there had been a gentleman, a Mr Wilkinson, and it was a long time since she had seen a gentleman in bed.

When they had crossed the stream they saw, on the path leading to the door of the ruined building, a set of footprints. They were truly horrid footprints, made by a spectre with only three toes, and they stopped suddenly as though the ghost who made them had got bored with walking and had suddenly become airborne.

'Oh, isn't this thrilling!' said Mother Margaret, clapping her hands.

'I wonder what happened to the other two toes?' said Sister Phyllida. Nurses are interested in that kind of thing.

Before they reached the door of the Abbey they had another treat.

'Look, Sister – bloodstains. I'm sure they are.' Mother Margaret bent down and dipped her finger in the red pool and sure enough her finger came away with a sticky dark spot.

'They must have settled in,' said Sister Phyllida. 'People don't make bloodstains, I'm sure, unless they feel at home.'

But when they reached the door of the bell tower, and pushed it open, the noises they heard did not seem to be those of a contented family of ghosts at breakfast.

The Shriekers were quarrelling as usual.

'And what exactly is that?' Sabrina yelled at her husband, throwing something soft and furry at his face.

'It's a dead shrew, you loathsome grub-pot,' screeched her husband.

'Oh ha ha, you've frightened it to death I suppose! Why don't you frighten something your own size? Don't lie to me – that shrew has been lying there for days. It stinks.'

'Of course it stinks. And you stink too. You've got rotten egg yolk oozing out of your ear hole.'

'I should just hope I do stink. I swore I would stink from the day of our Great Sorrow. I swore I would stink and suffer and claw and kill!'

Fortunately the nuns down below could not hear the actual words that the Shriekers were saying. They did, however, get the idea that their new guests were not completely happy and relaxed.

'Of course it's often like that with married people before breakfast,' said Mother Margaret, who knew that a lot of couples are best not spoken to before they have had their early morning cup of tea.

'And the journey may have been a strain,' said Sister Phyllida. 'Larchford is rather low-lying, it takes time to get used to the damp.'

So the kind nuns decided they would leave their new guests to settle in and call back on the following day. 'Though I would have loved to see the little girl. She sounded such a dear thing in her nightdress with her sponge bag and the fish.'

When the nuns had gone, the Shriekers went on

quarrelling and pelting each other with foul things they had found on the floor of the ruined abbey. Then suddenly they got bored and decided they were hungry.

The ghoul lay on a tombstone, quivering in his sleep.

'Wake up and cook something, stenchbag!' screeched Lady de Bone, twitching his rope.

'And be quick about it or we'll nail you up by your nostrils,' yelled Pelham.

As they screamed at their servant and jerked his rope, the ghoul became madder and madder, uttering his weird cooking cries and waving his frying pan to and fro.

'Fry!' he gabbled. 'Sizzle! Burn!'

As he ran about, the pan became less grey, more reddish . . . hotter. Suddenly it burst into flame and he scooped a dead owl from a rafter, tore its feathers off and threw it into the fire. Then he tossed two burnt thighs at the de Bones and collapsed again on to the slab.

Back in the convent, the smell of cooking came quite clearly to the Sisters.

'That's their breakfast now,' said Mother Margaret. 'They'll soon feel better.'

'There's nothing like a nice cooked breakfast to settle the stomach,' agreed Sister Phyllida. 'So many families just start the day with nothing but a piece of toast, and it's so unwise.'

They felt very relieved, sure now that the ghosts they had invited were going to lead a sensible life, and then they said goodnight to each other and went to bed.

But the Shriekers, tearing the flesh off the roasted

owl, were not exactly being sensible. Mind you, they had had a very difficult journey. The mouse had not agreed with the python, who had been sick, and the ghoul kept passing out at the end of his rope like a log. And when they had at last lost height and come down where the instructions had told them to, they had seen none of the things they had been promised. No great hall with towers and battlements, no writhing statues, no suits of armour or stone pillars or iron gates. Instead there were a few tumbledown buildings and a ruined abbey with the most awful feel to it – the feel of a place where people had been *good*.

And then when dawn broke they saw something that made them stagger back in horror: a row of nuns on their way to the chapel to pray!

'I'm not staying here!' Sabrina yelled. 'I'm not having that awful gooey goodness clogging up my pores. I can feel it between my teeth. Ugh!'

But they had been too tired to glide back at once. Now they decided to wait for a few days and gather up their strength.

'There might be a child we can harm,' said Pelham.

'How could there be? Nuns don't have children.'

'No. But they might run a school.'

The idea of scratching and strangling and smothering a whole school full of children cheered Sabrina up a little.

'Well, all right. But I won't stay for long.'

'Don't worry,' said Pelham. 'I'm all set to make those women in the agency wish they'd never been born!'

Chapter Eleven

A new and happy life now began for Oliver.

He woke to find Adopta sitting on the bottom of his bed and heard the other ghosts splashing about in the bathroom and thought how wonderful it was not to be alone.

They all came down to breakfast and made themselves invisible while Miss Match brought him toast and cereal. Just as she was putting it down, the budgie said, 'Open wide', and she jiggled her hearing aid and said, 'I'm not going to open wine at this time of day. Wine is for supper.'

'I'll bet she can't see us,' said Adopta – and before Aunt Maud could stop her, she flitted off into the kitchen.

'I told you,' she said when she came back. 'I leaned over her and said "Boo" and she just went on reading some silly story in the paper. We've got nothing to worry about there.'

But in any case, Miss Match was only supposed to leave out Oliver's meals. The rest of the day she spent in the village with her cousin. Fulton's plan to leave Oliver quite alone was turning out to be the best thing that could have happened.

The ghosts simply loved the house.

'Oh, my dear boy,' said Aunt Maud. 'These cellars . . . the fungus . . . the damp! It's a bit strong for me, but just think what poor Mr Hofmann would make of this place. How happy he would be!'

'Who's Mr Hofmann?' Oliver wanted to know.

'He's Grandma's boyfriend,' said Adopta. 'He lives in a bunion shop and he's got every ghost disease in the book, but he's terribly clever.'

The ghosts liked the kitchens and they liked the drawing room with its claw-footed chairs, and the faceless statues in the library. They liked the hall with its huge fireplace which you could look up and see the sky, and they absolutely loved the library with its rows of mouldering books.

'I bet there are ghost bookworms in those books,' said Adopta. 'I bet they're *full* of them. Can I look later?'

'Of course. I wish you wouldn't *ask*, Adopta.' Oliver sounded quite cross. 'If Helton's mine then what's mine is yours and that's the end of the matter.'

If they liked the house, the ghosts liked the gardens even more. The weeping ash tree with its drooping branches, the rook droppings on the stone benches, the yew trees cut into gloomy shapes . . .

'It's so romantic, dear boy, so cool!' said Aunt Maud. 'You can't imagine what it is like to be here after the knicker shop.'

When they reached the lake they found Eric staring down into the water.

'There is someone in there,' he said. 'Someone like me. Someone who has suffered.'

'There's supposed to be a drowned farmer,' said Oliver. He had been afraid of the body trapped in the mud, but already the ghosts were making him think of things differently.

Eric nodded. 'He died for love,' he said. 'I can tell

74

because of Cynthia Harbottle. She wouldn't go out with me even after I'd bought her a box of liquorice allsorts. It took all my sweet ration and she didn't even say thank you. And this man's just the same. People who have been hurt by women can recognize each other.'

'Can you call him up, dear?' said Aunt Maud. She was thinking how nice it would be if Eric could talk to someone else about being unhappily in love. When he talked to *her* about Cynthia Harbottle she got terribly cross. Mothers always get cross when people do not love their sons, and Cynthia had been a nasty piece of work, wiggling her behind at American soldiers and smearing herself with lipstick.

'He doesn't want to; not now,' said Eric – and Oliver couldn't help being glad. He didn't feel quite ready yet for a drowned farmer covered in mud.

But the farmer reminded Aunt Maud of something she wanted to ask Oliver.

'Now please tell me honestly,' she said, taking his hand. 'Don't be polite. But . . . how would you feel if . . . if someone came here, someone *appeared*, who was only wearing a flag? Would she be welcome?'

Oliver was quite hurt that she should ask such a question. 'Of *course* she would be welcome. Of course. A ghost wrapped in a flag would be . . . inspiring.'

After lunch (which was a sandwich for Oliver in the garden) the other ghosts said they would rest, and Oliver and Adopta climbed up the hill to look at the place where the two hikers had frozen to death.

'I can't *feel* them,' said Adopta. 'I'm afraid they may just not have become ghosts. Perhaps it's as well if they had bad frostbite. But I think you ought to

75

ask your factor to put up a proper cross or a little monument. It seems rude not to have anything.'

'I don't know if I've got a factor. What is it exactly?'

'It's a person who runs an estate and tells the shepherds and farmers what to do.'

'How do you know about factors? I mean you wouldn't have had them in the knicker shop or at Resthaven.'

Adopta shrugged. 'Sometimes I know things that I don't know how I know them, but please don't start on again about how I'm really someone else because I'm a Wilkinson and I'm me.' She glanced round at the wide view, the heather-covered hills, the river. 'Pernilla would love this. She feels so trapped in the shopping arcade.'

'Who's Pernilla?'

'She's a Swedish ghost – she came to look after some children and learn English, and some idiot in a Jaguar drove her home from a party and crashed.'

'Why don't you ask her to stay? And Mr Hofmann too. Anyone you want, there's lots of room here.'

'Could we? Oh Oliver, that would be great. Only we'd better do it properly through the agency or—' She broke off and pointed excitedly at a field below them. 'Look! Sheep! Hundreds of them. Come on!'

But when they reached the field every single sheep in it looked fleecy and cheerful and well.

'I could kill one for you, I suppose,' said Oliver. 'But I don't eat mutton and—'

'No, that would be silly. It might not become a ghost and then it would be a complete waste of time. You can never tell, you see. You can get half a dozen animals that just lie there dead as dodos and absolutely nothing happens, and then one suddenly rises up, and you're away!'

The day ended with a great honour for Oliver. He was invited to the Evening Calling for Trixie. They did it near the sundial and everybody linked hands and bowed to the north and the south and the east and the west and told Trixie that they wanted her and needed her and would she please, please come.

When it was over, Oliver asked if there was anything that Trixie had particularly liked.

'Something that we could put out for her, perhaps?' he said.

Grandma and Aunt Maud looked at each other. 'Bananas,' said Grandma. 'She'd have sold her soul for a banana. All of us would in the war.'

So Oliver ran back into the house and fetched a banana – a long and very yellow one – which they put on the sundial where it could be seen easily from above, and Aunt Maud was so happy that she rose into the air and did the dance that she and Trixie had done when they were Sugar Puffs – a thing she hadn't done for years.

Oliver fairly skipped along the corridor that night on his way to bed – and when he got to his room he had a surprise. While he was out with Adopta the others had done out his room. The man stuck full of arrows was gone, and so was the deer having its throat cut, and the rearing horses. Instead Aunt Maud had brought in some dried grasses and put them in a vase, and they'd hung up a cheerful picture of a garden they'd found in one of the other rooms.

And Oliver's inhaler was once again beside his bed.

'You won't need it,' said Uncle Henry. 'The air

here is excellent and anyway asthma's something you grow out of. But it might as well be there.'

Although ghosts usually haunt by night and sleep by day, they had decided to keep the same hours as Oliver, but when everyone had settled down, Oliver still sat up in bed with his arms round his knees.

'What are you thinking about?' asked Adopta sleepily.

'I was thinking about how much there is to find out. About ghosts and ectoplasm and why some people become them and others not, and why some people see them and others don't . . . I mean, if you eat carrots you're supposed to see better in the dark, so perhaps there's a sort of carrot for making you see ghosts? And if you really knew about ectoplasm, maybe you could change the things that ghosts are wearing. I bet it's the flag that's bothering your Aunt Trixie. Imagine if you called her and she could immediately put on a raincoat or a dressing gown. And wouldn't it be marvellous if people could *decide* whether to become ghosts or not.'

'And decide for their pets,' said Addie. It was always the animals that mattered to her.

Oliver nodded. 'I tell you, someone ought to start a proper research institute to study all this.'

'Not one of those places where they try to find out whether we exist or not. Ghost hunting and all that. Tying black thread over the staircase and sellotaping the windows. So rude.'

'No. This would be ghosts and people working side by side.'

Oliver's mind was racing. He hadn't wanted Helton, he was going to try and give it away. But now . . . Why not a research institute here – there was room enough.

'I wonder if I've got any money?' he said. 'I mean serious money for labs and people to work in them.'

'Why don't you write to your guardian? He seems a nice man, exploring places and trying to find the golden toads. I expect the lawyer's got his address.'

Oliver thought this was a good idea, but thinking about letters made him remember the one thing that still troubled him.

'What's the matter?' asked Addie, seeing the change in his face.

Oliver shrugged. 'It's silly to fuss when everything's turning out so well, but I had these friends in the Home . . .'

He explained what had happened and Addie frowned. 'Was it always Fulton who posted the letters for you?'

'Yes. He used to take everything down to Helton Post Office. He said it would be safer.'

'Hm.' Addie had never liked the sound of Fulton. 'Why don't you try once more when you write to your guardian and we'll take the letters to the box at Troughton?'

Oliver nodded. 'Yes,' he said. 'That sounds sensible. That's what we'll do.'

Chapter Twelve

The ghosts whom the kind nuns had adopted had been at Larchford Abbey for several days and the nuns were just a little bit disappointed and hurt. They knew that people needed time to settle in to a new place and they had made it clear to the ladies at the agency that they wouldn't bother the ghosts and that they didn't expect the ghosts to bother them.

All the same, a little friendliness would have been nice. They had looked forward to a glimpse of the child in her nightdress playing merrily in the bell tower or the old lady floating about in the rose garden, and having heard that Mr Wilkinson was fond of fishing, they had half expected to see him by the river, casting with a fly or tickling trout.

But there had been absolutely no sign of the family. Not one wisp of ectoplasm in the orchard, not a trace of a voice singing to itself in the dusk.

The ghosts were *there* all right. Oh yes, they were definitely there. Blood had oozed through the old abbey floor and they had found several sets of footprints with three toes. From time to time, too, there came the smell of frying meat – rather *strong* meat which did not seem to be absolutely fresh – and now and again they heard a gurgling moan, but no one had come forward to introduce themselves or to thank the nuns for giving them a home.

'One must do good without thinking of the

reward. One should not need to be thanked,' said Mother Margaret.

'Do you think we ought to write to the agency?' asked Sister Phyllida. 'I mean, there may be some little thing they are too shy to mention. Something we could put right?'

But Mother Margaret thought they had better wait a bit longer. 'After all, we don't know very much about . . . ectoplasm and that sort of thing. Perhaps there are changes when people travel, which have to right themselves.'

'Like air sickness. Upset stomachs and so on. Yes, that could explain a lot. Some of those bloodstains do look a little disordered,' said Sister Phyllida, who was the one that had been a nurse.

It wasn't just the Shriekers' bloodstains that were out of order. The Shriekers themselves were in a ghastly state. They were lying on the floor and kicking the air with their mouldering feet, and every time they thrust their legs out, they bellowed and whooped and howled and squealed.

They had remembered that it was the anniversary of their Great Sorrow. On an April day just like this one, the terrible thing had happened which had driven them mad with guilt and turned them into the ghastly, tortured and revolting creatures they now were.

'Oi! Oi! Oi!' moaned Sabrina. 'How could we have done it? How could we have been so cruel to our flesh and blood?'

'It is right to punish,' whined Pelham. 'People must be punished for doing wrong.'

'But not like that. Whipping would have been all

81

right, taking food away would have been all right. Thumping and scourging and walloping would have been all right, but not what we did.'

She began to moan again and roll about on the floor among the owl droppings and scrabble her feet in the filth. Even as she did that, the guilt and sin made her little toe go all wibbly and Pelham slapped her hard on the behind and said, 'Stop it! I too suffer. I too feel my guilt and my sin, but you have hardly any toes left and enough is enough. We must act. We must be revenged on the world. We must see that no other child is left unharmed to remind us of that ghastly day when our—'

'No!' shrieked Sabrina. 'Don't mention that name. Don't dig the knife deeper into my bosom.'

'You haven't *got* a bosom any more,' said Pelham. 'It's all skin and bone and—'

They began quarrelling again about whether or not Sabrina had a bosom. Then they sat up and tried to pull themselves together.

'It's true that we have to rid the world of children,' said Pelham. 'It's not till the sobs and moans of other parents mingle with our own that we shall get some rest. But there don't seem to be any children here, and in the meantime . . .'

He glided over to the window and stood looking out at the fields and stables and orchards which the nuns had tended so lovingly.

'In the meantime what?'

Pelham's scarred face was a grimace of hatred. 'Meanwhile, there are little lambs *gambolling*—' he spat out the word. 'And puppy dogs playing . . . and baby goats – ugh – leaping for joy.'

Sabrina came to join him. 'Yes,' she said. 'And you know what they call baby goats. They call them *kids* . . .'

Chapter Thirteen

'Bend over,' said Fulton Snodde-Brittle – and the small boy standing in front of him in his study bent over.

'Right over,' said Fulton, and the child doubled up over the arm of the leather chair. His name was Toby Benson and he was just seven years old.

Fulton went for his cane, and then frowned and put it back. Canes left marks and the school inspector was due in the next couple of weeks. Not that it mattered – by then he and Frieda should be living in Helton Hall and the school could go to the devil. Still, might as well play safe. He fetched his gym shoe out of the cupboard and bent it back. You could get quite a decent thwack with that, but it wasn't the same. Everything had become namby-pamby nowadays.

'You know why I'm going to beat you, don't you?' said Fulton.

Toby sniffed and a tear ran down one cheek. 'Yes, sir. Because I was eating sweets in the gym, sir. My mother sent me—'

'That's enough,' roared Fulton, raising his arm.

But when he had finished, and the little boy had hobbled out, Fulton didn't feel as cheered as he usually did after beating a child. His mind was on Helton Hall and what was happening there. Oliver had been alone now for nearly a week and he had hoped to hear that he had been taken ill or gone off

84

his head. Perhaps they should phone and find out what was happening? He went down to find Frieda, who was in the school kitchen telling the cook to remove one fish finger from every one of the children's helpings laid out for lunch.

'But that'll just leave one, Miss Snodde-Brittle,' said the cook. 'One fish finger's not much for a growing boy.'

'Are you telling *me* what growing boys should eat?' said Frieda, towering over the poor cook. 'You don't seem to be aware that over-eating is very bad for children. It makes them fat and gives them heart disease. Now let me see you take the extra finger away and put it in the freezer for next week. And I thought I said *one* tablespoon of tinned peas. She bent over a plate and began to count. 'I find it very hard to believe that twenty-three peas make up one tablespoon. I do hope you can count because—'

But at this moment Fulton appeared by her side and said he wanted to speak to her.

'I'm going to telephone Miss Match,' he said, when they were alone in the study.

So he dialled the Helton number and after a very long time Miss Match's voice could be heard at the other end. She had forgotten her hearing aid and her voice sounded croaky and cross.

'Helton Hall.'

'Ah, Miss Match. It's Fulton Snodde-Brittle here. I'm just ringing up to find out how Oliver is. How has he been?'

There was a pause at the other end. Then: 'I've never given him any beans. It's the wrong time of year for beans. Beans come later.'

Fulton tried again.

'No, not beans to eat. I want to know how he's getting on. Have you any news?'

'No, of course I haven't got any newts. Can't abide the things – slimy little nasties.'

Frieda reached for the phone. 'Let me try,' she said. 'I've got a more carrying voice.' She put the mouthpiece to her lips. 'We want to know how Oliver is,' she shrieked. 'How is he in himself?'

There was another pause. Then Miss Match said, 'Barmy. Off his head.'

A great smile spread over Frieda's face.

'Barmy?' she repeated. 'You mean mad?'

'Mad as a hatter,' said the housekeeper. 'Talks to himself, runs about waving his arms, won't come in for meals.'

'Oh that's wonderful – I mean that's terrible. But don't worry, Miss Match. We'll be back soon to take him off your hands.'

She put the phone down and the Snodde-Brittles stood and grinned at each other. 'It's worked,' said Fulton. 'Oh glory – think of it. Helton Hall is ours! We'll give him another three or four days to go off the deep end completely, and then we'll get a doctor and have him put away.'

Frieda flopped down in the armchair. The thought of owning Helton was so marvellous that she almost thought of telling the cook to leave the second fish finger on the children's plates. But in the end she decided against it. Happiness didn't have to make you stupid.

Chapter Fourteen

When the Wilkinsons had been with Oliver for a week, they called up the ghost of the farmer from the lake.

Oliver had been worried about this, but it turned out to be a very good thing to do. They called him up the way they called Trixie, telling him he was wanted and needed and that he should not wander alone in the Land of the Shades, and gradually there was a sort of heaving on the lake, and then a kind of juddering, and slowly the spirit of Benjamin Jenkins, who had run the Home Farm at Helton a hundred years ago, floated up and out of the water.

He couldn't have been nicer. He was simply dressed, in breeches and a checked shirt, and carried a gun over his shoulder because he had meant to shoot himself if the drowning didn't work, and the first thing he did in his pleasant country voice was to thank them for calling him up.

'I was getting a bit bogged down in there,' he said, 'but I couldn't make up my mind about coming out.'

Eric and Mr Jenkins took to each other at once, and in no time at all they were telling each other how badly they had been treated by the women they loved.

'Her name was Fredrica Snodde-Brittle,' said the farmer. 'She used to ride through my fields every morning on a huge horse and I was always there, holding open the gate for her. I was so sure she'd come to care for me.'

'That's what I thought about Cynthia Harbottle. I used to carry her satchel all the way to the bus stop.'

The farmer sighed. 'She was so *haughty*. She said no Snodde-Brittle could marry a common farmer.'

Eric nodded understandingly. 'Cynthia was haughty too. She used to blow bubble gum in my face.'

Fredrica hadn't done that because bubble gum wasn't invented in those days and anyway the Snodde-Brittles were too haughty to chew, but she had done other things, and soon Eric and Mr Jenkins took to wandering away into the woods, feeling very much comforted to know that they were not alone.

With Eric so much more cheerful, his parents could settle down to enjoy themselves. Uncle Henry went fishing, borrowing a rod from the lumber room and sitting peacefully by the river for hours on end. He didn't catch any fish – he didn't want to – he just liked to sit and be quiet and forget all those years when people had opened their mouths and showed him their teeth even on a Monday morning. And if anyone came and saw a rod stretched by itself over the water, they probably thought it was the branch of a tree.

Aunt Maud, meanwhile, took up her dancing again, hitching up her long tweed skirt and twirling and swirling on the rim of the fountain, and Grandma did housework. Miss Match never came upstairs, so that no one noticed a hoover snaking along the floor by itself or a feather duster shaking itself out. Even the budgie became a useful bird, helping the swallows build their nests and hardly saying anything silly at all.

There was only one thing which puzzled the ghosts. Why had Miss Pringle not told them that they were going to Helton instead of the nuns? And who was it that had offered to have the ghosts at Helton in the first place? Who had gone to the agency and offered them a home?

'It must have been Fulton,' said Oliver. 'He kept telling me ghost stories, but I didn't understand. I feel awful now, not liking him, when he was doing this marvellous thing for me.'

The Wilkinsons looked at each other. They weren't so sure about Fulton Snodde-Brittle. Why had he left Oliver alone for days on end – and what had happened to the letters Oliver had given him to post? Because his friends in the Home had *not* forgotten him. There'd been an absolute spate of letters answering the one he'd sent from Troughton. They meant to keep a sharp eye on Fulton Snodde-Brittle when he came – and he came, as it happened, on the following day.

'I'm afraid you'll find the poor little boy in a dreadful state,' said Fulton as he drove the car towards Helton Hall.

'Barmy,' agreed Frieda. 'Completely raving.'

Dr O'Hara said he was sorry to hear that. He was a young doctor with dark hair and a friendly smile, and not the doctor whom Fulton had hoped to bring to Helton. It was old Dr Gridlestone whom the Snodde-Brittles had chosen to put Oliver away, but he was ill. Dr O'Hara was new to the district and it was his day off, but when Fulton had told him that there was a child who might become a danger to himself and others he had agreed to come.

'Is there any mental illness in the family?' Dr O'Hara asked. 'Any madness?'

'Is there *not*!' lied Fulton. 'His mother thought she was a chicken and his aunt jumped off a cliff and his little sister had fits. Not the Snodde-Brittles of course – the Snodde-Brittles are perfect – but the family on his mother's side.'

'So you see how worried we are for Oliver,' said Frieda. 'He must be shut away somewhere and protected from the strain of running Helton Hall.'

Dr O'Hara was silent, wishing he hadn't come. The idea of picking up a struggling boy and carrying him off was not pleasant at all.

They turned into the drive and found Miss Match waiting for them.

'Well, how is the dear boy?' asked Fulton. 'We've been so anxious about him, but Dr O'Hara has come to examine him and we can get an ambulance in no time and take him away.'

'Best thing you can do,' said Miss Match grumpily. 'He gets sillier and sillier.'

'Is he in bed?'

'Not him. Rampaging round in the garden talking to himself. Won't come in for meals. Leaves bananas on the sundial.'

Fulton and Frieda exchanged glances. 'Bananas on the sundial, eh? That sounds serious, wouldn't you say, Dr O'Hara?'

'It is certainly unusual,' the doctor admitted.

'You'll find him by the lake,' said Miss Match, and stumped back into the house.

So the Snodde-Brittles, followed by Dr O'Hara,

crossed the lawn and made their way down the gravel path towards the water.

Even from a distance they could see that Oliver was behaving very strangely. He was running round and round, beckoning and calling, and suddenly he burst out laughing.

'I think I'll just go back and see about the ambulance,' said Frieda. She had remembered Fulton's description of the Shriekers and even in broad daylight she didn't fancy meeting them.

But at that moment, Oliver looked up and saw them.

Fulton expected anything except what happened next. Oliver gave a shout of welcome and ran towards his cousin with his arms stretched out.

'Oh thank you, *thank* you,' he said, hugging him round the waist. 'Thank you so much – so terribly much! I was so lonely and miserable and now everything's *lovely*!' He turned to Frieda, standing with her mouth open. 'And Cousin Frieda too! It's the best thing that's ever happened, you sending me the ghosts.'

Fulton loosened Oliver's hands and took a step backwards. He had left a pale, thin child whose eyes were too big for his face. Now he saw a boy with rosy cheeks and the glow that happiness brings. Was it a feverish flush? Yes, it had to be.

'What ... ghosts?' he stammered. 'I never sent any.'

'Didn't you?' Oliver was puzzled. 'That's strange. They said—'

'They? Who are they?' asked the doctor.

'Come and meet them. Please. They vanished when they heard the car because they thought they might be in the way.' He took Fulton's hand and reluctantly the others followed. 'Adopta's very excited because Mr Jenkins has dredged up a phantom prawn for her and she thinks it might cheer up the fish in her sponge bag, but we're not sure because it's quite a *big* prawn.'

Dr O'Hara sighed. This was madness all right – and he'd really liked the little boy.

They had reached the lake.

'It's all right, everybody – please appear again,' Oliver called. 'It's Cousin Fulton and Cousin Frieda and—' he turned to the doctor. 'I'm sorry, I'm afraid I don't know your name.'

'I'm Dr O'Hara.'

'Oh, a doctor! Uncle Henry will like that. He was a dentist and he's a very scientific person. Good – there they are!' One by one the ghosts appeared and Oliver introduced them. 'This is Aunt Maud . . . well, Mrs Wilkinson really, and this is Mr Wilkinson and this is Grandma . . .'

What followed kept Fulton and Frieda rooted to the ground. Dr O'Hara stepped forward and shook hands with – nothing. With air.

'Pleased to meet you, Mrs Wilkinson,' he said. 'And you too, sir.' He took another step and this time he raised his hand to his forehead in a salute. 'I was a Scout too,' he said in his friendly way. 'Though I never made it to patrol leader.'

'*Who are you talking to?*' shrieked Frieda. '*What are you doing?*'

Dr O'Hara turned to them, very surprised. 'But surely you can see them?' he said. 'This gentleman here in the army helmet and the old lady with the umbrella and—'

'No, we can't,' said Fulton, white-faced. 'You're making it up. You're playing a joke.'

'No, he isn't, Cousin Fulton,' said Oliver. 'Those are the Wilkinsons. They're my family. Look, there's Adopta now – you *must* be able to see her. She's my special friend.'

'Yes, you must surely see the little girl?' said Dr O'Hara. 'Her nightdress is quite dazzling.'

'You're lying!' Fulton was shaking with anger and fear. He had brought in a doctor who was as crazy as the child.

Oliver was very upset. 'Oh how unfair, Cousin Fulton! That's really rotten, you not being able to see the ghosts when it was you that gave them a home.'

But Addie didn't at all want to be seen by the Snodde-Brittles. She thought they looked horrible with their long yellow faces and bulging eyes, and she was more certain than ever that Fulton was up to no good. Dr O'Hara was another matter – and now the Snodde-Brittles saw the doctor bend down and cup his hands as though something was being lowered into them.

'Ah yes – how interesting! I've never seen a phantom prawn before. I think you'd be quite safe putting her in with your fish. It's a female and they only attack when they're laying eggs.' He straightened himself and put his arm round Oliver. 'You've certainly got a most delightful family,' he said. 'I haven't met such pleasant ghosts since I was a little boy in Ireland. Our house was haunted by such an interesting couple – a schoolteacher and his wife who drowned in a bog. They were the most wonderful storytellers.' He walked over to Fulton and Frieda. 'I can't see the slightest sign of mental illness in the boy;

he seems as fit as a flea, and for someone who's going to run a place like this, an open mind about unusual things is most important. You must be so relieved to know that you have nothing at all to worry about.'

But Fulton and Frieda had had enough. The last thing they saw as they hurried back to the car was a fishing rod lift itself into the air and drop into the doctor's hand.

'How very kind,' they heard Dr O'Hara say. 'I must say an hour's fishing would be most pleasant. It so happens that it's my day off.'

'It's your fault, you idiot,' said Frieda when they were alone again. 'You said you'd get ghosts that were going to frighten him into fits and look what you've done! Unless Dr O'Hara's mad. Grandmothers. Boy Scouts. Little girls in nightgowns. It's ridiculous!'

'It's not my fault – it's the fault of that stupid woman in the agency. She swore she had a pair of spooks that would frighten the living daylights out of people. There must have been a mix-up and I'm going to get to the bottom of it. I tell you, Frieda, I'm not finished yet. I'm going to Set My Foot Upon My—'

'All right, all right,' said Frieda grumpily.

She wasn't really in the mood for feet.

Chapter Fifteen

Colonel Mersham sat on a camp stool beside a meandering dark-brown river, reading a letter.

A turtle lumbered on to a sandbar, huge blue butterflies drank in the shallows, and in the rain-washed trees a family of howler monkeys caught each other's fleas, but the Colonel did not look up. He was completely absorbed in what he read.

'Interesting,' he said. 'An interesting boy and an interesting idea.'

He was surprised. He had agreed to be Oliver's guardian because he was sorry for the orphaned boy, but he loathed the Snodde-Brittles, who had been his mother's cousins, and never went near Helton unless he had to.

This boy, though, was different.

He'd come upon a family of ghosts and a child who cared with all her heart for ghostly animals, and he was asking for help.

'I want to set up a research institute for the study of everything to do with ghostliness,' the boy had written. 'I want to find out what ectoplasm is made of and what happens when people become ghosts – and animals too. Addie is particularly worried about the animals: she says you can tell people what happened when they pass on but you can't tell animals, and they get muddled and bewildered and she'd like to make Helton into a safe place for them to be. Not a zoo, just somewhere they can live in peace.'

Colonel Mersham put the letter down and looked upriver to where Manuel, the Spaniard who had helped him in his travels, had drawn up the canoe. They had journeyed two days and nights to the place where the fabled golden toads of Costa Rica had last been seen. They had searched every lily leaf, every clump of rushes, every stone, but they had come back empty-handed. The beautiful, palpitating, pop-eyed creatures, who had lit up the dark landscape like shimmering suns, were gone.

The Colonel had found it difficult to be brave about this. It was happening in so many places; marvellous animals that lived on now only as memories: the aye-ayes of Madagascar, the tigers of Bali . . .

And now the golden toads. It had been his dream to see them ever since he was a boy.

Had he given up too early, he wondered? If he could not find a living toad, might he perhaps find . . . its ghost? And if so, could it be brought back to Helton and cared for, so that people in the future would know what these marvellous creatures had been like?

The Colonel folded his letter and rose to his feet.

'Manuel!' he called to his friend. 'Get the canoe ready! We're going back!'

Chapter Sixteen

It was the worst day of their lives, both Miss Pringle and Mrs Mannering were agreed on that.

When Mother Margaret and Sister Phyllida came into Miss Pringle's office, Miss Pringle was delighted. She liked the nuns enormously and she hoped to get good news of her favourite family.

But one look at their faces and the question died in her throat. Mother Margaret looked as though she hadn't slept for a week; Sister Phyllida had obviously been crying.

'The most dreadful thing has happened,' said Mother Margaret. 'It has been the most terrible experience!'

'And frankly we don't understand how you came to do this to us, Miss Pringle. We only wanted to help.'

Miss Pringle was growing more and more frantic. 'But what *has* happened? Are you not satisfied with the Wilkinsons? Surely—'

'Satisfied!' Mother Margaret was no longer the kind and placid nun who had been to the agency before. '*Satisfied*! When we have two lambs with dislocated legs and a kid with a gash in its throat still at the vet! When we nearly lost our favourite calf and the chickens will probably never lay again!'

'But I don't understand. What has gone wrong? Please explain – I sent you the nicest ghosts in—'

97

Mother Margaret rose from her chair. 'The nicest ghosts! The *nicest*! I admit we are not worldly women but you had no right to play such a trick on us. If nice ghosts swoop down on innocent animals and scratch them with their fingernails . . . If nice ghosts wear evil pythons round their throats and tear the feathers off baby chicks . . .'

She couldn't go on. Tears choked her.

'And the man, Miss Pringle!' Sister Phyllida took up the story. 'That dreadful hoofmark, the vicious knees, the stench! He picked up a goat bodily and would have torn it limb from limb if Sister Felicity hadn't raised her crucifix. Not only that – poor Sister Bridget hit out at the lady with a rowan branch, and look!' She felt in the pocket of her habit and took out a small box which she opened. 'You can imagine how she felt when this dropped on to her head.'

Miss Pringle leant forward and her worst fears were confirmed. Quite clear to those who have an eye for such things, was the decayed and bloodstained toe of Lady Sabrina de Bone.

She covered her face with her hands and moaned. 'Oh heavens, how terrible. It was a mistake . . . a ghastly, ghastly mistake. Our mistake of course! We were asked for some really frightening ghosts for a stately home in the north and we sent the Shriekers. At least we thought we had. And you were supposed to get the Wilkinsons. I just can't understand it – we took such care to match you up.' She too was almost in tears. 'Thank goodness you knew about exorcism. I mean rowan twigs and prayers and so on.'

'We *knew* about it,' said Mother Margaret. 'But it is not a thing we liked to do. We wanted to welcome lost souls, not banish them.'

'Are they . . . the Shriekers completely . . . you know . . . destroyed?' asked Miss Pringle nervously.

'Not they! They just took off cursing and screaming, dragging that wretched blob along behind them. They were coming back to London, I believe.'

Miss Pringle was beside herself. 'You must let us make it up to you – the cost . . .'

But the nuns shook their heads. 'There is no money that can make up to us for the terror and the sadness. Our new litter of puppies simply won't leave their mother at all. They spend their time *underneath* her – and the bees will take weeks to recover.'

Though she was quite broken up by what had happened, Miss Pringle made a last plea for her favourite family. 'You wouldn't consider trying the Wilkinsons instead? They—'

But she had gone too far. 'Definitely not, Miss Pringle. Frankly, we are surprised that you can ask it,' said Mother Margaret.

And leaving Lady de Bone's toe on Miss Pringle's desk they went away.

When something bad has happened what one needs more than anything is a kind friend to talk to. But when Miss Pringle hurried across the corridor, she found Mrs Mannering as upset as she was herself.

'I was just coming over, Nellie. I've had that Mr Boyd on the telephone – the one from Helton Hall. He was absolutely furious. It seems as though we sent him the Wilkinsons, and he wants them out. He says they're namby-pamby and useless and he wants the ones he ordered at once. He wants the Shriekers. But where are they?'

'I'll tell you where they are,' said Miss Pringle.

When she had finished, Mrs Mannering had turned

quite pale. 'The honour of our agency is at stake, Nellie. We must find out how it happened. I quite definitely put the Shriekers' maps in a red folder and gave them to Ted.'

'And I quite definitely put the Wilkinsons' maps into a green folder and gave them to Ted.'

So they went into the little office at the back where Ted was sorting out the mail.

'Now, Ted,' said Mrs Mannering, 'there has been a dreadful muddle and we have sent the wrong ghosts to two lots of adopters. Do you remember my giving you a red folder to leave out for the Shriekers?'

'And do you remember me giving you a green folder to give to the Wilkinsons?'

Ted got to his feet and stood before them. He was blushing and looking very hang-dog indeed.

'Yes, I do. But . . . Well, I left them out like you said . . . Only . . . you see . . .'

So then it all came out. How he was colour-blind and had been afraid to tell them because he didn't want to lose his job.

'Oh, Ted, you should have told us; it was very wrong of you. We wouldn't have dismissed you just for that, and now look at the harm you've done.'

'We'll have to get a computer anyway,' said Mrs Mannering. 'But in the meantime we must put this right at once. Fortunately the Shriekers are still wanted at Helton, so I'll see if I can get hold of them and let them know.'

'And I shall go to the Wilkinsons myself and break the bad news. The trouble is the nuns have been put right off adopting any more spooks, so we can't do a swop. You're sure they can't stay at Helton too?'

'Quite sure. Mr Boyd's really taken against them. He wants them out at once.'

Miss Pringle dabbed her eyes. 'It looks as though it's back to the knicker shop for that dear, nice family. You know, Dorothy, sometimes I think that life just isn't *fair*.'

Chapter Seventeen

Miss Pringle arrived at Helton late in the afternoon. Addie and Oliver were out for a walk, but Aunt Maud was waltzing about on the head of the man trying to strangle a snake and she came down at once.

'Why if it isn't dear Miss Pringle,' she said. 'What a pleasure to see you. We should have let you know before how very happy and grateful we are.'

Grandma, who was having a little nap on one of the benches, now sat up and said, 'Yes that's right. It's a lovely place here; we're as snug as anything. It just seems like a bad dream now, that time in the knicker shop.' She called to Eric. 'Eric, here's Miss Pringle from the agency come to see how we've settled in.'

You can imagine how poor Miss Pringle felt. How she blushed and stammered and had to dash away her tears when she told them the dreadful news.

'A mistake?' said Uncle Henry, who had come to join them. 'What sort of a mistake?'

Miss Pringle blew her nose and explained about Ted and the colour blindness.

'You were meant to go to some nuns down in the West Country. Ever such nice people. And some quite different ghosts were ordered for up here. Rather fierce and horrible people but . . . suitable for such a big place.'

It was Uncle Henry who understood what she was trying to tell them.

'You mean you want us to leave here? To go away again?'

Miss Pringle nodded. 'The gentleman who ordered the ghosts for here was very angry and upset.'

The Wilkinsons could make no sense of this. All they knew was that they were not wanted.

'Of course we aren't headless,' said Aunt Maud hopelessly.

'I told you,' said Eric. 'I told you no one would want me. If Cynthia Harbottle didn't want me, no one else will either.'

'Now, Eric,' said Grandma. He'd hardly mentioned Cynthia since they came to Helton and here it was starting up again. 'It isn't you, it's me. It's because I'm old.'

'No, no, no!' cried Miss Pringle. 'It's just that Mr Boyd wanted fierce ghosts and he's very cross. It's to do with attracting tourists.'

But she looked round at Helton in a very puzzled way. There didn't seem to be any notices saying that the hall was open to the public.

Uncle Henry's ectoplasm had become quite curdled with shock, but he spoke with dignity. 'If we're not wanted here, we must leave at once. Go and catch the budgie, Maud, and I'll get our things.'

'Oh dear, oh dear!' Miss Pringle was getting more and more flustered. Still, she was running an agency; she had to be businesslike. 'Where is Adopta?' she asked, for the little girl was a special favourite of hers.

'She's out with Oliver,' said Aunt Maud – and when she thought of saying goodbye to the child they

103

had grown to love so much, she could no longer hold back her tears.

'Oliver? Is that Mr Boyd – the man who owns Helton?' asked Miss Pringle. 'Because if so perhaps I'd better stay and apologize to him myself.'

But just then the children came running down the path. Oliver had found another letter from Trevor in the Troughton Post Office and his face was alight with happiness. At least it was till he saw the ghosts.

'What is it?' he asked, suddenly afraid. 'What's happened?'

Miss Pringle came forward and introduced herself. 'I'm afraid I've had to tell them that they aren't wanted here at Helton. That they were sent here by mistake.'

The next minute, she stepped back a pace because the most extraordinary change had taken place in the little boy.

He had seemed to be a gentle sort of child and not at all bossy or strong-minded. Now his chin went up and his eyes blazed.

'Not welcome at Helton?' he said furiously. 'Not *welcome*! How dare you say such a thing! They're the most welcome people I have ever known. They're my friends. They're my family and they're not going away from here ever. I'll . . . I'll kill anyone who tries to take them away.'

The effect of Oliver's words was incredible. The ghosts' ectoplasm seemed to thicken and grow stronger. Grandma's whiskers, which had faded almost to nothingness, stood out clear and sharp again, and Eric smiled.

'Oh you good, kind boy,' said Aunt Maud, and came to put her arms round him.

Miss Pringle, though, was completely muddled.

'You see, dear, the man who owns this place—'

Oliver, usually so shy and never one to interrupt, broke in.

'*I* am the man who owns this place,' he said – and it seemed quite reasonable that this little boy, who scarcely came up to Miss Pringle's shoulder, should talk of himself as a man. 'I didn't want to but I do – you can ask anyone – and I hated it here till the Wilkinsons came and *I will not let them go.*'

Miss Pringle stared at him. 'But the person who came to the agency was a grown-up – a tall man with a long face and a moustache. And he said he wanted a very particular kind of ghost—'

'That wasn't the owner. That was my cousin, Fulton Snodde-Brittle, and it was very nice of him to order some ghosts because I was lonely. But whatever he ordered, these ghosts are *mine.*'

Miss Pringle had turned pale. She had just taken in what Oliver had said. 'You mean you really own this place? And you live here all the time? You sleep here at night?'

'Yes.'

Miss Pringle's hand flew to her mouth. Mrs Mannering had found the Shriekers cursing and raging in the meat store and told them they could go to Helton.

And the Shriekers had sworn to destroy any child that they could find!

'Oh heavens!' said Miss Pringle. 'How dreadful. Oh whatever should I do?'

Chapter Eighteen

'At last!' cried Sabrina de Bone. 'At last a place that's fit for us!'

The Shriekers stood in the hall at Helton, looking about them with their greedy, hate-filled eyes. It had become very cold; a fall of soot came roaring down the chimney, and a dead jackdaw tumbled out on to the hearth.

In the dining room, the pictures of the Snodde-Brittles fell to the ground and lay in a mess of twisted string and broken glass. A suit of armour crashed on to its side.

'Nice,' said Sabrina. She floated into the drawing room and drew her fingernails along the sofa – and the cloth ripped apart, letting the stuffing ooze out like clotted blood.

The hands of the clock began a mad whirring and an icy mist crept along the floor.

'Something's going on,' said Mr Tusker, down in the basement. 'Don't like the sound of it.'

'Better go and see if the boy's all right,' said Miss Match.

But Mr Tusker didn't think that was a good idea at all. 'Not me,' he said and bolted the kitchen door.

The Shriekers floated on through the grand rooms, dragging the ghoul behind them. Blue flames sprang up in the fireplace and terrified mice scuttled deep into the wainscot.

Then suddenly Sir Pelham stopped.

'Do you smell anything, snotbag?' he asked.

Sabrina's nose stump began to twitch. She turned her face this way and that.

'Oh yes, I smell something,' she drawled. 'I smell something . . . lovely.'

Sir Pelham yanked the rope and the ghoul gurgled and choked.

'Where is it, you slime gobbet?' he asked. '*Where is the child?*'

With his eyes still shut, the ghoul began to run wildly about. 'Child,' he muttered. 'Burn. Fry. Sizzle. Child.' He set off across the drawing room, through the billiard room, towards the staircase . . .

'The smell's getting stronger,' said Sabrina happily. 'And it's a *clean* child. A washed child. I do love hurting clean children.'

'Clean children are the best,' agreed Sir Pelham.

Dribbling with blood lust, they followed the ghoul as he panted up the staircase . . . across the Long Gallery . . . down the corridor with the grinning masks . . .

It was the crash of falling Snodde-Brittles which woke Aunt Maud.

'Is that you, Eric?' she called, for the farmer and Eric had decided to go camping in the woods.

But the noises which came from downstairs were not the kind made by her shy son. Squealings . . . rappings . . . and now the sound of a clock striking twelve . . . and thirteen . . . and on and on.

'Henry, I'm bit worried,' she began.

But her husband was already sitting up, and now Grandma popped her head out of the coffin chest.

'There's some hanky-panky going on somewhere,' she said. 'I can tell by my whiskers. They're as stiff as boards.'

'I'm going downstairs to see,' said Uncle Henry. 'You stay here.'

But of course there was no way the women would let him go alone.

They did not have far to go before they saw the intruders. A pair of crazed, blood-spattered spectres and, pulling them along, a quivering blob of jelly with foaming jaws.

'*Stop*!' Uncle Henry spoke like the brave soldier he had been in the war. 'This part of the house is private.'

The female spook tittered. 'You funny man,' she said. She unwound the python from her neck, and it hissed and swayed and shot out its flickering tongue.

But the Wilkinsons stood their ground.

'You can't come any further,' said Aunt Maud. 'You'll wake the children.'

Poor Maud – she realized almost at once that she had made a terrible mistake.

'Ah, *children*,' gloated Sir Pelham. 'Not just one child! One *each*, then. We won't have to share! I'm going to strangle mine.'

'I'm going to cut mine to ribbons with my nails.'

'No you aren't!' Grandma stepped forward and lunged out with her umbrella. Uncle Henry plucked a sword from the wall. They were ready to fight to the last drop of their ectoplasm, but then something so horrible happened that they stopped just for a moment – and that moment was fatal.

The budgie, trusting and stupid, had followed them. Now he landed, fluttering and squawking, on Aunt Maud's shoulder.

'Open wide,' said the bird in his friendly way. 'Open—'

But it was the python who opened wide. And as the Wilkinsons stared in horror, watching their beloved pet disappear into the jaws of the evil snake, the Shriekers passed through them as if they were morning mist and entered the room where the children lay fast asleep.

They lay head to feet as usual. Addie had become invisible. She always vanished when she slept.

The moon was full and the quiet room was bathed in a silver light.

'Child,' gabbled the ghoul, and collapsed in a heap on to the rug.

The Shriekers stepped over him and moved towards the bed.

'Ah, how sweet, a little boy in his pyjamas,' sighed Sabrina and stretched out her fingers, with their dreadful nails, to touch his cheek.

And in that instant, Oliver woke.

'Are you all right, Addie?' he asked sleepily. Then he fell back on the pillow and a scream died in his throat. Bending over him was a spectre so hideous that he couldn't have imagined it in his wildest dreams. She had no nose, her hollow eyes glittered with hatred, gobbets of raw meat clung to her hair.

It's impossible, he thought. I can't be seeing this.

Then he wondered if maybe it was a sort of joke. 'Are you in fancy dress, Aunt Maud?' he managed to say.

But he knew it wasn't so. From the appalling spook there came such a sense of loathing and danger that no one could have pretended it. And now, looming up behind her, was a second spectre even more gruesome: a man with a broken skull who raised the whip he held in his hand – and laughed.

'Well well, you look a nice healthy fellow, all safe and sound in your bed. What a pity your last hour has come!'

But as the female phantom's fingers began to move towards his throat, something happened to Oliver that was far worse than anything the spooks could do. His chest tightened . . . his breath came in choking gasps . . . the air he had drawn into his lungs stayed trapped. Desperately he stretched out his hand for his inhaler . . . he had almost reached it – and then the thong of the man's whip curled round it and dashed it to the ground. Even as the vile spectres prepared to throttle him, Oliver was turning blue in the worst asthma attack of his life.

He tried to cry out and warn Addie, but there was no hope of making a single sound. This is it, then, thought Oliver. This is the end.

But Addie was awake. Without bothering to become visible she went into the attack.

'How dare you?' she screamed. 'How *dare* you harm Oliver, you disgusting old spooks.' Kicking out at Pelham with one foot, she swooped down and picked up the inhaler. 'Breathe!' she ordered Oliver, putting it into his hand. 'Go on. *Do* it.'

'Who are you? What's going on here?' spluttered Pelham, who could see nothing.

'What's going on here is that I'm going to do you in,' yelled Adopta. 'I don't know where you come from, but I'm not scared of you, you silly old banshees.' She aimed a kick at the ghoul, lying on the floor, then swooped up to bite Sabrina in the neck.

110

'If you've hurt Oliver, I'll kill you. I'll turn your ecto-plasm into semolina; I'll grow maggots in your earhole.'

As she walloped and thumped and kicked, Addie was slowly becoming visible. Her night-dress was beginning to show up now, and her long hair.

'Well, go on,' roared Pelham to his wife. 'Do her in. Finish the little spitfire off. The boy's done for anyway.'

But Lady de Bone was standing quite still. Her loathsome mouth hung open and she was staring and staring.

'What's the matter with you?' yelled Pelham to his wife. 'What are you gawping at?'

'I feel . . . strange,' said Sabrina.

Addie was moving in for the kill. She rose into the air, ready to punch the female phantom's nose stump into a pulp – and as she did so, she rolled up the sleeve of her nightdress.

And Lady de Bone screamed once . . . screamed twice . . . and fell in a dead faint on to the floor.

Chapter Nineteen

Toby Benson, the little boy whom Fulton had beaten so cruelly, sat on his suitcase in the hall at Sunnydell Preparatory School and smiled. His parents were coming to take him away for ever and he was so happy he thought he would burst.

The inspectors had been to the Snodde-Brittles' school and said it had to be closed at once. The teaching was a disgrace, they said, and Fulton not fit to be a headmaster.

But if the boys had left, and the cook and the cleaning ladies and the sports master, there were other people who had come. The greengrocer who supplied the school with vegetables had come, waving his bill, and the butcher had put a ladder against the house and stuck his head in at the bathroom window and told Fulton he'd turn him into a plate of tripe if he didn't pay what was owing. Even now, a van from the electricity company had drawn up and two men got out, ready to cut off supplies.

'We're going to end up in prison for debt if this goes on,' said Frieda, looking down at the street.

'No we aren't. We're going to end up in Helton Hall. We're going to own the farm and the grounds and the forest and have proper servants to wait on us.'

'Well, I hope you're right. That horrible little boy seems to be spook-proof as far as I can see.'

'He won't be spook-proof with this new lot. I tell you, Frieda—' He broke off. 'Good Lord, look who's here! It's Mr Tusker getting out of a taxi.'

Getting out of a taxi was not an easy thing for Mr Tusker to do. He was too bent and his legs were too wobbly. But he managed it at last and then they saw that Miss Match was in the taxi too.

'This is it, Frieda. I just feel this is it.'

It looked as though he was right. When the housekeeper and the butler reached Fulton's study they were grey with shock and they had come to give notice. Mr Tusker was on the way to his sister in York and Miss Match was going to stay with a niece in Scotland and neither of them was ever going to spend another minute in Helton Hall.

'We tried to tell Mr Norman,' said the butler. 'But he's away and his secretary's a twitty little thing. So we came to let you know and to give back the keys.' He laid a great bunch of labelled keys on the table. 'We want you to sign that we've given them to you, and a month's wages is owing to us.'

'Yes, yes. Mr Norman will pay them when he returns. But why? Why are you going in such a hurry? What's happened at Helton?'

Mr Tusker started to wheeze and Miss Match hit him on the back. 'Everything. It's haunted. It's full of evil. Things fall.'

'Things burn.'

'There's a creeping mist in all the rooms.'

'There's screams to make your hair stand on end.'

'Oh dear, how terrible,' said Fulton. 'And the boy?'

'Gone!' said Mr Tusker.

'Dead, it's my opinion,' said Miss Match. 'Drowned.'

113

'Drowned! But how terrible! How ghastly!' Fulton's voice rose to a shriek. 'Tell us more! Tell us more!'

'We found his clothes by the lake. Shoes. And a shirt floating on the water. And the lake looks . . . funny.'

'But how appalling! The poor little boy. Have you told the police?'

'It's not our job to tell the police, Mr Snodde-Brittle. We've given back the keys and you've got our notice. And a month's wages is owing—'

'Yes, yes. You shall have them of course. I'll tell Mr Norman. Just leave your address.'

'It's happened!' shouted Fulton when the butler and the housekeeper had left. 'I told you! The woman in the agency said they were spooks to end all spooks. They've obviously frightened the boy into fits and he's run into the lake. I told you he wasn't stable.'

'Yes, but even if he's dead what are we going to do about the spooks? I'm not staying in the place with those nasties hanging round.'

'Now, Frieda, why don't you trust me? I wouldn't have set all this up if I hadn't had a card up my sleeve.'

'You mean exorcism and all that? Salt and rowan twigs and that sort of stuff? Because—'

'No. Nothing as feeble as that. It might work on those soppy Wilkinsons in their night-gowns, but it wouldn't work on the Shriekers. No, this is something different,' said Fulton gloatingly. 'This is *science*.'

He opened a drawer and handed her a newspaper cutting which she read carefully, and then read once again.

114

'I see,' she said, licking her lips. 'Yes. You don't think it will come expensive?'

'What does that matter? Once we have Helton we'll have all the money in the world. We can cut down the forests and sell the wood. We can bulldoze the farm for building land – we'll be rolling.'

'Yes.' Frieda put down the newspaper and looked down at the street. Toby Benson was just running out to meet his parents. They were going to take him out to Africa with them rather than send him to another boarding school. 'You don't think he'll . . . Oliver . . . he'll come up from the lake and haunt us?'

'For Pete's sake, Frieda, what's got into you?' He pushed the newspaper under her nose. 'You can read, can't you? There isn't a spook on the planet we can't destroy with what they've got there.'

'Yes.' Fulton was right. It was silly to think of Oliver lying at the bottom of the deep dark pit that was the Helton lake. No one got anywhere who let themselves get soft.

Chapter Twenty

The letters above the grimy redbrick building said *The Safeguard Sewing Machine Company*, but it wasn't sewing machines that they made in that sinister place. It was something quite different.

It was a liquid – as Dr Fetlock now explained – that you could spray on to ghosts so as to destroy them completely and for ever.

'We have to keep our work secret,' he told Fulton Snodde-Brittle. 'That story in the paper did us a lot of harm. You see there are feeble and soppy people about who might make a fuss. They might think that ghosts have a right to be around and then there would be questions asked and laws passed. So I have to tell you that everything you see and hear in this building is top secret. Will you promise me that?'

'Oh yes, yes indeed,' said Fulton. He had wasted no time in coming to see the doctor. 'I'd rather not have my part in this talked about either. In fact I'd like it if your men could come and spray Helton under cover of darkness.'

'There shouldn't be any problem about that. Now you will want to know what you are getting for your money, so let me show you round.' Dr Fetlock leant forward and stared hard at Fulton with his black pop-eyes. His long hair straggled down his back, he wore thick glasses and looked as though he hadn't been in the open air for years. 'But first of all I have to ask you something: can you personally see ghosts? Are you a spook seer?'

Fulton stroked his moustache. A piece of kipper had caught in it from his breakfast, but he didn't know this and thought he looked good. 'Well, actually, no. I can't.'

Dr Fetlock nodded. 'Perhaps it's as well. But it means I'll have to explain the experiments to you. I will have to describe what we have done to the ghost animals we keep here, so that you will see how amazing our product is. Now if you will just put on this white coat, we will go into the laboratory.'

He opened the door for Fulton and led him down a long dark corridor. 'You will find that everyone here is really keen on their work. All the staff of EEB Incorporated – that's what we call ourselves – have suffered from disgusting spooks. The lab boy who is looking after the animals has a gash down the side of his cheek, as you will see. He got it when a head on a platter came out of the larder of his mother's house in Peckham. Just a severed head and nothing else – well, you know how these creepy-crawlies carry on. He fell over backwards and gashed his cheek on the fender and he's got the scar to this day.'

'I'm sorry to hear it,' said Fulton.

Dr Fetlock opened the door of the animal house. What Fulton saw were rows and rows of cages with straw in the bottom and numbers nailed to the top. Beside the numbers were charts showing how much liquid the animals had been given and at what dose. A strange smell of decay hung about the room, and a murky fog clouded the windows.

'That's the dissolving ectoplasm,' said Dr Fetlock. 'We'll get the fan going on it in a minute. Now this

117

top row is the rabbits. Of course we had to drill a small hole in their brains and squirt it with EEB – that's the name of our product – so as to destroy their will power. Otherwise they'd just have glided through the bars – keeping ghosts caged up is the devil, as you know. The first three cages are the ones where we've destroyed the rabbits' left ears, and in the next row they've lost their right ears – it's a pity you can't see because it's a very neat experiment. Then below them we've got the mice. We've got rid of all the tails in the first batch and the second batch have got neither tails nor forepaws.' He turned round and shouted: 'Charlie!', and a youth in a spattered overall with a scar down the side of his face came out with a clipboard. 'Show Mr Snodde-Brittle the figures, Charlie.'

Fulton took them and ran his eyes down the pages. They seemed to be graphs of different strengths of the EEB mixture set against the loss of limbs and ears and eyes.

'Very interesting,' he said.

Dr Fetlock had moved to another group of cages. 'Now these are the hamsters,' he said. 'You see we've managed to destroy their pouches completely. That's only the beginning of course . . . we're going to make the spray stronger and liquidate their front ends alto-gether so—'

'Yes, yes.' Fulton was feeling a little queasy. 'But how do I know it's going to work on humans? The ghosts I want to exterminate are people – well, they were.'

Dr Fetlock seemed to be thinking. 'I think we'd best take Mr Snodde-Brittle to the rest-rooms, Charlie.'

The rest-rooms were just cubicles, rather like police cells, each with a camp bed, a grey blanket and a water jug.

'Perhaps you'd like to look in here?' said Dr Fetlock. 'If you're sure it won't upset you.'

'Nothing upsets me,' blustered Fulton. He stared at the empty bed and the folded blanket – and saw nothing else.

'He was only a tramp,' said Dr Fetlock. 'We thought it was quite right to use him for science. He was sleeping rough under Waterloo Bridge when he became a ghost. So we lured him in here – we said he could rest in peace and he *is* resting in peace!' He began to titter. 'What's left of him!'

'Er . . . what is left?'

'A shoe with a broken sole . . . half a sock . . . look there, hanging over the bed. We came at him while he was asleep – three squirts from one of the big aerosols and well, you'll see. We've got two more in the next rooms. The old bag lady is completely gone, but there's a drunk we found on the Embankment – his arms and legs have disappeared but his torso's left, if you'd like to have a look.'

'No, that's all right, thank you. I think I've seen enough,' said Fulton. 'But are you absolutely sure there's no effect on living people? I mean, I shall want to move back into the house when it's cleared.'

Dr Fetlock turned to Charlie. 'Go and get Number Five – it's just been filled.'

Charlie went away and returned with a large metal canister rather like a fire extinguisher, with a hose and nozzle. The letters EEB were written on it in red paint. Dr Felton put out his arm. 'Right. You can give me a full dose.'

Charlie pressed the nozzle. There was a hiss, and an evil-smelling liquid shot on to the doctor's sleeve. Apart from the smell and a damp stain nothing happened at all.

'Satisfied?' asked Dr Fetlock.

Fulton nodded. 'Yes, indeed. It's all exactly as I hoped. But . . . could one ask . . . what *is* EEB? What do the letters stand for?'

Charlie and Dr Fetlock looked at each other. 'Well, Mr Snodde-Brittle, we don't trust everyone with this, but . . . all right . . . we'll take you along to the preparation room. It isn't I who discovered the EEB, you see – it's Professor Mankovitch. But I warn you, the Professor is completely dumb. She's probably the most brilliant scientist in the world – a Hungarian; they're very clever in Eastern Europe – even the little children play chess – but she can't say a word. She lost her voice as the result of a frightful shock.'

'What was that?'

'She was picnicking with her boyfriend in a forest. They have a lot of forests over there. And suddenly a whole lot of white, shimmering creepies came out of the trees – wibbly, wobbly slithering ghoulies – they call them villis or tree spirits or some such thing. And they stretched out their awful arms and grasped her boyfriend and went off with him into the woods and he never came back. So she swore she would spend the rest of her life finding out how to destroy *things* that shouldn't be there. Come along; I'll show you.'

Fulton followed him. As they came closer to the lab he could hear a kind of bumping and gurgling, and the temperature rose. Then the door was thrown open and he saw an enormous vat which reached

120

from the floor to the ceiling. A great piston went thump, thump, thump, stirring whatever was inside; tubes came from the vat and curled round the walls. Beside the vat, a woman with a blank face and white hair was twiddling a dial.

'This is it, Mr Snodde-Brittle. This is the fruit of twenty years' work on the part of Professor Mankovitch. She has scarcely stopped to eat or sleep in all that time, but the result is success. Complete and total success. This vat is full to the brim of the most amazing discovery of the century. It is full, Mr Snodde-Brittle, of EEB.'

'Yes, but what *is* EEB? What's inside it?'

'You have heard of ectoplasm, surely?'

'Yes, of course.'

'And you have heard of bacteria? Of germs? The things that cause measles and chicken-pox and everything that's vile?'

'Yes.'

'Well, we have found out how to grow a bacterium that eats ectoplasm. The Ectoplasm Eating Bacterium or EEB. We are manufacturing it as *Rid A Spook* and soon every hall, house and mansion in the land will be free of ghosts!'

Fulton was convinced. He had come to the right place. But when they were back in the office he had a shock.

'How much would it cost to rid Helton Hall of ghosts? Completely?'

'Well, the charge is a thousand pounds a room. Which I'm sure you'll see is reasonable—'

'A thousand pounds a room! But Helton has got thirty rooms.'

'Then it will cost you thirty thousand pounds.

121

Which does not seem a lot to make sure that Helton is free of nasties for ever. And I'm afraid I have to ask you to let me have the money in cash. You won't believe it, but we completely cleared a castle for a well-known British lord and when we came to cash the cheque it bounced.'

Fulton was thinking, chewing on his moustache. How on earth was he going to get thirty thousand pounds? But once people knew that he was going to be the master of Helton, they'd lend it to him. After all, Helton wasn't worth thousands of pounds; it was worth millions.

'Very well, Dr Fetlock,' he said. 'You shall have it in banknotes, I promise you.'

Chapter Twenty-One

Addie perched on the arm of the sofa and glared at her long-lost parents. A night and a day had passed since the Shriekers had seen the birthmark on Addie's arm and realized that she was their daughter, and the change in the evil pair was staggering. They crawled about on the floor, they tried to touch the hem of Addie's nightdress, they wept – and all the time they begged and implored and beseeched their daughter to forgive them.

'We shouldn't have done it,' wailed Sabrina.

'We only meant to punish you a little. We didn't think you would jump into the lake.'

'We haven't had a moment's peace since that dreadful day we found that you were gone.'

'That's why we tried to strangle other children. We couldn't bear to see them well and happy while our Little One was lost to us.'

Addie took not the slightest notice. The python, with his sad bulge in the middle, had been hung on the towel rail in the bathroom and all she cared about was helping Oliver. He *said* he was all right; he'd wanted to go out and fetch the clothes he'd left strewn by the lake the day before when he was helping Mr Jenkins, but he still looked very pale, and the Wilkinsons insisted that he stayed indoors and rested.

Aunt Maud would have been ashamed to moan and grovel like the de Bones, but she had never felt more wretched in her life. She felt sure that she was going to lose Adopta. Addie might say now that she was a Wilkinson, but how could she stand out against two such grand spectres – spectres with titles, who knew about the upper classes? Sooner or later Addie would want to become Honoria de Bone, Aunt Maud was sure of that, and she felt as if her heart was breaking.

Uncle Henry and Grandma were almost as upset. They had known that they were only foster parents, but somehow they had not really thought that things would ever change.

All the same, Uncle Henry was a fair man and now he said, 'I think the de Bones must be allowed to tell their story. What was it that made Adopta jump into the lake and drown?'

So the Shriekers began.

'It happened on the night that Queen Victoria came to supper with us in our house near the Scottish Border. You must remember our house, Honoria?' said Sabrina.

'I'm not called Honoria,' said Addie, scowling, 'and I don't remember a thing.'

Sabrina sighed and went on with her story. 'You have to understand how important it was to us to have the great Queen in our house. She was the Empress of India, remember, and the Mother of the Country, and it was her husband who first brought Christmas trees to England.

'So we prepared a tremendous banquet. We slaughtered seven oxen and shot one hundred and twenty pheasants and killed five dozen salmon and—'

'Well I think that's disgusting,' said Addie. 'All

124

those animals killed just to stuff into the stomach of a fat little queen.'

'Yes, that's what you said. You were very angry. You were always an angry child – though we love you, of course – we absolutely adore you—'

'Go on with the story,' said Adopta.

'So de Bone Towers was decorated with flags, and the crimson bedroom was hung with fresh tapestries and there were flowers everywhere. It meant a lot to us, this day. You see, your father was expecting to be made an earl – people often were when they had the Queen to stay. But you had been getting crosser and crosser because of the dead animals. Of course we quite understood but—'

Pelham put up his hand. 'I will go on with the story,' he said. 'Queen Victoria arrived and we put on our evening clothes and our medals and our knee breeches. The footmen were in livery; the Great Hall sparkled with candlelight and the table was set with gold plates and crystal goblets and decanters of priceless wine. Queen Victoria sat at the head of the table and the ladies-in-waiting sat at the foot of the table, and the pheasants were just being brought in on great platters – all one hundred and twenty of them – when the long windows on to the terrace opened – and a cow entered the dining room.'

Addie was wrinkling up her forehead. 'Daisy?' she said dreamily. 'A cow called Daisy?'

'Yes, yes, yes!' cried Sabrina. 'Oh, my little darling!'

'Go on,' said the child. 'What happened next?'

'Daisy was a large cow, ready for milking. She came up to the Queen and mooed and pushed her head on to the table and the glass fell over and spilled wine on to the royal skirt. Then came Buttercup . . . and after Buttercup came Violet . . . and after Violet came Rose and Geranium and Marigold. All our cows were named for flowers. Twenty-three cows were herded into the dining hall, mooing and shoving their heads into the plates and . . . er . . . lifting their tails to spatter the ground with manure . . . And after them came the bull. The bull was called Hector – he weighed over a ton – and he began chasing Daisy. Daisy was his favourite. You can imagine . . . chairs turned over, people on the table, tails swishing . . . and the Queen, the famous Queen whose throne was inlaid with ivory and tourmaline and gold, shrieking and stepping in cow-pats and being butted in the behind by Daisy's horns.'

'And then came the sheep,' said Adopta suddenly. 'The cows were easy – I just shooed them up the steps – but the stupid dog couldn't get the idea of herding sheep *into* the house.'

Both the de Bones turned to her. 'So you do remember! It's all coming back to you,' they said excitedly. 'You see now that you are truly our child!'

Addie shrugged. 'I remember the cows and the sheep – and that silly Queen honking at the end of the table.'

'Anyway, that was the end of all Pelham's hopes of becoming an earl. The Queen left that night and never came back and we were very, very angry. So we locked you in the tower at the edge of the lake. We just wanted to keep you there for the night and make you realize what a terrible thing you had done. We never imagined you would jump into the water and try to escape. Oh, the misery and the guilt and

the wretchedness . . . After that I'm afraid we let ourselves go.'

'You certainly did that,' said Grandma, looking at
Lady de Bone's dress and the bare feet with their
mouldering toes.

'Even before we became ghosts we had become
hermits in the castle,' Sabrina went on. 'And we
decided that if our little girl was lost to us for ever,
no other children should sleep unharmed in their
beds. But now everything will be quite different if
only you will come into my arms and call me
"Mother".'

'And come into *my* arms and call me "Father",'
Pelham put in.

Addie twitched her nightdress out of his hand.
'You must be mad,' she said. 'Do you really think I
want parents who tried to kill my best friend? Not to
mention what your beastly snake did to the budgie.'

The de Bones sidled up to Oliver. 'We are really
very sorry, dear boy. Very sorry indeed,' said Lady de
Bone.

'On the other hand,' put in Pelham, 'you must
remember that we were particularly *asked* to come
here and do our most sinister haunting. We were *told*
to go to the tower room and pull out all the stops.
Mrs Mannering said that the gentleman who ordered
us most particularly *wanted* evil ghosts.'

Everyone now looked at everyone else. The de
Bones might be loathsome, but they seemed to be
telling the truth.

Someone – and it had to be Fulton – had wanted
Oliver harmed or even dead.

'*Now* do you believe me?' asked Adopta, turning
to her friend.

But Oliver still had trouble believing that anyone who had sent him the Wilkinsons could be totally evil. 'You don't think he guessed that the Shriekers were your parents and wanted to give you a surprise?'

'Oh for goodness *sake*,' began Addie.

But she caught Uncle Henry's glance and said no more. Clearly something would have to be done about Fulton Snodde-Brittle, but not till Oliver could be got away to safety.

'Mr Tusker thinks Oliver's drowned,' said Eric when Oliver had fallen asleep at last. 'I heard him going round the lake with Miss Match before he left. He's going to tell Fulton.'

'Good,' said Uncle Henry. 'In that case it won't be long before Fulton's back.'

'And we'll be ready for him,' said Sir Pelham – and this time the Wilkinsons were glad to hear the crack of his whip and see the hatred in his hollow eyes.

Chapter Twenty-Two

To decide that Oliver should be got out of the way was one thing; to get him to go was another. He didn't want to leave Helton even for a couple of days. He knew how worried Aunt Maud was about losing Adopta, and how Addie fretted about the budgie, and he wanted to be with them and help.

It was Grandma who persuaded him to go. 'I'm worried sick about Mr Hofmann,' she said. 'And if you mean it, I'd like to ask him down to Helton – and Pernilla too. But I want you to come too, so it'll seem like a proper invitation.'

What Grandma started, Trevor finished by writing to ask Oliver if he'd come up for his birthday. So they took the housekeeping money which Miss Match had left in the kitchen drawer and set off for London, and everyone in the Home was so pleased to see him, and so excited to have a ghost to stay, that Oliver couldn't be sorry he had come.

Now they were on their way to Mr Hofmann, but there was something Grandma wanted to show him first.

'Here we are,' she said. 'This is the place.'

Oliver stared through the plate glass windows at the knicker shop.

'Is this really where you lived?' he asked. 'Honestly and truly?'

'Honestly and truly,' said Grandma. 'Eric slept up

there above the bikinis and Henry was in with the Footsies and we put Adopta in the office – that's through that door there.'

Oliver was amazed. 'I didn't realize it was so small.'

'Small and stuffy and daft,' said Grandma, snorting at the Wonderbras, and they crossed the arcade and made their way towards the bunion shop.

Mr Hofmann sat in his wheelchair as he had done every day for years. His eyes watered, his chest wheezed, his head wobbled. Above him was a picture of a stomach with lumps on it. Bowls for spitting into and rubber tubes for pushing down people's throats and packets of bandages were piled round him. The leather bunion was still there, but dusty, and he was extremely sad.

Then the door opened and a boy came into the shop. He was a nice boy and he looked healthy and Mr Hofmann was sure he had come to the wrong place. But the boy came forward and smiled and said: 'I've got a surprise for you!'

And then there she was, slowly becoming visible, his dear friend, the only woman who understood him and his suffering! There were the cherries trembling on her hat, there were the kindly wrinkles, the umbrella . . .

'Is it you?' croaked the spectre. Tears sprang to his eyes; he tried to get out of his chair. 'Is it really you?'

'Now, Mr Hofmann, you've let yourself get in a dreadful pother,' said Grandma. 'Just look at you, you're the colour of cheese and you shouldn't be sitting under that stomach, I told you before.'

'Ah yes . . . but I am so weak . . . I am so useless . . . what matters it if I sit under stomachs or no.'

'It matters a great deal,' said Grandma sternly. 'And now listen, because I've come to take you away. This nice boy lives in a beautiful house in the country and he's invited you down to live with us. For good.'

But Mr Hofmann only shook his withered head. 'No,' he said. 'Such things do not happen to old useless German professors who are dead. I shall stay here alone and suffer. It is my fate.'

But Grandma wasn't having any of that. 'That's quite enough, Mr Hofmann. I'm coming back the day after tomorrow to take you down, so make sure you're ready. Pernilla's invited too, so we'll make a party of it.'

They found the Swedish ghost drooping over her harp in the music store. She was overjoyed at the thought of living where there were forests and fresh, clean air, but she was worried about the jogger on the A12. They had become friends and tried to Keep Fit together, and she felt bad about leaving him alone.

Of course Oliver soon settled that. 'He can come too, honestly,' he said. 'There's plenty of room,' – and the smile that came over her face was wonderful to see.

When they got back to the Home, Grandma thought she might have a little lie down or perhaps have a go with the Space Invaders games she'd learnt the day before, but it didn't turn out like that. The children clustered round her and pestered her for stories.

'Tell about the time you held down the Nazi parachutist with the tip of your umbrella,' said Trevor.

'And the one about how you pushed Mrs Ferryweather into a flower bed because she wouldn't draw her blackout curtains,' begged Nonie.

'And the one where the bomb fell and you found you were a ghost,' said Tabitha.

'Yes, tell about that,' cried all the children. That was their favourite.

Oliver, meanwhile, had been called into the office, where Matron and the two adoption ladies had been having a meeting.

Miss Pringle and Mrs Mannering had been frantic when they heard that the Shriekers had gone to Helton. They thought that if anything had happened to Oliver they would have to shut the agency and go and save whales or start a cat shelter, so when Grandma called in and explained that Oliver was safe, they were overjoyed. But like Matron they did not feel that Oliver should be at Helton with only the ghosts to protect him from Fulton Snodde-Brittle.

'Of course we could get hold of the police,' said Matron. 'But it's a strange story and suppose we hit on someone who doesn't believe in ghosts? There's no doubt in my mind that Fulton's a villain, but you can't really arrest someone for giving a home to spooks. I think we must somehow keep Oliver here till his guardian comes. That lawyer seems to be worse than useless. It's monstrous that the boy should have been alone there without an adult all this time.'

'Is there no news of the Colonel yet?'

'Well, yes. I sent a fax to the British consul in Costa Rica and it seems he's on his way back to Britain. Till then Oliver will be safe here and the children will love having him.'

But when she told Oliver what had been decided, he shook his head. 'I can't stay away that long; I just can't. Helton's my home now and Addie needs me.'

Matron looked at his troubled face. 'Yes, I quite

understand that, Oliver. Look, would you stay till Trevor's party? It's only a few more days and it would mean a lot to him.'

Oliver nodded. It meant letting Grandma go ahead with the ghosts, but Trevor had always been his special friend.

'Yes, I'll do that,' he said, and Matron was relieved. If Colonel Mersham had not returned by then, she would try to find someone to go down with Oliver.

When he went back into the garden, Oliver found the other children still sitting listening to Grandma, but Trevor had left the circle and was waiting by the climbing frame. Trevor was tough: he'd had to be, losing his parents, losing one hand, finding that his relatives in Jamaica didn't want him. He was a boy who hit out first and asked questions afterwards. But when Grandma came to the bit of her story where they'd found out that Trixie wasn't with them, he always got a lump in his throat. That poor spook in her flag lost in space for ever . . . It was more than anyone could stand.

'I'm staying for your party,' said Oliver. 'But after that I'll have to go even if Matron doesn't give me permission. I'll have to.'

Trevor nodded. 'Maybe I'll come with you,' he said.

Chapter Twenty-Three

'Think of roast kidneys dipped in icing sugar,' said Adopta. 'Or marshmallows fried in Marmite. Go on, think of them,' she ordered the snake.

But the python didn't. He was still draped over the towelling rail and he wouldn't be sick whatever she said to him. She could see the bulge where the budgie was, and since the python had swallowed him whole she was hopeful that he might be all right, like Jonah inside the whale, but whatever she said to the wretched snake he just hung there with a blank look in his eye, refusing to throw up.

Addie had spent a lot of time in the bathroom since the Shriekers came, because her long-lost parents were driving her mad. They popped up behind bushes begging her to call them 'Mother' and 'Father', or crawled about in the flower beds asking her to forgive them. Sabrina called her 'Little One' and Sir Pelham wanted her to sit on his knee. But what made Addie really angry was the way they kept on snubbing the Wilkinsons. They called Uncle Henry 'that tooth puller' and sneered at Eric's woggle, and they thought it terribly funny that Aunt Maud had been a Sugar Puff.

And she was missing Oliver badly. She knew it was right that he should be out of the way till they had dealt with Fulton, but life was not the same without her friend.

Uncle Henry now came in, as he had done each morning, to look at the snake.

'I could operate, I suppose,' he said, 'but there's always a risk.'

'Let's wait a bit longer,' said Addie. She was cross with the python, but it was hard to think of a hole being cut into his side. 'I'll go and see if Mr Jenkins wants any help.'

It was the farmer who was in charge of making it look as though Oliver had drowned. He saw to it that Oliver's shoes bobbed up occasionally, and that there were footmarks leading into the water such as might be made by a boy running in terror from something evil. Mr Tusker had been quite certain that Oliver lay at the bottom of the lake, and the ghosts were sure that Fulton would think the same.

But when she reached the water, Addie found Lady de Bone dripping bloodstains on to Oliver's torn shirt, and at once the fuss began.

'Ah there you are, darling Honoria,' she cried, trying to rub her nose stump against Addie's cheek. 'Have you come to tell your mother that you love her?'

'And tell your father that you love *him*?' said Pelham, rising from the bullrushes.

'No, I have *not*,' said Addie. 'Where's Aunt Maud?'

The de Bones looked at each other. 'She's in the walled garden smelling the flowers,' sneered Lady de Bone.

But Aunt Maud was only pretending to smell the flowers. What she was really doing was trying not to cry.

'Have they been beastly to you?' asked Addie. 'Because if so—'

'No, no. Not really. It's just . . . I mean, it's very silly of me not to know what a lobster claw squeezer is, but you see we never had them at Resthaven. And I didn't realize it was common to say "toilet". One should say "loo" but I never have, Adopta. And honestly I think it might be better if I just gave up and let them have you. I'm not really grand enough to haunt a place like this.'

'Now, Aunt Maud.' Addie was very cross indeed. 'That's enough. If I've told you once I've told you a thousand times that I'm a Wilkinson. You and Uncle Henry are the only parents I want and if they go on sneering at you, I'll do them in.'

But when they started to rehearse the attack on Fulton and Frieda, even Aunt Maud had to admit that the Shriekers were impressive. When they stopped grovelling to Adopta and did their proper haunting, the de Bones were something to watch. It wasn't just the flickering tongues of light and the evil stench with which they kept tradesmen and passers-by from coming to the Hall. Sabrina could raise her skinny arms and decayed owls came tumbling down the chimney in droves, and when Sir Pelham cracked his lethal whip, the hardiest person felt his skin crawl and the flesh shrivel on the bones.

And since they expected to ambush Fulton by the lake, when he came to make sure that Oliver was dead, they had their special outdoor effects. They could make great branches crack and fall; they could bring up a swirling fog that would blind any man, and call up shapes that writhed and snatched and gibbered in the undergrowth. The Wilkinsons meant to help, of course, but when it came to punishing

Fulton Snodde-Brittle once and for all, they couldn't do without the Shriekers.

But it wasn't Fulton who came next to Helton Hall.

The ghosts were all in the drawing room having a sing-song. Grandma had brought Mr Hofmann down the day before with Pernilla and the jogger, and he'd been resting ever since, but Aunt Maud thought they should have a bit of a party to show him how welcome he was. He couldn't eat – his intestines had gone completely to pieces in the bunion shop – but he loved music. Pernilla knew some splendid songs about mad trolls and screaming banshees, and though she would rather have been outdoors roaming in the woods, she stayed and sang to them in her lovely mournful voice.

Of course the Shriekers thought that sing-songs were vulgar – they didn't have them in de Bone Towers – but that didn't mean they stayed away and left the Wilkinsons in peace. Even the farmer had come up from the lake. Only the ghoul still slept on his tombstone in the church: every other ghost at Helton was gathered in that room.

No one looked out of the window. No one saw a red van with some dreadful words painted on the side draw up in front of the house. No one saw the people who got out: a woman with white hair, a youth with an ugly scar on his face; a man with pop-eyes and long black hair.

No one saw what they took out of the van: hose-pipes with nozzles, face masks, canisters of liquid gas . . . no one saw anything until the door opened – and then it was too late.

137

Chapter Twenty-Four

'Is this all yours, honest?' asked Trevor as he and Oliver made their way up the drive. The roof and towers of Helton in the sunrise looked like an ogre's castle in a book. 'No wonder you didn't want it. What a pile!'

Oliver didn't answer. Now that he was back, he was wondering why he'd been in such a panic to come home. It had come over him suddenly after Trevor's party; sitting up in bed it got so strong, the feeling that his ghosts needed him, that he'd started to dress almost without thinking. He'd meant to creep out alone and take the night train, but Trevor had ears like a lynx. It was horrid, deceiving Matron, but nothing could have stopped Oliver.

But why had he felt like that? Everything was peaceful and quiet.

'They're probably still asleep,' he said, and pushed open the big oak door.

It was *very* peaceful and *very* quiet. Addie would probably be in the bathroom trying to make the python sick, and Uncle Henry would be doing his exercises. He liked to get through them before Aunt Maud got up and told him not to strain himself.

Was it *too* quiet?

'There's a funny smell,' said Trevor.

Oliver had noticed it too. A sweet, sickly smell, drifting down the shallow marble steps towards them.

'Best prop the door open,' said Trevor and tugged at the heavy bolts.

Oliver did not help him. He was walking like a zombie towards the drawing room door. He had reached it somehow . . . opened it.

The ghosts were inside, all of them. And they were asleep. Oliver said this aloud so as to make certain that it was true.

'They're sleeping,' he said to Trevor.

He wouldn't ask himself why they were lying like that . . . like sacks waiting to be dumped . . . like those piled-up bodies he had seen in pictures of war.

Trevor put an arm round his friend's shoulders. He'd known at once what Oliver would not admit: that something was terribly wrong.

They began to move about among the ghosts; to call them.

Not one of them stirred. Not one of them opened their eyes.

Grandma lay under a carved wooden table. Mr Hofmann's sad old head was in her arms; she must have tried to shelter with him under the table like people did in air raids. But what had happened here was nothing as simple as a bomb.

Eric had slithered to the ground beside his father and both of them had brought their hands up to their foreheads in a salute, as if they wanted to meet what was coming like soldiers or like Scouts.

Only what *had* come? What had turned this room into a battlefield?

Aunt Maud lay close to her husband, her face turned towards him as it always was when she wanted comfort. Oliver picked up her hand and felt none of the lovely, slithery lightness he was used to. It felt heavy and curdled and when he let it go, it dropped like a stone.

'I can't bear it,' said Oliver, and gritted his teeth because he was being sorry for himself and there might be hope still, and something he could do.

He moved on to Sir Pelham. If anyone could survive an attack it would be him – but when he turned the hairy, pock-marked face towards him, the head lolled back and the sightless eyes were like black pits of nothingness.

'It's to do with that smell, I'm sure,' said Trevor. 'If we could get them outside into the air . . .'

But Oliver had found Adopta. She lay between Aunt Maud and Lady de Bone, and both spectres had stretched out their twisted limbs towards her as though even in their final agony they'd fought for her. No, he'd got that wrong. Their arms were sheltering her, not grasping. They had made an arch round Addie's head; they had had time to make their peace.

Oliver knelt down beside his friend. The sponge bag had dropped from her fingers; her tumbled hair was spread out in a halo behind her head. She was so frail that he could make out the pattern of the carpet beneath her shoulders.

'Addie, you can't go away, you *can't*. I need you so much. Remember all the things we were going to do? Please, Addie, *please*.'

As he tried to call her back, to prop her up, his tears fell on her upturned face. But nothing woke her, and to Oliver suddenly it was as though the end of the world had come. Everything bad that had happened to him: his parents dying, the year he had been shunted between people who didn't want him . . . everything got him by the throat.

140

'It's my fault,' he sobbed. 'It's because I went away and left them.' And then: 'I don't want to live.'

Trevor had been trying to comfort him. Now he got up and tiptoed to the door. 'Listen,' he whispered. 'Someone's just come in. Two people. I can hear them talking.'

Fulton and Frieda stood in the hall at Helton and gloated.

'We've done it! We've got rid of the spooks and Oliver is dead! Helton is ours, Frieda! It's ours. It's ours!'

But Frieda had stopped at the bottom of the stairs.

'Are you sure it's safe? They're all done for, the creepy-crawlies?'

'Of course it's safe. You heard what Dr Fetlock said when I handed over the money. "Wait till morning to make sure their ectoplasm's properly eaten and then you'll be fine," he said. And anyway the Ectoplasm Eating Bacterium doesn't hurt living people. I've told you.'

'No. But I don't want to bump into half-chewed legs and fingers and things. Even if we can't see them we might feel them. And there's a funny smell.'

'Now, Frieda, you're always whining. The spooks are done for and Oliver is dead! There's nothing to stop us now. Nothing.'

'Yes, Oliver is dead—' began Frieda. Then she stopped and pointed with a trembling hand towards the top of the stairs. 'It's his ghost,' she said with chattering teeth. 'It's Oliver's ghost!'

It was something anyone might have thought. Oliver was as white as a spectre and he held something that real boys do not often hold: a great throwing spear with a black wooden handle and a point as sharp and lethal as only the Indians of the Amazon could make it. An assegai which he had plucked from the wall and carried as if it weighed no more than Grandma's umbrella.

And he had gone mad. Trevor saw that at once. This slight, shy boy stared down at Fulton with such hatred that the Snodde-Brittles stood hypnotized like baboons in front of a leopard.

'I am not dead as you see,' said Oliver. 'But you will be in a minute because of what you have done to my ghosts.'

He lifted the spear and began to walk down the steps – and Fulton took a step backwards and fell over Frieda so that both of them rolled down on to the marble floor.

'I too am a Snodde-Brittle,' said Oliver, still in that level voice. 'And I Am Going To Set My Foot On *My* Enemies. *Now.*'

He took another step and lifted the spear, and as Fulton and Frieda tried to disentangle themselves, he brought the point down to touch Fulton's throat.

'No!' screamed Fulton. 'Stop! I didn't mean it. I'm sorry! Don't kill me, don't!'

'But I'm going to,' said Oliver. 'I'm just looking for the best place.'

Trevor had come round behind him. 'Here, steady, Oliver. They'll put you away if you kill him, and you don't want that.'

Oliver didn't even hear him. He brushed the tip of the spear against Fulton's throat and the scratch filled up with blood. No, not Fulton's Adam's apple – his heart . . .

Frieda was trying to scramble to her feet and

Trevor moved towards her and kicked her hard in the shins. If he couldn't stop Oliver, at least he could see that the woman didn't run away and squeal.

Fulton was grasping his throat, screaming with terror as his hand came away dipped in crimson.

Then from somewhere above them there came a . . . fluttering . . . the sound, faint as breath, of wing beats. And then a noise so unbelievable, so absolutely amazing, that Oliver couldn't believe his ears.

He turned his head only for a moment – but in that moment, Fulton and Frieda took to their heels and ran.

Chapter Twenty-Five

The van was back in the garage. The letters *Rid A Spook* had been painted out; it was just a plain red lorry now.

And the laboratories had been dismantled. The cages where the phantom mice had had their tails removed by the dreaded EEB had been sent back to the pet shop from which they came; the rest-rooms in which the tramp and the bag lady had been destroyed were once again ordinary cloakrooms.

'That should see it through,' said Dr Fetlock – who wasn't a doctor at all but plain Bob Fetlock, a man who'd failed every exam he'd ever taken but had a flair for tricking people.

'Six months in the sun!' said Professor Mankovitch, throwing her white wig on to the table and combing out her frizzy red hair. Her name was Maisie; she was Fetlock's girlfriend and they were off to Spain.

'What a sucker that bloke was,' said Charlie. His scar was real enough but he certainly hadn't got it when a head on a platter came out of his mother's larder in Peckham. He'd got it by roller-skating into a milk float when he should have been at school.

They'd worked on all sorts of scams, Fetlock and Maisie and Charlie, who was Maisie's nephew, but they'd enjoyed this one particularly.

'That was good, the bit about the villis luring my boyfriend away in the forest – I really went for that,' said Maisie, lighting a fag. 'Can you see me just sitting there while these white ghoulies pull off a bloke I fancied. I'd have kicked them in the teeth.'

'It's a pleasure to deceive such a nasty piece of work,' said Fetlock, who hadn't cared for Fulton Snodde-Brittle. 'Swallowing all that stuff. Ectoplasm Eating Bacteria! What a twerp!'

Fetlock had got the idea out of a horror comic and set the whole thing up. There hadn't been any phantom mice or rabbits or ghostly tramps, of course. The labs that Fulton had been shown round were completely empty and the great thumping vat that 'Professor Mankovitch' had been working on was left behind from a steam laundry. As for the stuff they'd squirted from their nozzles, it was a job lot of laughing gas they'd nicked from the back of the dental hospital. No one used it now for pulling teeth – it put people to sleep all right, but it made them so sick and silly and giggly afterwards that dentists had stopped using it.

'Well, that's it, then,' said Fetlock. 'Thirty thousand in cash should keep us out there for a bit. Got the tickets, Maisie?'

Maisie nodded and shut her suitcase. 'What'll happen to the spooks, do you reckon?' She was a person who could see ghosts, but she didn't care what became of them – she'd have done anything for money.

Fetlock shrugged. 'Same as happens to people, I suppose. Only with them being sort of looser and woozier than us, the gas'll get further into their brains. All the same we'd best be well clear of Fulton before they come round.'

And ten minutes later the premises of *Rid A Spook* were deserted – and as silent as the grave.

145

Chapter Twenty-Six

'Do I look all right?' asked Lady de Bone.

'Yes, Mother, you look fine,' said Adopta. She rearranged a piece of liver in the spectre's tangled hair and pulled her bloodstained skirt straight.

'What about me?' asked Sir Pelham. 'Does my hoofmark show up properly?'

Addie stood on tiptoe to examine the place where the horse had bashed in her father's head and said they both looked fine and everyone would be terrified and now it was time to start.

The de Bones were always a little nervous before the doors of Helton opened to the public and the long queues shuffled in to see the Most Haunted House in Britain. The visitors liked seeing Mr Hofmann's withered head coming out of the dining-room sideboard and they enjoyed Grandma whooping up and down the window curtains, but it was the Shriekers who made them go 'Ooh' and 'Aah' and hold on to each other in terror and feel that they had got their money's worth.

It had been Oliver's idea to open Helton to the public so as to get money for the work he wanted to do, and it was a great success. Trevor was in charge of the car park and Oliver showed people round and Helton had already beaten all other stately homes for attracting visitors.

Three months had passed since Oliver had turned

his head and seen the budgie giggling and laughing and falling about, and he and Addie were close now to fulfilling their dreams. Colonel Mersham had come to live at Helton and Matron had sent her sister down to keep house, and you couldn't have found two nicer people anywhere. As for Fulton and Frieda, no one had seen them since they scuttled away in terror from the hall.

The awful moment when the ghosts saw the nozzle of the EEB people come round the door and believed they were finished, had changed them all. In that ghastly moment, Lady de Bone and Aunt Maud had stopped fighting over Addie and sheltered her, and when they came round again the de Bones realized how wicked they had been and glided off to Larchfield Abbey to ask the nuns for forgiveness.

When they came back, a sensible arrangement was made about Addie. She spent the weekend with the de Bones, learning to say upper-class things and keeping her shoulders straight, and the week with the Wilkinsons, so that she stopped being a tug-of-war ghost and became a ghost with two sets of parents, which is a very different thing. And if she was always glad when Monday morning came round and she could be a Wilkinson again, she kept these thoughts to herself.

With the money they got from the visitors, Colonel Mersham and Oliver turned the stables into a Laboratory for the Study of Ghostliness. The Colonel was in charge of the work, with Uncle Henry to help him, and they made a splendid team. Already Helton was becoming the place to go if one wanted to know about ectoplasm and how it worked.

But the rest of the buildings and the gardens and

the grounds filled up with Addie's pets. Every phantom animal who did not understand what had happened to them was welcome and not one was turned away: not the ghost of the meanest water-flea or the skinniest tapeworm or the most beaten-up rabbit or pigeon with gunshot wounds in its side. The duck-bill in the zoo passed on at last and Addie brought it down to live in the shrubbery, and though she never found a phantom sheep she became quite fond of the python, who had been ill for a long time after the gas made him throw up the budgie, and needed careful nursing. And there was one animal so special and so famous that scientists came from all over the world to see it sitting by the fountain: the shining, pop-eyed and beautiful ghost of the golden toad which Colonel Mersham had brought back from the cloud forests of Costa Rica.

If Addie never turned away an animal in need, Oliver opened his home to every human spook without a place to lay his head. He had told the ladies of the adoption agency to send him any ghosts they couldn't place themselves, and soon the Hall filled up with bloodstained widows and actresses who had fallen through trapdoors and foolish people who had thrown themselves under trains for love.

There was one ghost, though, who did not appear.

However much they called her, poor Trixie never came to them. But one night as they were gathered round the sundial for the Evening Calling, a spectre did appear. A blowzy, raddled old spook with a puffy face and an out-of-date hairstyle who landed with a bump on the sundial.

'Coo-ee!' she called, waving a fat arm. 'It's me.

Don't you remember me, Eric? It's Cynthia Harbottle!'

It was the most incredible shock. Eric couldn't believe it. He'd remembered her the way she was, of course: a thin girl in a gym-slip with marvellous teeth.

'I told you,' said Aunt Maud under her breath. 'I told you she'd be old.'

Eric was speechless. He knew that if you love people you have to do it for always and perhaps he would have tried, but then Cynthia did the most awful thing. She snatched Trixie's banana, peeled it – *and threw the skin on to the neatly swept gravel path*.

That finished it. No Boy Scout could ever bring himself to love a person who leaves litter lying about, and in that moment Eric's passion for Cynthia Harbottle shrivelled and died.

Fortunately she was only passing, and after she went Eric was a new man. He whistled as he worked, he went for long tramps in the woods, and when Oliver's friends came down from the Home for the holidays, he showed them all the clever things he had learnt to do when he was a Scout: how to make a noise like a corncrake, how to splice ropes, and which kinds of sticks are suitable for skewering sausages and which are not.

'I expect Frederica Snodde-Brittle would be just as awful if she turned up now,' he said, trying to cheer up the farmer, and Mr Jenkins had to agree.

It was just six months after the *Rid A Spook* people had been to Helton that Miss Pringle and Mrs Mannering had a visitor who absolutely amazed them.

'You cannot be serious,' said Mrs Mannering when

149

the ghost who stood before them told them what he wanted. 'You want *us* to find you a home?'

The spook nodded. He had been an ugly man and he was a hideous ghost with his long, gloomy face and messy moustache and tombstone teeth. Not only that, but his forehead was peppered with gunshot wounds.

'I'm a ghost, aren't I?' said Fulton Snodde-Brittle. 'I've got my rights, same as everyone else.'

'No, Mr Snodde-Brittle, you have *not*,' said Miss Pringle. She was a gentle woman but she was absolutely outraged. 'You have lied and cheated and been a criminal spook-destroyer and you are not a person we would ever have on our books.'

'Well, I don't think that's fair. My sister ratted on me – she's gone all soft and I can't go on living rough on my own.'

The ladies knew what had happened to Frieda Snodde-Brittle. She had been so terrified when she saw Oliver's ghost that she had decided to stop being wicked and become a nun, and now she was down at Larchford with her head shaved doing humble things like mucking out the stables and scrubbing floors.

As for Fulton, when he found out that the EEB people had cheated him and that Oliver's spooks were not only well and happy but making him rich, he went quite mad. He found an old gun that his father had used for shooting rabbits, and took off for Spain to find Fetlock and force him to give back the thirty thousand pounds.

Fetlock and Maisie were in a disco when Fulton stormed in and started letting off his gun, and when he had shot three strobe lights and a potted palm tree, he tripped over a bongo drum and the gun went off and shot him through the head.

'I didn't ask to be a ghost,' said Fulton, who had been sent back from Spain in a body bag. 'I hate the things. But here I am and I want somewhere to live.'

Miss Pringle and Mrs Mannering turned to each other. Their eyes met. They smiled.

'Well, Mr Snodde-Brittle,' they said, 'there is one place which might just suit you.'

So that's where Fulton landed up – among the bikinis and the see-through nighties and the Footsies in the knicker shop.

Oliver goes to visit him sometimes when he and Matron's sister go to London, but it's a waste of time. Fulton just rants and raves among the underwear and tries to tear the Wonderbras to pieces with his teeth.

But for the Wilkinsons, his own family and the people who had made him so happy, Oliver, at the end of his first year at Helton, had a most wonderful surprise.

Aunt Maud had tried to share the Hall with the Shriekers, and not to worry when it was Addie's turn to be with them. But though they behaved so much better, they were still very snooty and she had never felt really at home among the huge knobbly furniture and the brown pictures of things being shot and the heavy fire irons. Oliver had seen this, but it wasn't till the farm turned in a profit and he'd done some accounts with his guardian that he saw what to do, and it was really very simple.

He rebuilt Resthaven in the gardens of Helton Hall. He built it exactly as it had been, with the bow windows and the stained glass in the bathroom and the pretty porch. He had the door painted blue

151

and the bird table with the rustic roof put up beside it, and found a mat with *Welcome* on it just like the one that had been there before.

So just fifty years after they lost their beloved home, the Wilkinsons moved into it again. And this time no bombs fell from the sky and the country was at peace.

EVA IBBOTSON

The Secret of Platform 13

Under Platform 13 at King's Cross Station there is a gump. Few people know that gumps are doors leading to other worlds. And this one opens for exactly nine days every nine years.

On the other side is a hand-picked team on a daring rescue mission. Odge Gribble, a young hag, together with an invisible ogre, a doddery wizard, a magical fey and an enchanted mistmaker, must bring back the Prince of their kingdom, stolen as a baby nine years before.

But the Prince has become a horrible boy called Raymond Trottle, who is determined not to be rescued . . .

EVA IBBOTSON

Which Witch?

Which of the most powerful witches will win
the right to marry Arriman, the awful Wizard
of the North?

The competition begins, and each witch in turn
pulls out of the cauldron her especially wicked
spell. But some go terribly, horribly wrong . . .